THE COUNTERFEIT FAMILY TREE OF VEE CRAWFORD-WONG

BY L. TAM HOLLAND

SIMON + SCHUSTER BFYR

NEW YORK LONDON TORONTO SYDNEY NEW DELHI

SIMON + SCHUSTER BFYR

An imprint of Simon & Schuster Children's Publishing Division
1230 Avenue of the Americas, New York, New York 10020

SIMON + SCHUSTER BFYR is a trademark of Simon & Schuster, Inc.
For information about special discounts for bulk purchases, please contact Simon & Schuster
Special Sales at 1-866-506-1949 or business@simonandschuster.com.
The Simon & Schuster Speakers Bureau can bring authors to your live event. For more
information or to book an event, contact the Simon & Schuster Speakers Bureau
at 1-866-248-3049 or visit our website at www.simonspeakers.com.
Also available in a SIMON + SCHUSTER BFYR hardcover edition.
Design by Chloë Foglia
The text for this book is set in Berling LT Std.
Manufactured in the United States of America
First SIMON + SCHUSTER BFYR paperback edition July 2014
2 4 6 8 10 9 7 5 3 1
The Library of Congress has cataloged the hardcover edition as follows:
Holland, L. Tam.
The counterfeit family tree of Vee Crawford-Wong / L. Tam Holland.
p. cm.
Summary: Vee's history assignment is to create a family tree, but he doesn't know anything
about his family beyond his parents' generation.
ISBN 978-1-4424-1264-4 (hc)
[1. High schools—Fiction. 2. Schools—Fiction. 3. Families—Fiction. 4. Chinese Americans—
Fiction. 5. China—Fiction.] I. Title.
PZ7.H70866Cou 2013
[Fic]—dc23
2012014542
ISBN 978-1-4424-1265-1 (pbk)
ISBN 978-1-4424-1266-8 (eBook)

FOR MY PARENTS

ACKNOWLEDGMENTS

Many thanks to my agents Molly Lyons and Joëlle Delbourgo, and my editor, Alexandra Cooper.

I received enormous support from Maury Zeff, Arthur Patterson, Jay Barmann, Anne Young, Joel Darnauer, and the fantastic MFA faculty at the University of San Francisco.

Thank you to Patty Tennant for always believing in me, and thanks to Michael and Kelly Conley for your thoughtful feedback.

To my students: You keep me inspired and humble.

And, of course, thank you to Wallace—for your unwavering love and belief in the value of all that I do.

Dad was like China, full of sad irony and ancient secrets. These were the words he used to describe the country he abandoned, and they were full of philosophy and poetry, like him, and I didn't understand them at all. I knew he grew up in a little village along the Yangtze, and I knew he left to become a freethinking American, and I knew he'd never been back and he'd never take me, but everything else I had to imagine. Which usually wasn't a problem, because I had a crazy imagination, but now it was a problem. Now I needed to know more, which was a big, big problem.

When I imagined Dad in China, I always saw the same thing: a hut, like ones I'd seen in *National Geographic*, perched on a muddy bank and about to tumble into the insistent current; and Dad as a raggedy, rascally teenager—in many ways just like me, the same slants and bulges, the same horrible sense of humor, the same awkward eagerness and lack of social skills. I always figured social awkwardness was a Chinese curse. I watched Dad putter around the edges of a social circle, never telling the right jokes at the right time, and using the wrong words and pausing in the wrong places.

Because of Dad my upper lip sagged a little and looked swollen, like I'd just been punched in the mouth. My teeth lined up too neatly. They were too small and flat for my mouth. Even though I played basketball, my shoulders sloped unathletically. I also had freckles. On my nose, my shoulders, even the tops of my knees. I had a mole on my left cheek, the cheek down there. It was galactic and had pulled other small moles and freckles into its orbit.

So a man goes to a doctor with a frog growing out of a lump on his head. The doctor asks: "When did this all start?" The frog replies: "It all began with a pimple on my ass."

Frog, lump, pimple, ass. These were words that spoke to me.

"What are you laughing for?" Dad asked. He stood in front of the stove and cracked eggs into a wok. I was supposed to be setting the table.

"Is that lump-o-stuff?" I asked. That was our nickname for fried rice.

"Yangzhou style," Dad said, "which comes from my very own village."

This wasn't true, or at least it wasn't true that his village invented fried rice. Fried rice, like gravity and cockroaches, had probably been around since the big bang.

He tossed me the empty egg carton and said, "I appreciate the flavor of irony. Yangzhou fried rice is not actually from Yangzhou."

I knew all this already. I stomped on the egg carton and put it in the trash. I watched the gunk in the pan—the egg congealing on the rice kernels and char siu and shrimp and carrots and cabbage, binding it all together. Lump-o-stuff.

"It's like French fries and Hawaiian pizza. People desire things that seem exotic, even if just in name."

I rolled my eyes. Most of the time Dad was an ophthalmologist, but sometimes he mentally time-traveled back to 1978 and all the philosophy he studied at Berkeley. Maybe whacked-out on drugs, too, but he'd never talk about that. Mom probably didn't even know what dope smelled like, and he wouldn't want to upset her. We didn't like to upset one another. That's why we couldn't talk about anything. That's why I didn't know anything. That's why I couldn't do my homework, which was why I was going to flunk history. It was all my parents' fault.

My history class at Liverton High, home of the Fighting Lions and two thousand fuckups, was a joke. Mr. Riley was a joke. He looked like a bellhop on safari: brown hair, brown skin, khaki pants, brown shirt every day. His suede loafers, brown of course, were scuffed at the instep, as if he played soccer in them. His skin was the color of dry dirt, the color of the first layer that you have to dig through to get to anything interesting and valuable. Sometimes he came to class with his Oakleys still on his forehead—his forehead, not in his hair or hanging around his neck—as if he were just stepping out of the sun-soaked pages of some men's outdoor magazine. He should have been a PE teacher; his peppiness only marginally covered up his dorkiness and his lack of academic inspiration. His favorite idea was "the story in history," so as we read about the Sumerians and Egyptians, he always wanted us to pause for a minute to appreciate the life of "Hatshepsut: The Noble Queen" or "Gilgamesh the King."

Normally, I loved ancient history and the little pieces of people's lives that they left behind without even knowing it; I loved digging to unearth those pieces and connecting them to make sense of a world that was utterly different from our own. Normally, I'd curl up on the couch with my *National Geographic* or *Archaeology* and read about the very same people and be in heaven. But I hated reading from our textbook, *World Societies, World Histories*, which weighed about ten tons and was written for a third grader. I hated that Mr. Riley didn't know any more than the textbook. We were an honors class. Honors, schmonors. He only loved coaching girls' basketball and riding his over-priced mountain bike. Every second I suffered through his class, I wished that Mr. Riley knew more and could get us out of our color-coded, outlined, memorizable textbook and into something complicated and real.

In order for us to "appreciate" history more—"appreciate" being a flimsy word meaning "talk about nicely without learning anything of substance"—he'd given us a week to write an account of our own family history. I considered starting with *Australopithecus*, going into great detail about gradual bipedalism and stone tool development, and ending with *Homo sapiens*, dot, dot, dot. That could cover the necessary five pages. Or I could write about Peking man, my seven-hundred-thousand-year-old

4

ancestor, a skeleton that had an outside chance of connecting prehumans to humans, who was dug up outside of Beijing and then lost when the Japanese invaded China during World War II. That would be more exciting, like a mystery and an adventure story all rolled into one life. Mine.

I could write some joke of a paper and risk flunking for being a smart ass, or I could blow a hole through my parents' happiness. I could keep the comfortable silence, or I could ask the impossible questions.

These were the impossible questions: What's the huge problem with our family? Why is our family history such a big, bad, dirty secret? Where are my grandparents and why can't I meet them? Why don't we talk about the past? Why don't we talk about your families? How come I know, without even asking, that I'm not allowed to ask these questions? That it's better, it's always better, to keep my mouth shut?

I only knew my parents in their current daily lives. I knew random things, like their favorite foods and what their sneezes sounded like. What could I possibly mine from their lives that would be a story worth writing about?

My parents met during Dad's residency in San Francisco, where Mom—my lonely, divorced mom—was a dental assistant. She must have fallen for Dad's brains, because she was tall and blond and from Texas, and he was a goofy, middle-aged Chinese guy. Despite all their differences, they went ahead and fell in love and for some reason decided to have me. Maybe Mom made

Dad more American, and Dad made Mom more exotic and cultural, and it was as easy as wanting what the other had.

Then why me? Why have a kid when you're not going to give him brothers or sisters or grandparents or cousins? And why name him Vee Crawford-Wong? Who names their kid after a letter in the alphabet, one of those weird ones at the end, one that in third grade no one ever practiced in cursive because it barely ever came up? What was wrong with something normal, like Michael or Joe or Fred? Couldn't they have guessed that I'd end up with nicknames like Veegina and guys making Vs with their fingers and sticking their tongues in between, which they did for years before I realized what it meant? And then Crawford-Wong. What was so special about either one? There were over two million people in America named Crawford. And Wong. How unique. Half a million in the U.S. and then truckloads more in China.

I was like that joke: If you're one in a million, there are a thousand people just like you in China!

I was most likely a mistake. They would never have gotten married if it hadn't been for me. I could imagine them going out for greasy Chinese, and they'd be using their chopsticks to pick mushrooms and snow peas off the lo mein. It'd be raining, because in movies it's always raining when people are serious and sad, and Mom's rubber-ducky scrubs would practically glow under the bright fluorescent lights. They'd both look crazy: Mom in her scrubs and Dad with his hair all wild because he'd have rubbed his head a million times.

Dad: Sometimes we choose our destiny, and sometimes our destiny chooses us.

Mom: Kenny . . .

My dad's real name was Ken-zhi, which meant "earnest," but he went by Kenny. Kenny Wong. A good old American boy.

Dad: Now that you're pregnant, we must do the right thing.

Mom: What is the right thing?

Dad: We will raise a perfect son who will play football and be popular and graduate magna cum summa summa laude magna laude, from Harvard of course, and then he will invent a new way of doing laser eye surgery that will revolutionize sight for the entire universe.

Mom: Well, okay. We could do that.

Mom was always agreeable. She tried too hard; she was almost too sweet; she never talked about her family or her ex-husband or anything else that wasn't wonderful. The only time she ever cried was once a year when she got a Christmas card from her parents. I'd learned to hide in my room when I saw the envelope leaning against the tacky Santa-shaped candles we could never bring ourselves to light and melt.

I couldn't stand watching Mom cry. Maybe when she found out about me, she had cried and then had covered up her sadness and done her best to make Dad happy, hoping that the lima-bean-like lump inside her would grow up to be a magna cum dream boy. And instead of a dream boy she got lumpy old me, who even at five preferred digging up the yard to studying Latin or doing whatever else a dream boy would do. Maybe she'd been trying to be happy for fifteen years, but here I was, bigger than her now, and still someone she'd never even wanted.

I prided myself on my investigative skills, my ability to navigate the past with the smallest of clues, but I was a total failure when it came to my family. All my imaginings—that Dad was Chinese royalty or some top secret intelligence official, that Mom's family in Texas were oil billionaires, that one or both of them was running away from a heinous crime or hiding out in the witness protection program—all of these ideas were straight out of HBO and I knew I couldn't believe them. I always had a complete failure of imagination when it came to my parents. They were simply Mom and Dad, and I was their weird, mediocre son, and there were endless things we couldn't and didn't talk about.

ontact sports were a constant negotiation of touching: where, when, how hard, and to what end. You had to find that shifting, invisible line between bully and fag and walk it like a high wire. So it was no surprise that no one jumped for joy or clicked his heels when word got out we were wrestling in PE.

PE, in general, was a bad way to start any day, particularly a Monday, even more particularly a cloudy October day that was otherwise filled with quizzes and oral presentations and looming essay deadlines. I wished we were playing basketball in the gym or flag football in the mud or that I could go back to kindergarten and have mandatory nap time.

The wrestling room smelled only slightly better than the locker room, which smelled like smelly ass all the time. We got in a circle and did push-ups and sit-ups and pull-ups and some strange yogalike stretches. The only reason I didn't give up entirely was because of Coach Wilson. He was our PE teacher but also the JV football and basketball coach. He'd cut me from each team last season, but I was planning on trying out for basketball again this year. I'd been running and doing some wind sprints (thirty-seven seconds from my driveway to the stop sign; twenty-two to the stop sign the other way) and playing pickup basketball most Fridays at lunch.

Coach Wilson suckered two guys from the wrestling team—Russell Reed, who could probably lift a truck, and Greg Haynes, who weighed about as much as Russell's left leg—to demonstrate the basic takedowns. Russell could have thrown Greg across the room like a Wiffle ball, but instead he half-assed the moves with a smirk on his stubbly face. Since most guys didn't give a shit about one another anyway, as soon as we broke into pairs to practice, everyone began to kung fu at each other, and Coach Wilson lost all control over us. Two guys had to leave and get ice for jammed fingers and scratched eyeballs, and someone punched Kyle Diamond in the jaw for grabbing crotch on a hold.

I didn't like most of the guys in my class, and I was a reluctant participator. Anytime I got my elbow folded into someone's armpit, I imagined I was doing it for a real reason: pulling someone out of a burning building, or forcing him down to dodge a bullet. But as soon as the other guy got adamant, I became the victim, the helpless one. I would sort of collapse on the mat like I'd been shot. The other guy could be the hero if he was really dying for it.

For the last ten minutes of class we came back to the circle and Coach Wilson called guys out, one on one, to wrestle in front of everyone. Of course Coach Wilson chose Greg Haynes to pick on Kyle Diamond; it was his teacherly way of telling

Kyle he shouldn't have grabbed crotch. It felt like a boxing ring, guys cheering and lunging in to egg someone on. I looked at the clock. Two minutes left. I looked at Coach Wilson, and he was looking at me.

"Go, go!" I yelled, and pumped my fist halfheartedly in the air. Panic engulfed me and sweat pricked my forehead. I tried to look involved and enthusiastic. I watched Greg crouch and go for Kyle's ankle. Greg pulled Kyle's legs out from underneath him. Kyle's back made a thudding noise on the mat. He slowly sat up and scooted to the edge of the mat, not even bothering to stand up.

"One more," Coach Wilson said. "Vee Wong and ..." He scanned the circle. I held my breath. "And Mark White. Last one, boys."

Coach Wilson, like most teachers, knew exactly who couldn't stand each other. And of course, he'd paired me with Mark White: the embodiment of everything I disliked.

My introduction to Mark White had been in Spanish class on the first day of freshman year, when Ms. Garcia came around and gave us Spanish names. They were translations of our regular English names. "*Juana! Isabel! Ricardo! Estéban!*" She sprinkled names down the aisles until she got to my desk.

"Hm," she said. "*Difícil. Veh.* Hm. *Veh.*" Every time she said "*Veh,*" her front teeth spit out her lower lip with a rush of coffee-scented air.

"But *Veh* is not a *llamo,*" I protested. I'd taken Spanglish all through junior high, so of course I still couldn't talk in complete sentences.

"Okay, okay, good. You pick," she said.

I wasn't ready with a good name. I hadn't expected her to let me protest.

"Hey." I felt the back of my chair dent with the force of someone's foot. "Hey, I want to be Paco."

I turned around to look at the guy behind me. His meaty face was spotted with freckles and zits, and he had on an Oakland Raiders jersey.

"*No, no! Es perfecto!*" she said, glancing at her seating chart. "*Mark es Marco.*"

"How come he gets to pick?"

I hated kids who did that. I hated the way teachers caved into this kind of bad logic. Life wasn't fair. Rules weren't fair. To her credit, Ms. Garcia ignored him and moved on to the next guy. I wondered, later, if she had caved in and let him be Paco, if things would have been different between Mark and me. If in some parallel universe we would have been friends or, better yet, polite strangers.

I wrenched my body around so I was facing him again, and I asked, "Hey, do you play football?"

"You?" he asked.

I nodded.

"You kidding me?" He scratched a zit near his ear.

"What? Chinese people can't play football?"

That made him laugh, and I smiled a little. Racist prick.

He sneered again and called me something—faggot, fat-ass—something mean and not at all clever. I decided he was an idiot who wasn't worth my time, but it turned out we were also in the same freshman honors history class. And this year, as sophomores, again we were together in Spanish and PE and honors history. He wasn't brilliant, but he also wasn't retarded, and this was what got under my skin the most. I was okay with the way the world was divided: the jocks, the nerds, the stoners, the emos, et cetera. Very few people were allowed to cross over, and Mark White wasn't special enough to be a football and basketball player (while I wasn't) and also an honors student. To make matters worse, over the summer he'd gone from big and zitty to solid and tanned (while I remained forever goofy-looking and soft around the edges).

Mark and I were like oil and water. Like iron and oxygen. Like Chinese and Japanese. I would rather have wrestled Coach Wilson, or Russell, or a rabid alligator, before facing Mark White.

Most guys cheered for Mark. As we squared off, he gave me a shit-eating smile. We grappled and his face glowed, his tan turning ruddy and mottled. My legs felt wobbly, like I might pitch over and collapse without anyone's assistance. My body lunged forward and my shoulder cracked against Mark's, and I breathed through my teeth. I got my hand on his elbow, but he snaked his arm around my waist. I leaned away so he couldn't hug me too tight, and I felt my foot slipping. One of my palms was up against his chest, and his fingers were digging into the skin around my waist. A kind of whine came from one of us. It sounded like a little kid about to burst into tears. It sounded weak and stupid. It made me mad. Stupid, popular prick. I felt him scratching for a foothold that would topple me, and I bent down and let him start to swing me, then I copied Greg's foot move and Mark went down like a sleeping giant. He had grabbed both my wrists on his way down, so I came down over and on top of him. My face hit the mat. I could feel him pushing me off him, and I rolled over and did the worst thing possible. I smiled. He glared at me, his nostrils bubbling with clear snot.

"Ugh," Mark said, pointing to my face.

I wiped my nose with the back of my hand. It came away sticky and red.

"Pinch it," Coach Wilson said. "Nice job. Get some ice."

That was as much of a compliment as anyone ever got from him. He'd remember this come basketball season. I smiled again and tasted blood.

Next stop: history. Out of habit I avoided Mark and ogled Adele Frank, the smoking-hot senior who was Riley's go-to basketball girl. She usually camped out in Riley's room during our history class, and I wondered if she had a free period or if she just never went to her own classes. This morning she sat in Riley's chair like it was her personal throne. Her bare feet, with blue polish on the toes, waggled on top of a stack of quizzes. Her yellow shirt, so thin and so tight that I could see the outline of her bra, rode up her back, exposing pale skin that puckered slightly near the top of her jeans.

"Wipe up your drool," Madison said.

Madison was both a genuine friend and a genuine pain in the

ass. Her life was full of pink: pink purses and scarves and fuzzy book covers. Also, she'd never gotten an A- in her life.

"Yo, Miao-ling," I said. Her real name was Miao-ling, but she hated her name almost as much as I hated mine. "Drool is attractive. Did you know that lionesses salivate in the presence of their mates? It's like a turn-on."

"Wow," Emily said as she drew a line of connected hearts on the front of her binder. Emily was Madison's unofficial sidekick. She had long, stringy blond hair, and she asked those questions that everyone in an honors class was too afraid to ask for fear of looking retarded.

"He made that up," Madison said. "Didn't you, Vee?"

"If you know the answer," I said, "why are you asking?"

Riley interrupted our fun by marching us down the hall to the computer lab and telling us to work on our family history essays. I hated him and his stupid assignment. We weren't learning anything. He was making the rich world of the past about as exciting as dry toast.

"Ughhh," I said. I grabbed the computer next to Madison even though, as fate would have it, that meant I was within spitting distance of Mark White. My nose throbbed and threatened to bleed again every time I turned in his general direction.

Madison's computer binged to life. "It's better than doing it at home."

"I forgot my log-in name," I said.

"Use mine," she said. "It's 'mingming38.' All one word, no spaces." She already had a new document up on her screen.

I stared at her. "Thirty-eight?"

"It's a good luck number."

"I knew that," I said. "How about 'mingming'?"

She chewed her forefinger, which she only did when she was embarrassed.

"As in Sun Ming Ming, that old, gigantic basketball player? Are you a secret basketball fan? How could you forget to tell me?" I loved basketball. I loved playing, and last year, even after I'd gotten cut, I sometimes went to the JV and always went to the varsity games. This year I'd make all the JV games—hopefully wearing those shiny orange warm-ups that reminded me of Syracuse's home jerseys. I also religiously watched the Warriors and March Madness. Dad and I sometimes even went to Berkeley to watch the Cal team thunder up and down the court. I liked the cold, empty smell of the gym and the squeak of shoes on the shiny floor. I liked the whooshing of the ball in the net and of course the cheerleaders with their bouncing smiles and smooth spandex crotches constantly flashing at the crowd.

"Basketball is ridiculous and barbaric," Madison said.

"I thought you said that about football."

"Football is also ridiculous and barbaric," she said. "Everyone just smashing around into each other, all nasty and sweaty."

"Just like a school dance," I said.

"Like you'd know," Mark said.

I should have known he'd eavesdrop on any conversation that involved sports.

"What are you even talking about?" I said.

"Like you go to dances," he said.

"I do." I went and usually plastered myself against the gym wall and bobbed my head for hours and hours, pretending to really be grooving to the thumping music.

"It means 'bright,'" Madison said. "Ming-ming. My parents call me that."

"I bet you just have your pick of dates to the Halloween dance," Mark said to me. "I just bet."

Riley came strolling around, and Madison started typing like a possessed secretary. She didn't even look at her fingers.

"I'm not a betting man," I said after Riley had finished his drive-by and returned to his desk. I stared at the blinking cursor on the screen. "But I'm happy to wrestle."

I almost flinched, expecting Mark to punch me in the face or tip the computer over and electrocute me. I stared at the pixilated screen and felt it burning tiny electric holes in my retinas.

"Who?" Mark said. "Who'd go with you?"

"Gosh," I said, "who wouldn't?"

Adele had followed us to the computer lab and was sitting next to Riley and texting on her phone. Occasionally she'd lean into him and make him read what she'd written. And he got paid for this? He called this teaching? I watched her comb her fingers through her hair. I knew I was staring, but I couldn't help myself.

"Uh-huh," Mark said. "Right. Adele Frank. You're shitting me."

He was right. I didn't even have a chance of taking Adele's dirty gym socks to the dance with me. I wasn't a stud football player or a party-hopping senior. Adele moved in another circle, and each circle at school was like its own fiefdom. Moving circles, breaking ranks, threatened the whole permanence of the system and made everyone uncomfortable. I was at most allowed to ogle her from a distance, which I did.

"I haven't technically asked her yet," I said. "Technically."

Mark snorted. Someone more intelligent might have used this opportunity to verbally abuse me into submission, but all he could think to do was snort. It fired me up. It reminded me that I'd thrown him to the ground this morning. I pushed my chair back and stood up.

"This is me doing my work," Madison said. "This is me not being distracted."

Mark said, "Does she even know who you are?"

"Of course," I said with confidence I didn't have. I sank back into my plastic chair. "I'm going to write about *Australopithecus*," I said.

"God, Vee," Madison said. "What do you not understand about family history?"

"Uhhhhh," I said. I hated my life. I hated brainless, cruel homework and the way I was supposed to figure out everything on my own. Other kids would have tough life stories: single parents, divorced parents, alcoholic parents, abusive parents, dead parents, all of the above. They'd be coddled and cooed over and given A's just for telling the truth. I wanted to tell the truth, I did, but there was no truth to tell. There was just this nothingness, this silence. I looked at Riley, who was still kicking back in the swiveling teacher's seat. This was all his fault. Disgust for him burned in the back of my throat.

Two minutes and seventeen seconds left in class. I closed down my blank document while other people printed out their finished essays. Adele sauntered by, still riveted to her phone.

"Hey, Adele, do you know who I am?" I asked in one rushed breath.

I heard Mark snort. Adele looked up from her phone and glanced at Mark, then me, then back at her phone. You could tell she liked the groveling question. "Of course," she said.

"Cool," I said. "Then how would you feel about going to the Halloween dance with me?" My mouth burned, as if the words were habaneros. My face flamed. I was making a total ass out of myself.

Adele laughed again. "Sure thing, babycakes," she said, and winked at me. "Call me later."

I gave her a shit-eating grin, which was completely for Mark's benefit. She wasn't even looking at me anymore. I didn't even have her number.

"I know it's crazy, but what if she means it?" I asked Madison at lunch. "What if she didn't just blow me off?"

"You're not totally ugly, anyway," Madison said. "That could have a lot to do with it."

"She's obviously drawn to the exotic."

"Vee," Madison said. "You're half Irish or something. You're not incredibly Chinese. You're just, I don't know."

"What?"

"Nothing."

"What?" I leaned forward and put my hands on the sticky cafeteria table.

"You're just confused looking. Like it's hard to tell what you are."

No one had ever said that to me before, but it made sense. I'd known it all along. I was awkward and strange. My height and my freckles and my black hair that was not as thick and straight and black as it needed to be. My lumpiness. Most Asian guys were built like chicken wire: stringy and strong. You could see Texas in my jowls and my thighs that made pants ride up and stick, folded, in my crotch if I sat down for too long. I wasn't fat. I was big and soft around the edges, like something left in the refrigerator too long that was starting to get soupy.

"You're cute in a kind of old-fashioned way," Madison said.

I rolled my eyes and concentrated on opening my Coke. "Whatever that means." I took a piece of lettuce from my taco salad and stuck it between two of my front teeth. Then I smiled all big at Madison. She rolled her eyes. I wanted to snort, but I held it back. "What?" I asked. I looked around me. "What?"

"Nothing," Madison said. "You don't have anything in your teeth."

"Okay," I said. I took the lettuce out of my teeth and swallowed it. "Fine. It's very difficult to make you laugh. But you're going to realize someday that a sense of humor is a genetic advantage. Practical jokes are part of what allowed humans to evolve past the ape stage."

"Really?"

"Sure. Humor takes sophistication and superior brain power."

"Really."

"Jokes, or things that require irony, show a complex intellect." I sounded like Dad. But I was also right.

"Really," she said. She licked her lips and narrowed her eyes at me. Her eyes were puffy, and her upper eyelids shimmered like she'd painted them with Vaseline. With narrowed eyes and saliva-smooth lips, she smiled at me.

I recognized the look, the glinting tilt of a debater's upper lip when she's going for the jugular. It brought back bad memories. In junior high I was forced to join the debate team. I hated it. I accused my parents of trying to turn me into a cheap knockoff version of a nerdy Chinese kid. Madison, however, loved debate. She was on the debate team. I didn't want to get into a debate just because I was trying to be funny.

"Where's Emily?" I asked cheerfully.

"Student council meeting. She says she wants to run for treasurer, but she actually has a crush on Darren Thomas." Darren Thomas was our sophomore class president. He ran student council meetings.

"Treasurer?" I said. "Are you kidding? She's only in geometry." Madison didn't even bother to roll her eyes.

"How's your dim sum?" I asked. "Or is that chicken feet?" She sighed.

"Braised sea cucumber?" I'd seen this in Chinatown, and though Dad had promised me it was bland, I had no interest in trying something that looked like a wart-covered penis.

Madison picked up her turkey sandwich to take a huge bite.

"She didn't mean it," I said. "Adele, I mean. I'm not that stupid."

"You never know," Madison mumbled, but her voice had no fight in it.

We finished our lunches, then we walked across the soccer field to get to biology. The sun was so bright it hurt, and we walked slowly, soaking in the warm afternoon, delaying the inevitable return to cold, hard desks and fluorescent lights and teachers who expected us to enjoy sitting inside.

3

Adele Frank knew that I was alive. That was enough for me, that and the off chance that Mark White believed she'd actually go to the dance with me. I slogged through the week and waited for Adele to notice me again. In my head she was always catching sight of me in my best moments: me, standing self-assured in the middle of history class; me, high-stepping it off the basketball court after an intense lunchtime pickup game; me, relaxing and laughing with friends. In my head she was always grabbing me and pulling me into the nearest supply closet and ripping at my clothes. I knew every place on campus she could take me to where no one else would find us.

At night I imagined her in my bed. I was confident and uninhibited, and she smelled sweet and clean. She put her hands under my shirt, warm and smooth, and I touched her breasts, which felt like balloons but heavier, soft like an earlobe but fuller. At night I was emboldened by the weight of my dark blue comforter, by the safety of the small pockets of air that contained our breath. Her bright shirt was on my carpet, her breasts against my cheeks and lips and then my own chest, then she slid over me, all this slick, tanned skin, breasts bigger than a handful, her hands on top of mine, her lips telling me she wanted more. She was naked and on top of me, all skin and breath and no more coolness, no more flirty bounciness, but friction and heat and need. The comforter in my mouth is soaking with saliva, and I gag on my own desire and press the pillow over my head and hump the mattress alone in the dark because I am alone but the bed is her, she is climbing on me, she is on me and I am on my bed, which is her. I am on her and the comforter is off the bed and she is pulling me up, and she keeps whispering and it sounds like swarms of bees, like waves breaking, and I am tireless, and she's gasping and her breath is mine, and she is everywhere, and there's this endless, sweet pressure that is hers and then it's mine, she's mine, I am with her and she is mineminemine.

In my daydreams, aside from being a total sex maniac, Adele also understood what was going on with my family. And at some point she'd pull Riley aside and explain to him that I couldn't, I just couldn't, do this essay.

But that was my daydream. In reality I'd done nothing, but I couldn't let myself just get a zero. I was good at history; history was my thing. I couldn't just roll over and let Riley win. He was a dumb-ass. A dumb-ass and a jackass, and he obviously didn't care about any of us. On Thursday night, the night before the essay was due, I procrastinated until Mom and Dad were sound asleep, and then I sat at my computer and stared at the screen in desperation. At midnight, with no one left to instant message, I did a Google search for "bad family stories" and "family tragedies" and "China family history tragedy." Just for some ideas. I found some stuff about Taiwan and Tibet and one blog where this guy was ripping on Marxism. Also, there were about a jillion adoption websites where white moms proudly clutched big-headed Chinese kids. If I weren't so much like Dad, I could believe that I'd been adopted.

I got on a Wikipedia page about the anti-Japanese resistance war and the Nanking Massacre, and I read about how Japan invaded China in 1937 and killed over two hundred thousand people. And how they denied it and portrayed the event in their textbooks like it was no big deal. That was bullshit. Nationalist bullshit. Bad things—murders, invasions, wars, bombs, holocausts, torture—were always true. People dying, and the massive piles of skeletons they left behind, were real and undeniable.

My grandparents could have been there. They could have died there. We were from Yangzhou, which was just across the river from Nanking. My grandparents might have watched what the website said was mass execution, rape, looting, burning, shooting, stabbing, decapitating, eviscerating, drowning, and castrating.

If my grandfather had been working in Nanking in 1937, he would have tried to escape across the Yangtze while dodging bullets and watching fifty thousand bodies pile up in the river. It was all true. It had happened to someone, maybe even to my grandfather. Not knowing didn't make it untrue.

I could see my grandfather in the muddy river, his head going under while the air above him exploded like firecrackers. I could feel the heavy panic pressing on his lungs and deepening the darkness in the corners of his eyes. He might have thought he was already one of those screaming souls finding his way toward his next life. He might have known even then that he wasn't going to watch his grandson grow up or have someone to tell his stories to.

My eyes got hot like I was about to cry. My teachers had no clue about me. They wouldn't understand what I was doing. They looked at me and saw a tall, soft, smart-mouthed mutt. I didn't trust their opinions of me, and I didn't trust my ability to correct them.

Friday morning Adele was wearing a blue shirt that was a Carolina blue, and I wondered if she was a UNC fan. I'd always been more of a Duke guy. I imagined heated, basketball-centered conversations with her while I turned in my essay and while Riley talked on and on about the glories of Greece and Rome. He'd had too many Jolts; he was too pumped about everything. He probably thought the Romans were as immortal as their huge marble statues, fascinating like their sophisticated senate and the feasts where they'd eat and eat, then puke so they could eat some more. Pretty sophisticated, I'd say. Lots of girls here were just like that, but they got sent to the counseling center.

At the end of class Adele got up from her permanent perch on Riley's desk and walked into the hallway. With me. "Hey," she said.

I wanted everyone to notice that I was walking down the hall with Adele Frank. Where were all the hotshot jocks? Where was Mark or Madison or even Emily? Where was everyone whose opinions counted? The high school equivalents of kings and landowners and slave owners? The hall was full of serfs today. Ugly prepubescent boys and girls who didn't properly acknowledge that we were all in the divine presence of royalty.

Adele and I wedged our way through loitering groups. "You didn't call me," she said with a flirty smile. "But anyway, I didn't want to embarrass you in front of your friends. I'm not planning on going to the dance. My boyfriend . . ." She flipped her hair around her shoulder and began to comb it with her fingers. "Anyway, you can't bring older guys, so I'm out, you know?"

My face felt hot and I couldn't locate my tongue. I could see the door to my Spanish class, so I slowed down.

"I don't have your number," I finally said. "I couldn't call you."

She laughed. "You are so hilarious. It was a joke. You were being cute, so I was being cute back, right? That's how jokes work."

"Right," I said. "Thanks for that."

She smiled and said, "No, thank *you*."

Me (*casually, at lunch*): Adele is so down with the Asian thing. She was trying to help me save face in front of Mark. Not that I needed it.

Madison (*sounding bored*): I could have told you she wouldn't go with you.

Me: She's not going at all. Plus, I don't care what he thinks.

Madison: Emily doesn't have anyone to go with, so I told her you'd be her date.

Emily? Emily had stringy hair, a flat chest, and an annoying, whiny voice.

Me: What about Darren Thomas?

Madison (*snorting*): Yeah, in her dreams.

What did it matter now? We could go together and leave together and ignore each other the rest of the time.

I said: Do you need me to find you a date?

Madison (*scoffing*): Yeah, dances don't help with my SAT scores, so let's just say my parents consider them a royal waste of time.

Madison's parents were very smart and very polite and very strict. We weren't even allowed to watch R-rated movies at her house, so she and Emily came to my house to watch stuff like *Alien* or *The Silence of the Lambs*.

Me: What about Nick? You could go with him. His parents are dentists too. Your parents would like him.

Madison: Seriously, Vee.

Nick was skinny and bug-eyed and smelled like French fries left over the weekend in someone's locker.

Me: If she really wants to go, I guess.

Madison (*sincerely*): Yay!

Me (*not sincerely*): Hip hip hooray.

4

On Saturday morning Mom and I took Fannie into the shop for new tires. Fannie was Mom's car, a 2005 Toyota Camry with a dull orange custom paint job and an awkward, swollen trunk that seemed to sag toward the tailpipe. When Mom had brought her home, Dad had said that from the back she looked like an overweight orangutan. She was the car I'd learn to drive.

Mom said that today she'd teach me to change a tire. In mid-December I could get my learner's permit, and there was a foot-long checklist of "Things Vee Needs to Do Before He Can Drive." Changing tires was one of the easier ones. Mom wanted me to be able to change the oil, too, and learn to drive manual (even though both our cars were automatic), and Dad wanted me to get a 3.5 GPA and take an accelerated Earth sciences class at Burnett Community College. They considered driving to be the big, juicy carrot that dangled less than two months away, and until then they were going to push me as hard as they could.

The tire place was in a strip mall, and we had to park in front of Ann's Fabrics. Mom paused outside the display window and studied the headless, nippleless mannequin who had some blue and brown swirling fabric draped around her like a sari.

"That's nice," Mom said.

I'd never seen Mom use a sewing machine before. I tucked my hands under my armpits. It was cold and foggy, and I hadn't brought a jacket. "You sew?" I asked.

"A little. Maybe Madison would like something," she said. "For Christmas." Her fingers were on the glass.

"Mom, Madison goes shopping for her clothes. She's fine."

"Of course," she said, and turned away from the window.

I was a jackass. Why couldn't I just keep my mouth shut? If she wanted to sew, she could go ahead and sew. I wasn't going to body-block her. And Madison was the kind of girl who'd probably wear whatever Mom made, however ugly, and really pretend to love it.

I was just being pissy about the dance tonight. Why did we need dates at all? And who was Adele's older boyfriend who was too old to sneak past the deans? I was an idiot for trying to talk to her at all. Of course she had an older boyfriend and better things to do. I was a sophomore who couldn't even drive.

Tom's Discount Tires had squares of rubber on the floor and rows and rows of tires stacked on long metal tubes stuck into the walls. A man with blue coveralls and a name tag that said SAL asked us what we needed. Sal was built like a wrestler. He ran a thick, dirty hand over his greased-back hair and tried to upgrade us to something studded and high performing, but Mom said we didn't drive in snow, and I wouldn't be doing doughnuts in parking lots, so basic tires were just fine.

"But you know," Sal said, "this one stabilizes tread, it's really good for the first-time driver, he feels the difference, more smoother and more control, you know." Sal lovingly stroked the rubber. "And for the hydroplaning, he's gonna be driving in the rain, you know, it's better for that, for channeling water." He dug a finger into one of the deep grooves. Then, while Mom was thinking, he picked at his nose hairs.

"Are you saying your cheaper tires aren't safe?" Mom asked.

"Oh, no, no, no, ma'am," Sal said quickly, shaking his head and his hands. "These are just more improved, better for all the problems you could have on the road with conditions not always predictable and your son here learning and everything behind the wheel."

"Mom, cheap is fine. We can paint fireballs on them if we need an upgrade." I didn't like seeing her get badgered.

Mom smiled and put her arm around me. "Sal has a point here, honey. You might be driving in the rain. You'll have basketball games at night sometimes, right? I don't want anything to happen to you." She was talking so Sal could hear us, and then she kissed me on my temple, and I smiled like I really enjoyed the cloying display of maternal love. Sal figured out the price difference using a handy calculator he kept in the pocket of his rough blue jumpsuit. Then Mom gave him the keys, and he screeched Fannie around and pulled her into the garage. We met him there and watched him roll the new, performance-enhanced tires around to their appropriate places.

"Watch," Mom told me. Then she told Sal, "He needs to learn to change a tire."

"Yeah," Sal said, not looking at me. "Well, we're gonna put it up here and get them all going at once, but that's not how you do it for real out on the road. You wanna have a lesson on it first?" Sal glanced up at me, his hands on the bolts of one of our old, smooth tires.

I looked at Mom. She nodded. I looked at Sal and nodded. He barked something in Spanish to the two other mechanics, and they scurried back into the store. Sal apparently had no real responsibilities. Or maybe he just liked showing off. He got the jack out of the trunk, and I expected Mom to speak up and tell him she'd already taught me this part. How to put the jack under the metal and crank it up, then loosen the nuts, then crank it up again. But Mom just stood there primly, holding her purse with two hands, the big belly of it almost reaching her knees.

Sal handed me the heavy, greasy wrench and said, "You look strong, like you can loosen them some, just right here and here." He pointed to the nuts that looked like they were trying to burrow into the hubcap. "And here and here," he said, tapping the other two.

"Thank you," I said. For pointing out the obvious.

I put the wrench up against the bolt and pushed. Nothing. I stood up, leaned over, and put all my weight onto it. All 155 pounds. Nothing. I pulled, in case I'd been going the wrong way.

My nose, still tender from its Monday morning encounter with the wrestling mat, throbbed and threatened to run.

"Come on," Sal said, "use those muscles, you're tall and strong, you must play some sports, right? Like what?"

"Ping-Pong," I said. The sport made for Asians.

Mom laughed. "Vee," she said, "come on now."

"I do a lot of work around the house," I said, which was not at all true, but Mom wasn't going to call me out twice in front of Rico Suave.

"That's good, that's good, you look after your mom. Boys gotta do that." Sal took the wrench from me and loosened each bolt with quick pops. "You gotta get the torque, that's all, good job." Then he pocketed the wrench, and we shimmied the new tire on and I slowly tightened the bolts, just half a turn, Sal pointing to each one until I clumsily wrapped the wrench around it.

It took Sal less time to do three tires than it did for us to do just one. Of course, he had the mechanical lift and the electric bolt looseners, but he also moved in a blur, like he was on some NASCAR pit crew. Adele's older boyfriend probably looked a lot like Sal: someone muscular and into cars. Someone almost too greasy to be sexy, unless you wanted that older-guy look, which Adele did. I wondered why she bothered kissing up to plain, nerdy Mr. Riley so much. He was like an REI poster child.

Sal washed his hands, finally, and rang us up, and Mom kept thanking him over and over, like he'd just performed open-heart surgery to save my life.

"Yeah, thanks," I said carefully, trying to act sincere without sounding too gung ho.

Sal shrugged as he handed us our receipt. "You know," he said, "I've got my sister who has a son and the father died, you know, and it's hard raising them without that, like, role model, you know, so I go over and teach him stuff, like working on the car and fixing things like that up. I like to do stuff like that."

Mom nodded and blinked. "I'm so sorry to hear about your sister," Mom said. "We appreciate your help very much."

"My dad's at home watching ESPN," I said.

"Oh," Sal said.

"We appreciate your help *very* much," Mom said. Once we'd turned away from the service counter, she hissed, "How *could* you, Vee? Did you think at all about what you were saying?"

"He thought Dad was dead."

"He was trying to help."

"You can't just assume things like that. He was stereotyping. He thought you'd only be in here if we had no man of the house."

"Don't be ridiculous."

A kid toddled in front of us, and his father, a tall guy with sideburns and a Bob Marley T-shirt, came chasing after him. The kid ran for the glass door and began smacking it with an open palm. "Sorry," the dad said. "Sorry about that." He scooped up the kid with one arm and pushed the door open for us with the other. Mom nodded and thanked him. I motioned for him to go first, but he said, "No, we're staying in. Go ahead." And then I

had to thank him and duck through, even though the kid man-
aged to get a whack on my head with his slimy palm.

I caught up with Mom. "He thought you were helpless and
stupid about cars, and you let him think that."

"I let him help," she said. "There's nothing wrong with that,
Vee. I let him help us. He probably looked at me and saw his
sister. He probably took great joy in helping. He was a good man.
Why couldn't you let him do that? You embarrassed me."

"You embarrassed me!" I said, which was kind of an exaggera-
tion, but my words had already blipped out into the world like
an irretrievable text message, and I watched her turn her head
away from me as if I'd slapped it.

"Get in the car," she said. "I'm going to look at sewing
machines, and I certainly don't want to embarrass you any more
than I already have." She tossed me the keys, and I caught them
awkwardly against my chest.

I got inside Fannie and turned on the ignition so I could
turn on the radio. Mom always had things tuned to public radio
stations, so I had to flip through static and Mexican and classi-
cal and more static before finding something remotely decent.
She'd be fine in the fabric store because it'd be full of women
who needed hobbies and needed to feel needed. She could fall
back into a normal momlike role and no one would know that
our family was abnormal, that strangers guessed that parts of
us were dead or missing, and that when they did, we weren't
allowed to correct them.

5

I'd been a clown, a vampire, a pumpkin, Spider-Man, Anakin Skywalker, and a mummy. In eighth grade I was a grave robber, but it was pretty lame—a black ski mask and some dusty clothes—and people thought that I was a ninja. I had to keep saying: "I'm Chinese, you idiots. Ninjas come from Japan."

This year, though, I was a gladiator. And Emily was my Roman mistress. Emily and Madison had gone out midweek to get costumes, and all I'd said was as long as I could have a sword impaled in my chest, it was an okay costume. At least we didn't go with their first idea, which was a geisha and samurai couple. Asian is Asian, huh? Why don't I go as a Vietcong soldier or a starving Korean guy? Emily could be my Thai prostitute.

My gladiator costume did have a plastic sword and scabbard, but it also had a plastic chest plate with molded pecs and washboard abs and a skirt—a *skirt*—that was deliberately tattered. I almost called Emily and canceled right then, as soon as I saw it. But she was picking me up in an hour, and it was my fault for not looking at it sooner. The mask was a rip-off of Russell

Crowe's mask in the movie *Gladiator*. It itched my forehead and chin, but it was freaky looking in a good Halloween kind of way. Plastic spikes came around my cheekbones, covering up a zit I had near my ear, and if I tilted my head down, it was hard to tell who I was. I found an old toy dagger lying around, and I broke it and glued it to my chest plate, the hilt sticking out of my plastic super abs like I'd been mortally wounded. Then I put some fake blood at the base of the dagger. I staggered down the stairs.

"Dad!" I moaned. "Dad, help, HELP!" I collapsed at the base of the stairs, being careful not to land on my impaled dagger or on the sword at my side.

Dad was laughing. He stole my sword off my belt and jabbed and cut the air like Zorro. "It's all fun and games," he said, striking a kung fu pose, "until someone gets a sword through his chest."

The chest plate dug painfully into my belly if I slouched. It hid my hairless chest and soft stomach. I made a bellowing sound like a warrior's yell and pounded lightly on the chest plate. It rattled hollowly, like an empty plastic Coke bottle.

I hoped Emily's costume was cute, not because I liked her or anything, but just so I'd look like I was meant to be with someone, like, *Sorry, ladies, I'm already taken for this evening. Line up and get a number.*

The doorbell rang and I opened the door, and there stood Emily, but she didn't look like herself. Her hair was piled on top of her head, and her makeup was garishly blue and purple around her eyes, to match her plum-colored, floor-length gown with one long sleeve and one bare arm. I poked her bare shoulder with the tip of my plastic sword.

"A lion got your sleeve," I said.

She rolled her eyes and laughed. "I'm not a *gladiator*."

Emily's dad, a tall guy with bushy blond arm hair and a beige Hawaiian shirt, came up the walkway, and the parents did that parent-introduction thing, and then I shook his hand, and Emily shook Dad's hand, and Mom messed everything up by wanting to give Emily a hug. Then she wanted to take pictures, and I insisted that in every picture I should be stabbing the Roman lady as if she were a huge threat to national security. Emily let that happen for a few poses, even playing up looking death-stricken, but then she stole my sword and actually hit me pretty hard on the head with it.

Then we got in the car, and as we were driving to school, I worried that we didn't look like we went together. People were going to think I came up with this outfit idea all on my own. I stared out the window, feeling sick.

The teachers, guarding the door of the gym, had on vampire teeth and Afro wigs, and I wanted to tell them that picking a few random things from the bargain box at the Halloween store didn't make a good costume. But who was I to talk, me with my big plastic pecs.

The girls in line were intimidating. I couldn't recognize them as my classmates. Pixies, nurses, pirates, go-go girls, cheerleaders, Charlie's Angels. They all had costumes that required fishnets and high heels. They giggled and clutched at one another, and I stood quietly next to Emily, not touching her, not laughing and cracking jokes, just wishing I'd never come. I hated Halloween. I hated this dance and the way Madison, who wasn't even here, had dragged me into it, and the girls with all their trussed-up flesh, and the thumping music inside, and the teachers, and Emily, and my stupid plastic chestplate and sword.

I didn't have a ride home for three more hours, though, so I followed Emily into the gaping, dark gym. Strobe lights. Bodies. Unbearable noise and stale, humid air. My mask itched and I sweated under my chestplate. We found a space against the wall. The music was so loud it put everything else on mute. There was nothing to do but watch and sweat and itch.

Emily tugged my arm and screamed something at me. I shook my head and shrugged my shoulders. She left and eventually returned with two tiny plastic cups of punch. I looked around and wondered who was spiking his friends' drinks with a little flask he had somewhere in his costume. This was what the cool kids did, what they'd been doing since sixth grade. The guy in the referee shirt with the Afro, he had a flask. The pimp, too, with a limegreen jacket and no shirt underneath. What did they say when they greeted their teachers? How could they be the same people tonight as they were in daylight, in class, or at home, having dinner with their families?

Emily looked at me and fixed her curls.

I raised my cup a bit. "Good punch," I said. It was watery red Kool-Aid.

"Yeah." She looked into her cup. "Do you want to dance?" she asked.

I took a deep breath. "Okay," I said.

We left our half-full cups on the bleachers. She put her hands on my plastic shoulders, and I put my hands on her velvet waist. She'd used a million bobby pins to get her hair to do what it was doing, and her scalp looked tight and ragged. My impaled dagger kept hitting her, which embarrassed me, so I peeled it off my stomach while avoiding eye contact with her. I didn't want to dance all close to her or anything; I just didn't want to look like an idiot.

Through the strobe lights I saw Mark. He was about twenty feet away, dressed like a gladiator too, but without all the plastic. His chest gleamed like he'd oiled it. My face felt hot. I'd kicked his ass. I'd kicked his ass in PE, yet here I was with awkward Emily, and he was dancing all nasty with some leggy volleyball player. What made him better than me? What did people like about him, or what did he like about himself, that made the difference?

The song ended, and another one started, and I watched Mark get sandwiched by two girls. The one in front of him was dressed like a Playboy Bunny. As she turned around to back her ass up, as the song was directing, I saw who it was. Adele.

She was here.

"Oh," I said. It was like getting punched in the gut.

"Huh?" asked Emily.

Of course she was here, and of course she'd lied to me. She

would never have considered me. How could I be Hugh Hefner, anyway? More like Jet Li's brother in a velvet bathrobe. She and Mark must have set me up to the whole thing. Planted the idea in my head and played me, laughing the whole time. The older boyfriend was just a fat, meaningless lie.

I wanted Adele to see me, to know I was in on it now too. I wanted another go at Mark. I edged Emily closer to Mark's posse. The strobe lights kept blinding me, and I was sure and then unsure, sure and then unsure, that it was Adele grinding herself against him.

I turned my back on them. I still had the broken plastic dagger in my hand. I tossed it behind me, a no-look pass à la Larry Bird, and I swear I heard it slap against Mark's meaty chest. It was only cheap plastic, though, and it couldn't do any permanent damage.

I turned away and tried to keep dancing with Emily but also disappear into the nearest crowd. Emily, not surprisingly, gawked at me in confusion.

"What was that all about?" she said.

"It's just a little inside joke," I said. "Don't worry about it."

Then someone punched me in the back. And punched me again, hard, right under my shoulder blade, my costume biting me.

Mark. The dagger had damaged his pride. His chest gleamed. Wiry hairs sprang from his small, sweaty nipples.

"Wuh, wuh," someone chanted. Emily backed away.

Mark waved the jagged plastic at me. "You little fucker," he said.

"Oh, *there* it is," I said. "Wardrobe malfunction over here." I laughed, but it came out too high pitched. I looked for Adele but couldn't see her. I sounded like a pansy.

"What's your problem?" he said.

I thought: *Where to start?*

I said, "I'm sorry I bruised your ginormous ego, but I didn't mean to throw that at you." Liar. I was a bad liar too. My face flamed with guilt.

Suddenly we were swinging at each other. We both wanted to. He wanted to take my head off. I wanted to knock him to the ground, give him the bloody nose this time. I connected with his shoulder—then his swing connected with my plastic mask. Plastic spikes dug into my cheek.

I crouched on the balls of my feet. He grabbed a corner of my mask and shoved. Plastic scraping on flesh. Scratching, crumpling, punching. I punched at his stupid, bare, sweaty male titties. He grunted and tackled and fell on top of me, cracking my hollow costume down the front, one of my pecs bright and broken, and he picked it up and chucked it at me.

My fist to his jaw. His fist to my shoulder.

I wanted the dagger. The dagger. Stabbing him right through the heart, blood spurting out in joyful, hissing streams. I wanted to kill him and eat him alive. I wanted to put his head on a stake. I was smiling and he didn't know what to do about it. I was smiling and laughing and I got a few good ones in.

His. Mine. Blood. Sweat. Joy.

We connected again and again.

• • •

Chinese monks were praised for their hard, fast fist fighting. Mayan athletes competed in ball games and the losers were slaughtered. Gladiators were expensive slaves, fighting to make others rich. Were we really any different? People circled around us, some football guys pushing gawking nerds back to clear the floor, these jocks acting like kings, like coaches, telling us what to hit next, where to grab, how to hold. Girls clutched their dates, and their dates, like referees, tried to decide who was winning.

I observed all these things—monks, Mayans, football players, kings, girls, gladiators—as I ducked and swung and missed and connected.

And then Coach Wilson was tearing us off each other and hauling us into his office. After the sultrily lit gym, the long, fluorescent bulbs on the low ceiling made us glow like ghosts. Mark was glaringly pasty except for the meandering scratches that ran like veins down his bare chest.

I refused to make eye contact with either of them.

I thought about Adele. Had she seen us? Had she seen me kicking Mark's ass?

I wondered what happened to Emily. She'd disappeared before I'd even thrown one punch.

I thought about my body, how it hurt. How I just wanted to lie down and go to sleep.

I did not think about my parents. I did not think about my parents. I tried not to think about my parents, about how they were going to lose it, about how they would put me under house arrest. About how proud they'd looked as I marched out of the house just a few hours ago, my date on my arm, my sword in the air, Dad laughing and Mom putting her arms around his waist. Had they thought about me while I was gone? Had they worried? They'd worry now. Oh, they'd worry.

"I don't care what you did," Coach Wilson said.

I looked up. He was standing in front of us and directing a pointer finger at each of our chests. I thought about pulling it, though he didn't seem like the kind of guy who would appreciate a fart joke.

I wanted to say: Guess I won. The odds were on him, God's gift to JV sports, and I survived, so I won. Right?

I wanted to say: I don't even know how it happened. It was spontaneous. It was an act of God.

I wanted to say: Please, please, please don't call my parents.

"I don't care what started all this," Coach Wilson said.

Didn't he feel some sense of responsibility? This all started in his PE class. He was the one who first made us fight. We didn't want to touch each other. I wanted to bring this up, but instead I nodded and sat up straight. Why was I so obedient in the face of the littlest bit of authority? It was like the Chinese parts of me rose to the surface whenever I felt threatened. I thought about an experiment I'd seen in a tech museum: You took this powerful rectangular magnet and stuck it in sand mixed with charged metal pieces, the pieces so small and smooth that they were like black sand. The powerful magnet sucked up the black sand, leaving the white sand behind. You could mold the black, mag-netized sand however you wanted, but it always turned back into the brick shape of the magnet whenever you let it go. The force was that powerful. The goody-goodiness in me was like those charged little particles: buried deep until something called to them, then *fwooooop*, all of them to the surface, all of them molding me into this stupid, polite smile and nodding head and prim posture and ass-kissing everything.

I thought: *I know more about China than you can imagine, Dad. I know more about our family than you think. You can't hide it from me. It's buried in me. It might be what's eating me up inside and causing me to act like a maniac.*

"Your parents are coming to take you home, and you'll be facing suspension, depending on what Dean Matthews has to say. I'd sure as hell suspend you."

"But Coach—," Mark said.

"*Don't* you 'but, Coach' me right now."

They sounded like father and son. Hah. Mark would be such a disappointment to him, fighting with someone like me.

Like me. Me. My parents coming to pick me up. I couldn't remember the last time I'd been afraid of them. I felt cold even though my skin burned. Something near my left eye was leak-ing, and I didn't touch it. I didn't want to bring attention to anything that might look like crying.

Coach Wilson handed me a tissue. "You're bleeding," he said, and pointed to my eye.

I could hear Mark breathing. It sounded like he was going to cry. Hah. I could hear everything he wanted to say through the whine of air that came squeezing out of his throat.

Coach Wilson terrified him. He was going to have to face this big, mean man every football and basketball season, and always he was going to be the kid who got into a stupid fight with a nerd. Because it *was* stupid. And also fun in some sick way. And if it weren't for my parents, I'd do it again.

Coach Wilson had no power over me. He'd cut me twice last year, and this year I'd show up as that guy who had fire in him, who wasn't afraid to fight. I'd just improved my odds.

"He started it," I said quickly, before he could cut me off.

"Shut up," Coach Wilson said.

"He did," I said.

Coach Wilson got right up in my face and I could smell his dead-air breath.

"Did you hear me?" he said. "Shut your mouth. I said I didn't care, and I mean it."

I met his eyes and said nothing. My silence made him back off. A little power play going Vee's way. I turned my face into a cold, expressionless mask. Silence had power. No wonder my parents buried their past in it.

Voices from the outer office. Both my parents coming in. They looked so mismatched, Mom with her thick, trimmed blond hair, and Dad already going bald and splotchy. Mom the all-American; Dad the Oriental. Mom the worrywart. Dad the silent observer. Why did they have to get here first? Why couldn't they have a big, chaotic family to distract them from always focusing on me?

I tried to look like a victim. I slouched some and let the blood-dotted tissue float on my open palm. I tightened my neck muscles to get my blood flowing, hopefully to get the blood dripping off me. It'd be great if it could fall onto the floor, too, leaving a little trail as I limped to the car.

Coach Wilson motioned for me to get up.

"Okay, tough guy," he said. The bastard. His sarcasm stung like acid on my sensitive, gaping wounds.

I wanted to say something, to defend myself, but that would look even worse. Must not disrespect teachers, Vee. Must not bring shame. Must not talk back. Make some joke. Laugh. Keep polite.

"Dean Matthews will call you to set up a meeting," he said to my parents.

He walked us to the car, like I was going to try to make a break for it. He even opened the car door for me. I paused and waited for my parents to get in.

I looked at Coach Wilson, I met his eyes, and right before I sank down into the depths of my parents' backseat, I said quietly, for his ears alone, "He started it, and I won."

6

The silence in the car was the silence of outer space or of being buried under tons of wet earth. We were in a vacuum. My parents didn't talk to me. They didn't ask me for my story, and they didn't tell me what was going to happen.

The silence scared me. I worried that I was a loose cannon, that maybe they were afraid of me, the way parents in horror movies watch their possessed children grab bloody knives and head toward them.

I was afraid of myself too, because of how I'd lost awareness of everything—Emily, Adele, the teachers, my own blobby body— and how I'd honestly wanted to kill Mark. Was it people like me who made school lockdown drills necessary? Would we have one on Monday now that everyone knew what I was really like?

When we got home, Mom gave me a box of Band-Aids with a tube of Neosporin and told me to go to bed.

"We'll talk to you tomorrow," she said.

Dad, behind her, nodded.

The Band-Aids were Power Ranger Band-Aids, and I studied

the pictures of the bug-eyed superheroes. I unwrapped Band-Aid after Band-Aid, affixing them to my arm in parallel strips, littering the tiled floor with their little waxy wrappers. I unwrapped more, and pulled down my pants and stuck them on my penis. It didn't hurt much, not even when I tore them off and stuck them back on again. I tried to imagine what could have happened: Adele turning and realizing she'd rather be dancing with me; Adele moving toward me in her little Playboy Bunny outfit. I tried to concentrate on this, but I could hear my parents downstairs, talking about what the hell to do with me. I couldn't keep my mind on anything sexy with my parents' voices as the soundtrack.

I could only hear murmurs in their different pitches, but I could imagine it:

Mom: Why does he want to embarrass us?

Dad: (*Insert lame joke here.*)

Mom: For heaven's sake, Ken. That's not helping.

Dad: Maybe he's taking drugs. I'll talk with him about that.

Mom (*clutching at her heart*): Drugs? Why? Why would he do that?

Dad: I cannot believe we don't know our son anymore.

Mom (*nodding, looking sad*): Mmm. Mmm-hmm.

I wanted to yell downstairs to them: You've NEVER known me! You have no clue what it's like to be me! Do you think I even know?

The next day what they actually said was, "Clearly, you have too much freedom. Too much free time. What are you not doing right at school? Are you getting all A's? You don't think so? You don't *think* so? How can you not know? You don't have your tests? They don't give back essays? What kind of a school is this? I'm going to call your teachers. Don't 'but, Mom' me. Do not 'but, Mom' your mother. It's too late for discussion. Discussions happen before fistfights."

And then they let me talk and pretended to want to know what was *troubling* me, who the other boy was, why we couldn't be friends.

I wanted to say: It's not about Mark. It's about stupid, condescending teachers. It's about this girl I'm obsessed with. It's about my soft belly and my unsoft penis. It's about cliques, and sports, and PE, and stupidity, and my name, and my grandparents, and your silence, and you will never, ever understand what I mean.

"It's just this guy who doesn't like me."

"Why would someone not like you?" Dad asked.

I wanted to laugh. He'd said it like a serious question. How could I begin to explain to them that I wasn't who they thought I was? That I wasn't this nice, popular, all-American guy? That I lurked around the periphery of "normal" and "cool," dangerously close to the "nerd" and "geek" zones, generally pretending like those titles didn't matter? I shrugged. "That's kinda just how it is. No reason."

Then we talked about good ways to resolve conflicts that didn't involve fists, and I felt like I was back in the summer before third grade, watching Dad get into a punching match with another Chinese guy at a barbecue. At first I thought they were fighting over a piece of chicken, and I was about to get up from my plastic chair and offer them mine when Mom's hand snaked out to block my path. Soon after, we left, and we ate cold turkey sandwiches for dinner, and then I got a big lecture about how Dad had been wrong to fight and why. *I* got the lecture. I was too young to know much, but I was smart enough to know that it had something to do with being Chinese. I assumed it had something to do with my family, those people far away who couldn't be talked about. Of course if you wanted to talk about them, you'd have to use your fists. It made perfect sense to me.

In the spirit of open communication, which was number one on Mom's "How to Avoid Fistfights" list, she e-mailed all my teachers and copied me on every one.

For example:

To: mckinley@LUSDCA.edu
Cc: BPsavant06@gmail.com

Dear Mrs. McKinley,

Vee has mentioned so many nice things about your class. We are concerned right now about his progress in Spanish. Please let us know how he has done regarding his grade and his written work. Has he turned in all work? Is his attitude positive and respectful? Does he participate in class? Thank you so much for your time.

Sincerely,
Pam Crawford and Kenny Wong

She sent it out Sunday afternoon. I wanted to pretend I didn't care what my teachers thought about me, or what my parents did, so I didn't even go near my computer until after they'd gone to bed. When the strip of light under their door had been dark for half an hour, I closed my door and turned on my computer and waited and waited for all the updates to stop, then I logged on to e-mail and waded through the Viagra and Rolex deals from GentlemanPharmacy@qzodkx.com and realwinNOW@29wKNfjk.net.

I couldn't believe that my teachers checked and responded to their school e-mails on Sundays, especially long-weekend Sundays. Losers.

Who hits reply all without knowing who "all" really is? Maybe they thought BPsavant06 was Dad. It was the e-mail address I'd made up for myself when I was in sixth grade. I got it from an article I'd read in *World Magazine for Kids*. The article, "B.P. Savants: Archaeologists See the Future," was all about famous archaeologists who knew about the world before the present. I loved the word "savant" because Dad used the phrase "idiot savant" while talking his big philosophy talk. And, in sixth grade at least, I thought I was hot shit. Like I'd grow up to be this incredible thinker, this famous digger, someone whose e-mail everyone would know because my e-mails would get forwarded around like those good luck chain letters. It was an e-mail address fit for a grown-up, it was a name I could grow into, which was why I got to see what my teachers really thought of me.

You should never be able to find out what your teachers think of you.

For example:

To: PamCr@frybergdentistry.com
Cc: BPsavant06@gmail.com

Mr. and Mrs. Crawford-Wong,

Thank you for expressing concerns over Vee's progress in Spanish II. He has regularly been failing our oral examinations. Perhaps think about getting him a tutor, or supervise his study time. Language acquisition works best when a student practices and memorizes vocabulary on a regular basis.

Thank you,
Marianne McKinley

She didn't sound like this in class. I was amazed that she'd written in English. It made me realize even more how much I hated her *I'm talking to you like you're a puppy* voice. I could actually care about Spanish if she'd adopt her e-mail voice in class.

I wondered when Mom would check her e-mail again. Should I tell her first about the orals? Should I get ready to explain what "failing" really meant, that it was a kind of pass/fail that was completely unfair to the person answering the questions? And that I'd always been answering questions, I never got picked to be the asker, and I never got called on even though I raised my hand, and maybe Mrs. McKinley didn't like me, or maybe she thought I was the one making trouble, when it was always people like Mark doing stupid shit and getting away with it?

Then this:

To: PamCr@frybergdentistry.com
Cc: BPsavant06@gmail.com

To Vee's parents:

Thanks for the heads-up on Vee's issues. He really is a great kid, real enthusiastic, but there may be other things going on with him outside of school (e.g., the fight)? He's struggling on quizzes, but his paper about his grandfather was first-rate. If he's struggling, I'm totally willing to help out however I can. My door's always open. Have a great rest of the weekend.

Yours truly,
Neil Riley

Why couldn't he be out on an epic mountain bike adventure? It was a random three-day weekend. Why couldn't he be taking a long vacation, or getting into a scuba-diving or a hang-gliding accident and never coming back to school?

I quickly shut down the computer. I was flunking Spanish. I'd cheated in history. I could get suspended. I thought about breaking the computer or hacking into my parents' e-mail and deleting the messages. Only in my fantasies, though, was I some great computer hacker. In reality I was a stupid fuckup, and there was only one person in the entire world who didn't completely know that yet.

I went downstairs to call Madison.

"Hey!" Her tinny voice was full of pep. "Ohmigod, how was the dance?"

"You haven't talked to Emily?"

"Are you and Emily together? Ohmigod!"

"Ohmigod," I said, "stop saying ohmigod. Adele was there. I saw her."

"At the dance?"

"No, at the zoo."

"So she must have changed her mind. People can do that."

"You're right." She was right. Nothing about Adele had anything to do with me.

"Are you going out with Emily?"

"She was dancing with Mark."

"Emily?"

I sighed a big, breathy, melodramatic sigh into the receiver.

"I'm in deep shit," I said.

"Honestly?"

"Yeah."

"Tell me."

"It's complicated," I said.

"Yeah," she said. "Tell me."

So I told her everything about the dance, the fight, the lecture, the e-mails to teachers.

"At least your parents didn't flat-out kill you," she said.

"Not yet." I peered into the dark dining room and the living room. No parents in sight. I crouched down behind the desk in the den, just to be safe. "Not until they hear from my teachers."

"Why? You're smart."

I couldn't tell her I was flunking Spanish. I couldn't tell her I'd invented my grandfather for the sake of a history paper. School and grandparents were sacred to Madison.

"My teachers all hate me," I said.

"They don't hate you. You're just a wiseass sometimes."

"Me?"

"Very funny." She paused, and the line hummed. "We'll do something," she finally said. "We'll start a rumor. We'll give you an excuse for acting like an idiot."

"A rumor? About what?"

"I don't know yet. Something that'll get Mark and your parents off your back."

It sounded great, but how would I start a rumor? "Okay, Mulan," I said. "I'm with you."

"Of course you are," she said. "I told you you weren't stupid."

7

I wasn't stupid, but Madison was a freaking genius.

Our plan was deceptively simple: Mark was a racist. The rumor that Madison spread by calling Emily and a few other people, who then texted more people, who had Facebook friends that Madison barely knew, was that Mark had called me Nuprin at the dance.

"Nuprin?" I asked Madison when she called me back the next night. "What's that?"

"You've never been called that?" she said. "You know, 'Little, yellow, different.'"

I cracked up so violently that Dad looked up from his wok. I should have answered the phone in the den, but now that I had Dad's attention, it would be awkward just to disappear.

"I think that's more of a joke than an insult," I said.

Dad was still looking at me. I mouthed, "What?" and shrugged at him.

"Obviously you've never been called that by someone who

means it," Madison said. "Anyway, practice looking insulted. Tomorrow's a big day."

The next morning I trudged through PE, avoiding all eye contact with Mark and Coach Wilson, and by the time I walked into history class, I actually did feel like a victim. My lower lip jutted out, practically dripping with my self-invented emotional pain.

Emily came running up to me. "Vee, I'm so sorry about what happened at the dance. I was going to call you, but, you know, is everything okay?"

"Fantastic," I said.

Her smile faded a little, and I felt like a jackass. I could at least be nice. She wasn't the one who'd insulted me. I slumped into my seat. I couldn't look at Adele, who was wearing black today—an odd color choice for her. I couldn't look at Riley, either, whose peppy sympathy I'd never asked for.

At least he wasn't lecturing us again today. He handed back our essays—lots of stars, lots of A pluses, full credit for everyone. I should have known that this was one of those freebie assignments that honors kids needed in order to pad their grades. Get them their required A pluses. After we all congratulated ourselves, we moved on to in-class work. Again. We'd finished with the collapse of Rome and were now in the dim and muddy Middle Ages. Of course, Riley—with his simpleminded approach to world history—only wanted to study wars, so we were focusing on the Crusades. To get us warmed up, he'd handed out a work sheet. It said: "Creative Assignment! Imagine you are on a Crusade. Write a letter home explaining your thoughts and feelings"... blah, blah, blah. What it *really* said was: *I am a shitty teacher who likes to give busywork. I know more about playing with my ding-a-ling than I do about history.*

I was good at reading between the lines.

Riley was talking to someone in the hallway, and a hulking blond kid everyone called Thor leaned over and asked, "What's yours on?"

"I'm going to be that guy who gets wankered his first night out and falls on his sword and dies before he's even left his village."

"Wankered?" Emily turned around. "Did you say 'wankered'? What's that?"

"Wankered. Sloshed. Smashed. Shit-faced. Inebriated."

"Oh," Emily said. "I've never heard 'wankered' before."

"It's a term that was common in the Middle Ages," I said.

Madison snorted.

"Bullshit," Thor said.

I smiled at him and shrugged. "Okay. But I'll be getting the A for effort."

"Your guy can't die his first night out. How's he going to write his letter?" Emily asked.

"Details, details. We'll jump off that bridge when we get to it."

She nodded.

Of course she did.

I decided that my Crusader guy was actually going to be an attendant to a really snobbish, flamboyant English lord. Lord

Stockingstuffer, I'd call him. And my poor guy, called Guy, would be writing home and telling of the hardships of riding his mule so far every day and having to satisfy Lord Stockingstuffer's every whim. Poor Guy got roped into going on the Third Crusade because he couldn't afford the Saladin tax that everyone had to pay. You paid, or you got put in prison or excommunicated. Guy was a modern man and didn't really care about excommunication, but getting excommunicated was like getting cut from the basketball team or getting suspended: It was an embarrassment. It was socially awkward. It sucked; even if he didn't really care, other people made it suck, so he got guilted into going to war. He didn't want to kill infidels. He thought the Muslims, with all their advanced medicine and uncorrupted sense of justice, would make solid friends. He secretly hoped that he'd have a chance to save some Muslim dude, and they could become friends, and their friendship would bring peace to both sides. His dream was like a Disney movie, but he was allowed to dream, and he wrote about it all to his wife, named Antoinette—she was a hot French lady—in this letter.

What would Riley think about my letter? He'd say it wasn't creative enough. Or that it was too creative. He probably just wanted a regurgitation of our history book. I got so frustrated that I couldn't even write a word, even though I had the whole story figured out. Why start something when you know it's going to get torn apart?

Mark and I continued to say nothing to each other. We didn't even look at each other. With my back to him, I smirked. I really did win, if this was how things were going to be from now on. I'd never wanted to be friends with him anyway. I should have beaten him up earlier.

With five minutes left in class I got called to the dean's office. So did Mark. I stood up and stuffed my binder in my backpack and glanced at Adele. She was looking at me. She'd lied and led me on. Even if I meant nothing to her, she probably understood that some of this was her fault. I hoped she felt bad for that.

Everyone watched us leave, and the room started buzzing even before we'd made it to the hall. We walked down opposite sides of the hallway until we were in sight of the polished wooden door that we both had to walk through.

"You threw your fucking sword at me, okay?" he said.

I glanced at him. He was walking in a strip of light, and the air around him looked dusty.

"You're the one who called me Nuprin," I said.

"So what if I did?"

I tripped over my own feet. He didn't seem surprised by the accusation. Madison had made it up, but obviously he liked the idea of having said something like that to me. He was a racist. My pretend hurt turned real, and my insides turned over and around on themselves. I swallowed the spit that seemed to fill up my mouth.

When we got to Mr. Matthews's office, he asked us what had happened. He seemed bored, and we answered "yes" and "no" and "I don't know" like we were making polite conversation. We might as well have grunted in response, or tried to speak like

Neanderthals, with slushy, deep, vowelless voices. He didn't ask about the Nuprin comment, and we didn't bring it up. He didn't ask about PE, and we didn't bring it up. We talked for five minutes, and then he gave us a two-day suspension and reminded us that fighting was wrong.

Mark and I walked back to class, and I thought of all the names I could call him. Jackass. Racist. Cracker. Honky. Homo. Faggot. Asshole. Ass pirate. Ass muncher. Ass monkey. I started cracking myself up. I snorted, and then Mark heard me and started laughing at me, but I was still thinking of things like ass monkey and butt monkey and butt weasel. His laugh that was supposed to be cool and hurtful was even funnier, and eventually he stopped laughing, which made me laugh so hard I was crying.

Then, abruptly, I realized nothing was really funny and I stopped.

"That sucked," I said.

"That did suck," Mark said. "Matthews sucks."

"He's an ass monkey," I said.

Mark laughed. For the first time he wasn't laughing at me. "Yup," he said.

We weren't going to apologize to each other, or hug and kiss and make up, but it felt a little bit like a truce. My fists connecting to his stomach and shoulders was a language he was used to. He understood that I'd said enough was enough and finally I'd really meant it.

8

After school I had to wait for my parents to have their own meeting with Mr. Matthews. I sat in the car with all the windows rolled up and watched them begin to fog with my breath.

Mom and Dad both got in the car, and Dad said, "Buckle up."

Since when did I need a reminder to buckle up?

When we got home, they asked me to sit down with them at the kitchen table and get out my school binders, and then I knew they'd read the e-mails. They leafed through all my sloppy notes, my math tests, my lab reports, my Spanish paragraphs, my history papers. Each binder, with its crackling spine broken open, laid bare more of my shortcomings, my private thoughts, my laziness and averageness and shame. It was anthropology at its worst, like dissection while the specimen's still alive and squirming.

They saw my sketch of Adele's bra on one of my biology handouts.

Mom pulled out a family tree I'd made for Spanish, and she fell silent as she looked at the way *madre* and *padre* grew like a vine into *abuelo* and *prima* and *sobrino*, the words climbing all over the page, people with names like Victor and Bartholomew and Yinyang and Hongwu all connected to me.

"It was okay to be a little creative," I said.

"She gave me an A," I said.

"I wanted to get a good grade." This was true. It was also maybe true that I'd gotten carried away.

They waited for more.

"I wouldn't have gotten a good grade if it had just been the three of us."

Mom's eyes got watery. "It *is* just the three of us, Vee. Honey."

Silence.

They pulled out my history binder and saw the "fuck off" and "yeah, right" I'd written on my notes, my silent dialogue with Mr. Riley. They read, in painstaking silence, my essay. My essay that Riley loved enough to write to my parents about it. I should have written about Neanderthals. I should have turned in nothing and taken the zero.

"I don't know what to say about this," Mom said. "You can't do things like this."

"Mom," I said. I didn't know what to say next. "Did you guys even talk to Mr. Matthews?" I asked. "Did he tell you what Mark called me? That's why I hit him. I didn't want to tell you before. I didn't want to upset you."

"I see," Dad said.

"What did he call you?" Mom asked.

This was the moment I'd been waiting for. Of course Mr. Matthews hadn't told them about Mark's insult, because we hadn't told him. And I couldn't have told them during our hash-it-out session; Madison hadn't invented it yet. But now I had a bombshell, a wild card, that would make them as indignant as I was. I remembered Mark's smug look in the hallway and conjured up my best hurt expression. "Nuprin," I said flatly.

"Nuprin?" Mom said.

"See, everyone thinks I'm Chinese, but I'm not. I'm not really. Eating fried rice doesn't make you Chinese. Having a weird name doesn't make you Chinese. That's why I hit him. I can't talk to you about anything. What was I supposed to do?"

"What's Nuprin?" Mom asked.

"Are you kidding? It's ibuprofin. It's an insult. You know the slogan, 'Little, yellow, different.'"

I looked at Dad. Dad looked at the ceiling, then at me, and then he cracked up completely. Watching him laugh and wipe his eyes made me want to laugh, I felt it bubbling up in my belly and throat, but I coughed and tried to think about the deep shit I was in. I tried to hang on to that hurt part of me that swelled up like a pimple or a bruise when Mark was around. I looked at Mom. She was not laughing. She looked like she'd inhaled a fly.

"What is the problem with being little, yellow, and different?" Dad asked.

"Dad, it's an insult. It's like calling someone the n-word."

He pulled at his ear hair. "No, it is not. This is inventive and doesn't have a combative socioeconomic history. If he calls you Chinaman, or Chink, or coolie, these have more serious connotations. Nuprin is creative. I like it."

"It's meant to be an insult," I said. "It doesn't matter what you think."

"Vee," Mom said, "we live in such a culturally sensitive world that these so-called insults get blown out of proportion. I mean, your father and I have seen much worse." Mom glanced at Dad and folded her hands on top of my essay. "For instance, growing up, we had the corner Chink store. Everyone went there after school to buy homemade doughnuts and bubble gum cigarettes. You couldn't have something like that now. But it never bothered anyone then."

"How do you know?" I asked. "How do you know it never bothered anyone?"

"And when I first started school here," Dad said, "all the time I had people asking me directions to Chinatown."

"That's not an insult," I said. "That's asking for directions."

"There is an assumption. Many people look Chinese but are not FOB, right?"

"Oh, and the Frito Bandito," Mom said. "I don't think you had Fritos in China. Anyway, I remember the Frito Bandito, this cartoon Mexican who would steal your Fritos. We loved him. He was a racial stereotype. But no one was offended. And remember that time after we were married? When we were buying that sofa?" Mom's hands hovered a few inches off my essay, then settled back down. "The salesman said to us something like: 'You're Chinese, right? The cheap stuff's in the back.'"

"We laughed the whole way home." Dad rubbed his eyes and smiled at Mom.

It was like I wasn't even in the room. Was this their idea of the good old days? When everyone was racist and thought that no one cared? Did my parents have no emotions and no common sense? No sympathy?

"So you probably think it's all right to have, like, Aunt Jemima and Uncle Ben's rice," I said. "And . . . and the Washington Redskins. And the Atlanta Braves. That's all okay, huh? Go ahead and insult black people and Native Americans."

Dad stuck his finger in his ear and dug around. "Your skin is thin," he said. "You need to think big picture."

"I can't believe you don't care that some white guy tried to insult my Chineseness."

Dad shrugged. "You decided it was a convenient place to take out your frustrations. If you had laughed, he'd have lost advantage and there'd be no fight and no suspension and no discussion right now."

"So it's my fault," I said.

"This is not about fault. You choose your own actions. You choose your own happiness."

They were choosing to ignore the insult. They didn't know it was made up, but that didn't matter anyway. What good were parents if they didn't defend their kids? If they didn't even try? They might as well be wolf spiders, eating their babies. They might as well kick me out and make me live on the street.

I pointed to my essay, which was under Mom's elbow. "None of this would have happened if I knew my family," I said. "Like, my whole family. Like, grandparents and stuff." I held my breath.

I didn't know what to call them. Grandma and Grandpa? Mr. and Mrs. Wong? Mama and Papa Crawford? Madison called hers Yeye and Nainai, but she knew them. She'd met them. I'd watched movies in her living room, which was filled with portraits of her big, uncontainable family.

Finally silence. I'd crossed the line from joke to no joke, and it was in the exact place I'd always suspected it would be. Not around race or violence or grades or honesty. The line ran directly through our family. It was like I'd slapped my parents in the face—I could see it in their expressions—and I imagined this line like a fault line running in spidery cracks all the way to Texas and China, splitting desert dirt and misty granite peaks with crumbling fissures. Gashes like wounds, and the earth like skin, torn and bleeding. This was what I'd done by crossing the line. I might as well have punched Dad in the nose or taken a knife to Mom's pale, freckled skin.

Dad reached over to touch Mom lightly on the elbow. She jerked back like he'd slapped her, and he smoothly slid my essay out from under her arm. Slowly he picked up my essay and read aloud: "'My grandfather swam to the east bank of the Yangtze and saw Japanese soldiers marching through the boulevards and having stabbing contests on both ancient and innocent civilians, such as grandparents and very young girls.'" He looked up at me. "It's not even good. I know you write better than this," he said. "Why do you choose to write about a man you know nothing about?"

I stared at my binder until it blurred into a fuzzy orange

puddle. "That was the assignment," I said. "I didn't know what else to do." The truth felt like an open wound. "I had to find a story because otherwise I had nothing to write."

Mom put her face in her hands, and Dad's expression collapsed into something naked and soft. This was worse than if they were angry. They loved me. I knew they loved me. And I was lying and inventing in order to protect them and their silence, and they finally understood that their lives were ruining mine.

"I do not know," Dad said slowly. "I honestly do not even know if your grandfather was there."

I held my breath and waited for Dad to say more. I didn't want to scare him away. It was like trying to coax the neighbors' cat, Boomerang, out of the hedges. If you moved too fast, he'd flick his tail and retreat. You had to crouch down and breathe slowly. You had to wait for him to appear before you could put your hand out and remind him you were there.

"We didn't ever talk about the past," he said. "Ever. It was dangerous." He looked at me and put my essay facedown on the table. "I left home because of this fear. I was young, and that meant trouble for everyone. It's impossible for me to live in a place where I cannot say what I mean and know that others are doing the same. And all China was like this during Mao."

"Right," I said. "Of course. The Communist Revolution. The Little Red Book and all that." I wanted to sound like I knew a lot of Chinese history. I did know a lot about things like the Terracotta Army and Peking man because those were fascinating and old. Peking man died seven hundred thousand years ago. The Terracotta Army got buried two hundred years before Jesus was even born. But my grandfather and Dad as a child were from another era too, and I knew almost nothing about their world.

Dad got up from the table and motioned for me to follow him upstairs. When I looked back for Mom, she smiled and shooed me away. She seemed content just sitting at the paper-strewn table. We left her staring at my essay and my wild family tree like she was trying to decode them.

Dad led me to their bedroom, which I hardly ever entered anymore, and it smelled like laundry detergent and drying flowers. My room always smelled like dirty socks.

Dad sat down on his side of the bed and patted the place next to him. He looked small, sitting there with his brown shower slippers just brushing the top of the carpet, sitting there quietly without any jokes or big declarations about humanity or happiness.

The bedside table had a little wooden drawer built into it, and the drawer was open. He pulled out a dingy Ziploc bag. Inside the Ziploc was a silk pouch. The silk pouch was black with tiny red dragons stitched onto it. I put my hand on Dad's shoulder and leaned in to look at it.

Dad stroked the pouch with his thumb. "He used to read so many books. He would say, 'The world belongs to you. China's future belongs to you.' That was right out of Mao's book. But then he would say, 'Your future belongs to you.' That was very subversive. I didn't know how dangerous that was. When I was older, he could not say those things."

He pulled the red cords on the black silk pouch, put his hand inside, and pulled out a carved wooden box the size of his fist. A drawer, a bag, a pouch, a box. What next? It was like those Russian dolls that kept opening and opening until the last one was just some tiny blob of paint.

"What's that?" I asked. I pointed to the lid of the box. A polished Chinese character rose out of the rough, carved wood. Lines from the carving tool radiated away from the symbol in little overlapping trenches. The character looked like a spindly jack-in-the-box.

"*Gu*. It means 'old.' And 'dear.' It is almost like 'mister,' but it shows affection. Nothing is a simple translation."

"Why put it on a box?" I asked.

"My father made it."

It was one of those answers that sounded right but didn't explain anything.

"Why did he give it to you?"

"I didn't know then. And still I'm not sure."

"It wasn't for your birthday or Christmas—I mean, not Christmas, that's stupid—I mean Chinese New Year or something?"

"It was after a very difficult day," he said. "I was ten. It was spring, and we should have been celebrating the Lantern Festival, but it was too traditional, too backward, and the government had forbidden it. I was making a lantern anyway, and my father asked me what I would say if a student activist—that is what we called the Red Guards then—asked me what I was doing.

"'This is just for our table,' he told me to say. 'This is not for a festival.'

"He made me repeat it a few times, and then he left the room. Two minutes later he came storming back in like a thundercloud, kicked the lantern and broke it, and picked me up by the shoulders and shook me so hard."

Dad was holding the wooden box in both his hands, and he kept flipping it over and over, like he was turning over cards in a poker game.

"He shook me again and asked, 'What do you say?' Because I was scared, I had forgotten, and I said nothing, and so he shook me again and again and said, 'What do you say? Tell me, what do you say?' When I began to cry, he stopped the shaking and said, 'Forget everything. Do not go near it again.'

"After he left, I remember learning that our old schoolteacher was being punished—I don't know why, you never knew why—but they marched him down the main street of our village naked, made him walk through ladies' living rooms and the commons and the fish market of my father. I did not go outside, but to hear about it was almost more than I could take. I loved that old man."

"God," I said. This was the kind of story you'd read about in a textbook, if textbooks ever bothered with China, or on the Internet, on some Chinese kid's blog or Facebook page, but now it wasn't someone else's story. It was my dad. It was his teacher.

My hand was still on Dad's shoulder, my knee on the bed now, my weight balanced against his, and I worried that I was leaning too much on him.

"He gave you this box after that?"

"Yes."

He opened the box, and nestled inside was a creased picture of a middle-aged man standing in a small boat, holding a fish and grinning. The man in the picture looked like Dad. He looked vaguely like me.

"My grandfather," I said. I felt dizzy, like I'd been holding my breath.

Dad lifted out the picture and held it up so that the lamplight glowed through it. "He was a good man, a very good man. He was scared, everyone was, and he wanted to protect me. I didn't understand that for a long time. I took offense and was angry. And we could not talk. It was a bad time. It was too easy to do unforgivable things."

"But you didn't," I said eagerly.

"I felt mistreated and untrusted. He had always been so . . . what is the word? Understated. Gentle. And from this point on he was not. He couldn't be."

Dad lowered the photograph. He looked at me and wiped his cheeks.

"I believe," he said, "he was trying to save me from seeing that ugliness. I was so frightened by him that when Lao Zhou marched by, with everyone screaming and pretending to support what the students were doing, I did not see it. You always had to look like what you were doing was right. Even later I had to joke with my friends—friends who had loved our teacher too!—about how right it was. Anything that showed sympathy made you the next target. And from that point my father showed no sympathy toward me, no kindness or gentleness, as if keeping me at arm's length would keep us all safe."

He closed the box.

"How do you trust power after that?" he said. "How can you want to grow up and live in that place? So many people have forgotten, or they have forgiven and work their entire lives to make China what they think it should be now. I don't trust it. I don't trust myself. Things do not change so quickly."

"But," I said, "what about the box? He gave it to you. Doesn't that mean something?"

He nodded and kept his eyes on it. "It does," he said. "It's something small to keep the heart warm. It's good not to forget that."

I shifted my weight off him. "You were just a kid. You were just messing around."

"When you're young, you do not always know what you're doing."

"But how could just making a lantern be that unforgivable?"

"Fear isn't logical. I don't blame my father. Maybe I used to, but I have had many years to think about this and understand it. And forgive him."

"Right," I said. I had thought I wanted this heart-to-heart kind of talking, but his emotions were so close to the surface that it was starting to make me uncomfortable. It was okay for Mom to cry, but not him. Guys didn't do that. Dads didn't do that.

I bounced a bit on the bed. "If I ever do anything unforgivable, by mistake I mean, you wouldn't give me the silent treatment forever, would you? You'd forgive me, right? That's what dads do."

He looked at me and smiled, but it was a lips-only smile. His eyes were still sad.

"If I agree to that," he said, "there is an inherent contradiction. I can't forgive what is unforgivable. That is theoretically impossible."

I had said it all wrong. I didn't want him to get all gushy again, but I didn't want a debate, either. Didn't he know what I meant? Couldn't he just say yes? Isn't that what fathers were supposed to do?

"Right," I said, "you're too smart. I almost got you."

Dad took one of my hands and turned it palm up. He placed the photograph in the middle of my open hand. "This is for you," he said, "for you to feel like you know your grandfather, as much as anyone can be known. I've thought about telling you all this for a while now, for a long while."

"No," I said. "No, it's yours. I don't want it." I did want it, but I didn't want him giving it to me just because he felt guilty for having such a screwed-up kid.

"Then hold on to it for me."

I stared at my grandfather's grainy smile. "I can try to do that," I said. My hand quivered, my grandfather's face blurred, and I got up awkwardly.

"I should find somewhere safe to put it, I guess," I said. Dad handed me the box. "This should work," he said.

"Thanks."

"You don't have to thank me. What's mine will someday be all yours anyway."

I rolled my eyes. "A buff guy like you? You're going to live forever." Finally I got a real laugh out of him. I felt my heart rate return to normal, though until that moment I hadn't realized it had been pounding the whole time.

9

Being suspended wasn't so bad, except Mom made me write apology notes to all my teachers. She made me get up like I was going to school, and she laid out six note cards and envelopes.

"Mom, Señora McKinley doesn't know I got in a fight," I argued. I was watching the red coils burn the edges of my toast. "And she doesn't know I don't have a huge family."

"This isn't about her," she said, "and it's not just about the fight."

I jiggled the handle of the toaster, but smoke began floating out of it. "It's not about me, either."

"If you give me lip, you can forget about an iPad. Don't start a fire in here."

I'd been asking for an iPad for months now.

"I don't care about an iPad," I said.

"Well, that's easy, then. Show me the notes when I get home. And clean up the counter."

After she left, I crumbled my charred toast in my fists and let the crumbs trail around the kitchen like little black ants. Then I stomped into the living room and sat on the couch and stared at the dust motes floating through the air around the TV. Then I walked up and down our street dribbling my basketball, but I didn't have enough energy to practice any shots or moves. Eventually I went inside and got out the little carved box that Dad had given me. I studied the photograph of my grandfather. His chin and ears looked like mine. I wondered about his butt, if he had any moles on it, and if he had wide, flat feet. If I ran into him on the street, would I recognize him? Or would he just be some wrinkly old Chinese guy who smelled like sour mushrooms and chicken fat?

The edges of the photograph were soft and framed in white. I brought the picture up to my nose, but it smelled like nothing, like paper. My grandfather might have touched the edges, where my fingers were now. How could Dad not know if he'd fought in the war? How could my grandfather never have told stories of his escape? I suddenly realized that Dad didn't tell stories either. He told jokes and stories about other people, but I didn't know what he'd done as a kid: where he liked to play or what his friends were like or what he was afraid of. It was as if Dad had been born as a seventeen-year-old in San Francisco, and everything in China was stuff that had happened to someone else, someone he didn't know or didn't want to remember.

Mom, too. Mom was the same way, but Texas was a million times closer than China, a million times more difficult to ignore, what with the Dallas Mavericks and Texas Tech and the

Cowboys and the Astros always on ESPN. She didn't have any wars or crazy Communists to chase her away from home. Her parents had to be criminals. Maybe they were in jail. That was why we couldn't see them. They were in jail for murder. Or drug trafficking. Or smuggling illegal immigrants across the border. I came back to the kitchen and cleaned up every crumb of toast I'd thrown around, and I even scrubbed the blackened wok that lay soaking in the sink. Poor Mom. Poor Dad. Poor me.

I felt so sorry for all of us that I even wrote the notes.

Dear [insert teacher name],

I want to apologize for my lackadaisical attitude in your class so far this year. I am truly sorry for being suspended. With your help and patience I am learning to achieve, and I appreciate your support in this endeavor.

Sincerely,
Your student, Vee Crawford-Wong

I had to channel Dad for each one. A peppering of ten-dollar words that made bullshit look like caviar.

Dear Señora McKinley,

I want to apologize for my lackadaisical attitude in your class so far this year. I also want to tell you that my árbol

*genealógico was a bit overzealous. I do not actually have
any aunts or uncles, and only one grandparent that I
sort of just met. I understand if you need to flunk me on
this assignment. I did not treat it professionally and I am
eternally sorry. With your help and patience I am learning
to achieve, and I appreciate your support in this endeavor.*

Sincerely,
Your student, Vee Crawford-Wong

Maybe she wouldn't care that I'd invented a family for
myself. Maybe everyone did, since it was just a big game to get
us to use our vocabulary words.

I wanted to forget about Riley. The note hung over my head
all day, the way a rain cloud will follow a cartoon character
around, constantly pouring on his head while everyone else is
out in the bright sunshine.

"Dear Mr. Riley," I wrote.

After that I stared at the raised gold lines that edged the card.
Then I wrote:

*I want to apologize for my lackadaisical attitude in your
class so far this year. I also want to tell you that my history
paper, the one I wrote about my grandfather in China, is
not quite true. I do have a grandfather in China, but I'm
not sure about anything else except that the government
oppressed him, which was just the way it was back then.*

*I'm not sure why you're so clueless about what's important
in the world, or why you insist on being so nice all the time.
It gets me in all kinds of trouble, especially when it's that
sort of peppy niceness I can't trust. I wish you knew more
about history, too. It's not enough just to be nice. But I will
take some pages from your book and try to do the same,
even though most of the time I feel like I'm going brain-dead
in your class.*

Most sincerely,
Vee Crawford Dash Wong

I wrote this and read it over a few times. Then I folded it up,
went upstairs, and stuck it in my address book, the babyish one
with astronauts floating in deep blue space on the cover, and
stuck that in the bottom drawer of my desk. I felt a lot better.
Until I remembered that I had to write one for real, one that
he would read, one that would get me busted to high heaven,
because of all the things a real historian could do, the worst was
to make stuff up. Historians were slaves to truth. And anthro-
pologists were the best kinds of historians, and I'd turned on
everything I wanted to be, everything I'd admired, just for a stupid grade. How could I admit to that?

I was missing lectures leading up to an essay test, so I went
downstairs and got out my textbook and pretended to study,
with Animal Planet playing in the background. Everyone we
learned about was either white or some sort of predecessor of

the white, Christian world—as if the Stone Age, Bronze Age, and Iron Age were just Greek and Roman stepping stones. As if everyone outside of Europe was still grunting and digging for grubs. As if China, centuries before Jesus started squalling in his crib, hadn't already kicked Europe's ass in technology and art.

I watched a great white bite the back of an elephant seal. A calm British voice announced that people have an irrational fear of getting bitten by a shark.

Maybe, no matter what the essay question, I'd write about Attila the Hun. He was a guy who got a lot done by pretending to be savage. His slitty eyes and round face got him no respect in Rome, but still he had women falling all over him, and he always just took whatever he wanted. Not that his story was in *World Societies, World Histories*. I had to learn real history all on my own.

I stared listlessly at the textbook, which I'd let fall open to a page on the French Revolution. We'd probably get to that in May, at the pace we were going.

Six p.m.

Mom's footsteps on the porch. *MythBusters* blaring in front of me.

I turned the volume down and refocused on the history book.

"Hi," she said. She leaned against the TV stand. She was wearing her scrubs, the ones with teddy bears on them. They looked comfortable, like pajamas, not like what you wore to work all day, but there was a reason she wore them—in case blood or drool or grosser things exploded unexpectedly out of people, the way they did in TV shows.

"How was your day?" she asked.

"Okay." I shrugged.

"Do you want enchiladas for dinner?" she asked.

"Okay."

I wasn't trying to be rude.

She walked over and gave my shoulders a squeeze. "Things will be fine, honey."

I nodded my head and kept my eyes on the jumble of words in front of me.

She scratched the back of my neck. "Your dad and I are worried about you."

I nodded. My throat felt thick. I worried them. I made them old and sad. It made me mad, but mad at myself, which was the worst kind of mad because the problem was always there, like a shadow or a cartoon rain cloud.

That night my parents read the apology notes one by one but never said a word about the missing one for Riley. Either they'd forgotten about him or they'd forgotten about my essay. Or the fact that I had to make up my family history, create it like a Wikipedia collage, had become a dirty family secret too. Why make more shame if you don't have to?

Madison called to tell me that history and math and biology were boring without me, and to remind me that tomorrow was her birthday. "I can't believe you're missing it. I hate you," she said.

"Crap," I said. It made me furious at Mark and Riley and Mr.

Matthews all over again. "You'll get something super fantastic on Thursday."

"Yeah," she said, "like an essay test?"

My second day at home alone I felt blurry and bored. The house seemed too big and bright. In the afternoon I baked Madison a birthday cake. Mom had bought me yellow cake mix and white frosting, and I baked the cake in two separate pans. When it cooled, I spread frosting on one and put the second cake on top. It looked like a cream cheese sandwich.

That night Madison called to tell me what her parents had given her for her birthday.

"A computer?" I guessed.

"Wrong."

"A panda bear," I said. Madison loved panda bears.

She giggled. "You'll never guess," she said.

"Never is a long time," I said.

"Oh, shut up. A trip to China."

"A what?"

"A trip to China," she said again, "to visit my *yeye*."

Madison's grandfather had emigrated to the U.S., had lived in a huge house in Fremont for forty years, and after his wife died, when Madison was seven, he'd decided to move back to his hilly hometown near Beijing. They were going to go at Christmas and stay at his house for two weeks and play mahjong and go see the Great Wall and visit gaggles of second cousins twice removed, strangers really, but suddenly family if she could meet them with her *yeye* by her side. She talked so fast I could barely keep up with it all, and a few times I wondered if she was babbling in Chinese.

When she paused for a breath, I said, "I think you're near some digs, too." She'd told me before that her grandfather drank ground-up dragon bones—actually the fossils of woolly mammoths and three-toed horses and ancient rhinos—for the cancer in his kidney or his pancreas, or maybe his liver. This would put him near a Paleolithic site.

"Digs?" she said.

"Hello?" I said. "Burins? Disc cores?"

"Hello?" she said. "In English, please?"

"Stoooone tooools," I said. "Flints and arrowheads. Ancient weapons for killing giant pandas."

"Vee!" Madison said.

"Kidding," I said, "sort of. I'll do some research for you. I don't want you getting bored."

"I won't get bored."

"Playing mahjong all day? Yawn."

"I won't get bored. It's not about mahjong."

I understood this. It was about a grandfather who actually lived in China, whose kidneys or pancreas or liver was failing him, and it was about the exotic adventure to visit him before he went the way of the woolly mammoth. This grandfather sent boxes of candies and money wrapped in red paper for Chinese New Year. He was more exciting than her other grandparents, even though they lived in San Francisco, in the middle of Chinatown. I had always pictured Chinatown as exotic and touristy and not somewhere people actually cooked and slept and studied. Madison went there all the time, for moon festivals and ghost festivals and boat races, and once, when she was seven, for her aunt's funeral. She told me about the burning incense and the prayer money, an old uncle who recited all night, and oranges and candy that sat on the grave and then got passed around and eaten. She was a good storyteller, though I couldn't tell if she had a knack for remembering or a knack for embellishing to make herself sound sophisticated and cultural.

"China, schmina," I said over the phone.

"Like you're not jealous," she said.

I didn't want to go to modern China. I had no *yeye* waiting for me, and I couldn't get excited about mahjong and incense. If I could go to China, I'd go back in time to a China where I could be the badass guy who knew all about the earth's axis and the rotation of the planets. I could be the adviser to the emperor, and day after day I'd tirelessly track the heavens and record them on bones and stones and tortoise shells. I'd whisper into the emperor's ear about the next solar eclipse. I'd tell him a story about a dragon devouring the sun and plunging us into midday darkness. He'd shower me with titles of nobility and red-lipped concubines, and of course if I ever got an eclipse or meteor shower wrong, he'd chop off my head. It was just how the world worked back then. The rules were clearer. You knew what you were getting into.

"You totally wish you were me," Madison said, "but you don't have to admit it."

"I admit it," I said. "I wish I could be you for the essay test tomorrow."

"Ugh," she said, and then we said our good-byes and hung up to study on our own about hulking white people who came from places that meant absolutely nothing to either one of us.

10

I wrote about feudalism, which was the most boring and straightforward topic the textbook had hammered on—and therefore, I figured, what Mr. Riley had droned on about during my absence. I kept the foil-covered cake under my desk until the essay test was over. As we walked to our third-period classes, I presented it to Madison.

"Voilà," I said.

Emily oohed and aahed.

Madison beamed and clapped her hands. "Yay!" she said. "But why'd you put the frosting in the middle?"

"It's a Twinkie."

"A what?"

"You know, like Nuprin, but different. A Twinkie—"

"Isn't that what Mark called you?" Emily asked. "Wow, that's harsh."

"Emily," I said, "it's not harsh. It's funny."

Madison held it out until I took it back. She took a few steps backward. "I know what a Twinkie is," she said.

"What did I do?" I asked her.

"Nothing."

She was walking fast, and I had to hold the cake and dodge oncoming traffic.

"You didn't get it, huh?" I asked. "It's supposed to be a joke."

"A joke?" She stopped and turned so suddenly that her thick ponytail whipped around into her face. "Just because I was born here, and my parents were born here, that does not make me a Twinkie."

"But you—"

"I don't care that you think I'm whitewashed. I mean, you should be the one to talk. But I'm not . . ." And here she wadded up her list of French verbs and threw it right into my chest. It bounced off my sweatshirt like I was wearing my gladiator plates again. "I'm not different on the outside than I am on the inside. I'm not. Maybe you are. But I'm not."

"But it was a simile thing!" I said. "*Comparing* you! I never said you *were* a Twinkie!"

But her back was already toward me. Everything was going wrong.

"Good one," Emily said, and swung her backpack around like a weapon.

"What did I do?" I asked her. On principle, I tried to avoid asking Emily for help, but I was desperate.

"You called her a Twinkie," she said.

"I know I called her a Twinkie. It was supposed to be a joke." I couldn't tell Emily that Madison had invented the Nuprin rumor, that I thought I'd been cleverly escalating the inside joke.

She looked over her shoulder as she walked away from me. "Don't you think everyone who says stuff like that thinks it's just a joke?" Her remark lost some of its bite as she ran into the football player in front of her. She giggled and called out, "Sorry! My bad!"

"Can you tell her I'm sorry?" I asked.

"Tell her yourself, Twinkie man."

I ate lunch alone and contemplated Madison's sudden loss of a sense of humor. She worried about being whitewashed. She wanted to be authentically Chinese. Chinese-from-China Chinese. She wanted a label. She wanted to be vanilla pudding or scrambled eggs or lemon squares. Yellow on the outside and yellow on the inside. It was probably because she got letters and packages from people over there. She knew for sure that her DNA was more than a string of letters climbing up a twisted ladder. It meant something. It connected her to people, a pair of people, then two more pairs, and then branching out and out until it connected her to a whole town and valley and continent. China was her family. All 1.3 billion strong.

It made me lonely. All afternoon I imagined Madison flying to China and getting off the plane and a giant, surging crowd of people picking her up and carrying her over their heads. They'd toss her in the air and absorb her fall. They'd slaughter bulls and suckling pigs in honor of all their common ancestors, and they'd crown her Miss Chinese Culture and I'd never see her again.

Dad picked me up after school. The car shuddered away from the curb. Our Honda Civic. Our Japanese car. Some kind of Chinese we were. The shameless kind. Dad wanted to be American, which meant trying to be a little bit of everything, which really meant that we were nothing. We connected with no one and belonged to nothing, forever suspended in a cultural no-man's-land. We were like those kids of average intelligence who got all Bs, belonged to no clubs, played no sports, and whose names teachers were always mixing up and forgetting.

Dad chose to be forgotten. He'd jumped ship on his family and continent and DNA. He'd made a choice for himself, and all along I'd been thinking he'd chosen for me, too.

"I want to call my grandparents," I said.

Dad stopped tapping on the steering wheel. His hand went to the knot of his tie. "You will have to ask your mother," he said.

"Not them. I mean your parents. The ones in China."

Dad put on his blinker and carefully made a turn.

"Or I can e-mail them," I said.

"E-mail? They don't have computers. Maybe even no telephones."

Of course. How stupid. "How about a letter?" I asked.

"What do you want to say to them all of a sudden?" Dad drummed his fingers on the steering wheel.

"I don't know. Anything."

"I left. When I left, I became dead to them."

"Seriously?" I said. Being dead to someone was worse than

being hated. It was nothingness. It meant being utterly, permanently forgotten.

"It is a serious insult to be the only son and leave your parents because of something you want, some ideal of freedom. And to not promise, even if you don't mean it, to come back."

"They didn't want you to be happy?" I said.

Silence.

"You're joking," I said.

"I do not joke about family," he said.

I thought about the Crawford Christmas card we got every year. From my room or the top of the stairs I would hear Dad reading it aloud in a falsely dramatic voice. Mom would laugh until she started crying. The card always had something religious in it, and Dad would read the scripture like it was some kind of punch line. No jokes about family? That's all we did. That's the only way we knew how to talk about these people who were dead to us, or who acted like we were dead. And there were different levels of jokes. Humor, like dirt, had layers. Jokes about the Crawfords were dark and muddy. Jokes about fried rice were like topsoil, like dust. Jokes about the Wongs didn't exist, or they used to exist but had gone extinct, or they would exist only after I wrote them a letter.

Dad was quiet, probably hoping I'd give it up. I stared out at the rows of glistening cars crawling toward the stoplight.

"They don't know about me, do they, Dad?"

A passing shower sprinkled the window with little, sparkling drops.

"They do not," he finally said.

"They should know about me," I said. "They'd like me if they knew me." They'd send me boxes of candy on Chinese New Year. They'd want me to visit them. I could sit in their cozy hut and watch the muddy Yangtze swirl past outside. We could visit places like the Great Wall and Dragon Bone Hill, and I could explain all about oracle bones and underneath those, three quarters of a million years earlier, the bones of Peking man and other *Homo erectus*. Our ancestors. Everyone's ancestors.

"Do you have their address?" I asked. "I could write a nice letter. Madison said she'd translate for me."

This was a lie, but Madison had been going to Chinese school her whole life. She spoke Mandarin at home. And she was my friend. Maybe. Maybe after today she wasn't. Even if we weren't friends, I could probably get her to do me a favor if it had to do with China. I could kiss China's ass, and that would charm the frilly pink socks off of her.

When we got home, I flopped on the couch and Dad wandered room to room. After a few minutes he appeared in the doorway and said, "You are my son." He'd taken off his tie and was now wrapping it around and around his hand like a tourniquet. "If you really want this, I don't think it will go anywhere, but I'll translate for you."

I thought about the man in the photograph, the proud man in the boat with the squiggling fish, getting a letter from America and his grandson. How could he not be happy to hear from me? How could he think about rejecting me? I scrambled to get a pen, envelope, and paper, then I sat at the kitchen table and fiddled with the pen until Dad came back downstairs wearing his old jeans and faded slippers and looking more like a grandfather than an eye doctor.

He pointed to the envelope. "They translate at the border, so just write in English. Okay. Ready? Zero, six, six, zero, zero, zero."

"What the heck is that?" I asked.

"The zip code."

"What about their names? You're going backward."

"This is the Chinese way. Maybe this is forward and you have been doing it backward your whole life."

I nodded. I really didn't know anything about China. I wrote quickly, but Dad was taking his time, and it made me crazy. I was ravenous; I wanted to ask my grandparents everything; I wanted to know everything; I didn't have time for envelopes. I wanted to exhume my ancestors and make a museum display of their old jade platters and ceramic cups, their shells and bones and fabrics, the diary of their lives. I wanted my hands in the dirt, digging.

"Next line, Hebei Province."

"How do you spell that?" I asked.

"H-e-b—"

"Wait," I said, "Dad, wait. Hebei Province? What happened to Yangzhou? You know, Yangzhou fried rice? Where's Hebei?"

He smiled like we were sharing an inside joke. "My passport says I am from Yangzhou, so I am from Yangzhou."

"Not a fun riddle, Dad."

"It was a better decision that I come from a place more to the south. Hebei is north and near Beijing, which is a political place, which is no good."

When he got stressed, his English fell apart.

"So we're not from Yangzhou?"

"My parents are not from Yangzhou."

I slapped my forehead with the envelope. "Dad, you can't just make up where you're from!"

"Sometimes you can. Sometimes there is a need for it."

It was no wonder he hadn't gotten mad at me for my invented history paper. History, to him, could be invented. Passports, birth certificates, names, tax records, memories, life stories, how far did the malleability go?

"Okay," I said. I didn't want to argue. I didn't want him to change his mind about writing this letter, even though I couldn't even trust that I had grandparents anymore, that they were actually Chinese, that they lived in a real place and were doing something real this very second—sleeping on cots in a mud hut, or fishing in a river, or eating small, spicy dishes with their fingers while kneeling at a dimly lit table.

"China, Hebei Province," I wrote, "Yihuangkou Town, Lulong Road West 10005, Wong An-wen Xiansheng."

"Now you put our address, the same way, on the lower right. It does not have to be so big."

Maybe we could be from somewhere more exotic than Liverton. Maybe I could put San Francisco or Hollywood or

Niagara Falls. I didn't, though. Dad was watching. I put: "The Wongs, 12 Meadow Street, Liverton, CA 94500." Then I gave the pen to Dad, and he slid the paper in front of him.

"Dear Grandma and Grandpa," I said.

"It is better to write more traditional."

"What does that mean?"

"Start with 'Mr. and Mrs. Wong.'"

He scratched out a few characters. I'd seen him write in Chinese before—grocery lists or little sticky-note reminders to himself. When I was little, I used to imagine that they were secret notes that would lead to a treasure. I used to collect them and restick them in secret places—on the chairs in the dining room or under the toilet seat lid.

But this was different. This was no scavenger hunt. He was taking my words and turning them into characters, pictures my grandparents could understand.

"How do you say it?" I asked.

He said something that sounded like a song. It was a rushed song, like he was pushing to get to the chorus, and full of staccato notes, like he'd taken a violin bow and was skipping over the strings.

"Which one's the 'Wong'?" I asked.

He pointed to a character that looked like a playground set. "This one, sort of," he said.

"How are you going to do my name?" I asked. "Have you put my name yet?"

"Not yet. First I am giving you an introduction."

"What does that mean?" I was leaning over his shoulder, breathing in the sunlit smell of laundry detergent and lemony furniture polish.

"They should know who you are before we give them your name."

"Why?"

"I have to write your name in pinyin."

"*Why?*"

He paused to finish a character. "Your name has no translation."

"What do you mean? You can't even make it a character?" I asked.

"No," he said. "There is no *v* sound."

I didn't even exist in Chinese.

"Why'd you do that to me?"

"It was a conscious choice. We wanted to unburden you from the commitment to artificial meaning that comes with a family name."

"In English, Dad."

"That is English."

"I don't get it."

"For example, my name, Ken-zhi, means 'earnest,' yes? So I go through life with earnestness, living up to my name. And maybe earnestness is against my nature, maybe I'm not earth. Maybe I'm fire. I do not choose my name, and it should not choose me."

"My middle name is Ken-zhi too."

"You make it mean what you want," he said.

"But, Dad," I said, "of course I'm going to be like you."

Out of everyone in the world, he was the person most like me. I knew I had Mom's DNA in me too, but he was a guy, and he was goofy and Chinese. And I didn't understand Mom and what all her niceness meant, and I was afraid of upsetting her if I tried to find out.

"It's imprinting," I told Dad. "You're the first thing I saw after I was born, and now I can't help following you around."

He laughed, his teeth and gums exposed by his recessed lips.

"I should have brought Jackie Chan to the hospital with me. I knew this," he said.

"Jackie Chan! What about Harrison Ford? Or Sean Connery?"

"Not enough Nuprin." He cracked himself up again.

"We saw a video in biology where this duck imprinted on a human. Anything's possible."

"Exactly," he said. His pen hovered over the paper. Rain began dripping off the gutters outside the window. "Anything is possible. Back to my first point. You have a name with no translation, so you are one hundred percent original."

"Dad, you'd make a horrible debater."

"Why?"

"Just because."

"Good. It's one more thing you did that you never learned from me."

"Dad?"

"What?"

"I sucked at debate too."

"Oh."

He shrugged and turned back to the letter. I watched him write. I gave him lines when he asked for them. "I am fifteen and like to read archaeology magazines and watch movies with my friends. I would someday like to visit China and meet you." Every few characters he'd pause for a long time and stare out the window, and I was afraid to interrupt. Like maybe he'd throw down the pen and say, Forget it, they won't read it, forget it, just forget about it. I imagined him imagining his parents getting the letter and reading it. They'd think about him, of course, because I was out of their realm of imagination. I would be a mini Kenzhi. I would be his spitting image. Accepting me meant accepting him, and if he was dead to them, what would they do? They could reject me, too. I felt the pain of it even as I watched him work on my words.

He took so many pauses that I wondered if he was making it all up.

Maybe the letter read: Greetings, Mr. and Mrs. Wong: I am honored to humbly present to you in my most earnest fashion a grateful young boy by the name ¿#*!&%! who desires to know all about you.

Maybe the letter read: Greetings Mister and Missus Wong. I regret to inform you that you have a grandchild. You somehow have a half-white grandson, ¿#*!&%!, even though your son is dead to you.

I was nervous. Nervous for Dad the way I was usually nervous for Mom and her wild sadness about her own family in Texas. I didn't want him to become an old man who cried a lot. I didn't want him to get rejected by his family all over again because of me.

I almost wished I could go back to the silence, back to when we never talked about grandparents, back when my family tree was a lonely little triangle, back to when I could imagine the horrors of my parents' childhoods and then dismiss them as products of a lonely, overactive imagination.

I *almost* wished all this.

He put down the pen and stretched his hands toward the ceiling. He picked up the paper and read my letter to me, translating as I followed his pointer finger character to character along the page. What he was saying didn't sound like me. It was worse than my history paper. It sounded like him, like Dad, like Ken-zhi, all earnest and full of philosophy, all full of apology and sadness. It was his letter, not mine. Maybe everything I felt and wanted to say couldn't be put into characters, couldn't be translated.

The letter was a jumble of black lines—all except for my name, which he'd written in English. I realized that my grandparents would see the opposite—the characters would all make sense to them, and my name would just be a pile of sticks, strange and useless and impossible to say.

11

I had grandparents now, and a letter going out to them, and the real place in China where my father was from. The apology letters to my teachers felt like footnotes, like captions to something that didn't need excusing or explaining. My history paper felt like a joke, and I knew my parents wouldn't give Riley the punch line. How I'd taken my grandfather's life right off www. chinawarblogviews.com. How this was our Wong family history: a history of secrets and invention.

History *was* invention—wasn't that Riley's whole point of "the story in history"?

Riley was writing on the whiteboard at the front of the room. He was drawing something, maybe a map, maybe amoebas or some kind of note-taking exercise. Emily tapped me on the shoulder to ask if Saladin captured Jerusalem in the Second or the Third Crusade. We weren't having a test; we'd just had a test; she just got nervous about not knowing things.

"Actually, it was the Seventeenth," I said.

"The Seventeenth!" She started flipping through her book.

"That was the most important crusade. I can't believe you don't remember it."

She looked at me as if I'd hurt her feelings.

"Okay, just kidding," I said. "I don't know."

"God, Vee," she said. "You always do that."

"Embellishing," I said, "that's all it is. I'm making history more interesting."

I knew Madison had heard me—she was sitting just on the other side of Emily—but she didn't laugh. She didn't even roll her eyes. We hadn't talked since last week when I delivered the Twinkie cake. It was her problem if she couldn't take a joke. She could choose her own damn happiness, as Dad would say.

I thought about my letter speeding across the Pacific in the belly of a gigantic plane. I thought about my grandparents standing in front of their hut, waving to the mailman as he biked by in his wide straw hat. I had other things going on. I didn't need Madison and her racial sensitivities.

I turned my head to watch Mark White saunter into the room thirty seconds before the bell. His hair was slicked back from PE, where we'd had to run in the rain. I felt completely indifferent to him—he was pretty much dead to me—and then he stopped at Riley's desk, above Adele, who was wearing low-riding Liverton Lions sweatpants and a tight, black, scoop-necked sweater.

"You ready for basketball?" he asked her. He was probably getting a great bird's-eye view of her cleavage.

"Heck yeah," she said.

"Me too," he said. "The hurt starts today. Bring it."

She smiled at him like he'd said something clever.

Basketball. I'd brought my stuff, but I was having last-minute doubts about tryouts. Most of the guys would be coming back for their second season. My wind sprints and pickup games were too slow. And then, of course, there was Mark. And Coach Wilson. And Riley there with his gaggle of girls. I didn't want to see any of them at all, but they were unavoidable. I couldn't quit history. If I made the team, I'd have to deal with Mark and Coach Wilson, but at least I'd be playing basketball. If I didn't make the team, I wouldn't be exempt from PE, and I'd still have to hang out with Coach Wilson while running the mile and playing Wiffle ball and doing other stupid PE stuff. It was sort of a lose-lose, so I could at least try to have fun. And basketball was so much fun. Maybe I'd even get more respect from Riley if he saw me shooting three-pointers every afternoon.

Mark was still lurking over Adele, ogling.

"Sweet," Adele finally said. "Basketball rocks."

Mark laughed. It was the most irritating sound on the planet. I dug my pen into one of the gang signs scrawled on my desk. I should have mentioned basketball to her. But now if I did, I'd be unoriginal, a loser, and Adele would think I was trying to be like Mark.

Riley started class and tried to engage us in laughing at his map of Europe. Hardy-har-har. He wanted us to come up to the board and draw the Crusades. He wanted us to use big, fat colored arrows to represent the movement in Europe, the urge to get down to the Promised Land and fuck some shit up.

Who was going to be the class superstar today? The teacher's pet? All the girls already had their hands up. Adele admired guys who went ape-shit. I could talk basketball with her. I could go ape-shit. I raised my hand to go first. If you went first, you got credit for trying, even though that was the lamest concept ever.

Riley called on me. Woo-hoo. I chose a red marker. I drew a fat line from England, the blobby island in the upper left, to the Middle East.

"Numbah One," I said in my best Chinese-man voice. "Numbah One Crusade."

People laughed. Adele laughed. Good.

Riley nodded and opened his mouth to say something. I grabbed a green pen.

"Numbah Two," I said. I nodded at the class. "Numbah Two Special."

More laughter. Madison was looking down at her desk. Thor started clapping. Mark looked bored. Adele was watching me.

The green line went from Germany and France and down to a spot on the map just up and in from where Riley had put Jerusalem, about where I thought Damascus was. It was a shitty map.

"Okay," Riley said. "Thanks."

But I wasn't done.

Blue. Blue lines flew out of England, France, and Germany, down the coast of the Mediterranean Sea, almost to Jerusalem. Saladin, in bold black, marched in from the right. I wrote "Saladin" above the black streak.

"Saladin capture city," I said. I said it in my Chinese-man voice, so "city" came out sounding like "shitty."

"In Turd Crusade white men no get shitty."

Laughter. This was honors-level humor. Intelligent potty mouth. I gave a stiff little bow and hustled back to my seat. Through my peripheral vision I could see Adele waggling her feet at me. Then Riley cleared his throat and everyone abruptly stopped laughing.

"Interestingly enough," Riley said, "Vee's got most of it right." His voice was carefully even, like he was cool, like he could out-cool me, like this was exactly how he wanted class to go today.

Who cares about any of this? I wanted to scream. *Give us something real to talk about! See me go ape-shit!*

He called on Madison to put dates on my arrows. Madison stood with her back to the class and calmly annotated my map. Next to her neat, bubbly numbers, my lines looked wild and random, like I'd been making it up as I went along, like it was sheer luck I'd done anything right. She even erased one of my lines and drew it more neatly. She didn't make any Chinese-guy jokes, and by the time she was done, Riley was genuinely smiling again. Was that all it took? Was that all everyone wanted: to color inside the lines and make the teacher smile? It made me sick. It made me feel like maybe Madison and I had never really known each other at all.

12

ryouts. Day one. Surrounded by the humid, old-sock smell of the locker room, I doubted myself all over again. Guys pulled on Under Armour shirts and clumped around in their bright Air Jordans and scratched their butts. Most of these guys had played together last year, and then had played football in the fall, and they sat together at lunch, and probably sat together in remedial math, and probably drank beer and hooked up with different girls every weekend. How was I ever going to be friends with any of them? I wished my parents had pushed me to join Little League and Pop Warner football and Jr. NBA. I wished I'd grown up with stories of Dad's walk-off hit or touchdown or slam dunk. Dad was more likely to go on and on about some old lady whose halos he'd corrected, some old lady who wanted to make him the poster child for LASIK surgery.

Most of all, I wished Madison and I were still friends, so that if something horrible did happen this afternoon, at least I'd be able to laugh about it later with her.

I could do this. I could do this. I pulled down my mesh shorts until the waistband of my boxers appeared. All I had to do was show up and work hard. I was big and stubborn. Plus, Mom's family was from Texas, and everyone from Texas had a knack for basketball. It was a cultural fact. Maybe I was just the tiniest bit black. Maybe someone in Mom's family history had crossed the shaky racial divide and inserted some wily, hoops-loving DNA into my bloodstream. I prayed for a bit of racial luck. I'd show Madison I didn't need her nerdy Asian love. I'd have my homeboys.

The orange, overpainted locker room doors spit us out into the gym. We squeaked our way to the middle of the waxy floor, and Coach Wilson said, "Welcome to tryouts, ladies. You've got five days to impress the hell out of me. I'm taking roll. Last name, then first name. For example: Wilson comma Coach." He laughed at himself. Then he glared at us. "Why are you standing around? Line up!" he barked. "And get alphabetical."

Coach Wilson made his way down the line. He had a sarcastic comment for everyone.

"Burge comma Charlie."

"Yes, sir."

"Charlie."

"Yes, sir?"

"Just checking. You go by Charlie?"

"Yes. Yes, Charlie." He said it like he wasn't sure anymore.

"All right. Casey comma Blake."

It was the boy standing next to me.

"Casey." Coach Wilson lowered his clipboard. "Brian's brother. How's he doing?"

"Good. He's good."

"Riding the bench for the Buckeyes now, isn't he?"

"Yes."

"How's his season looking?"

"Real good. He said to say hi."

It was the kind of inane conversation meant for other people to listen in on. His brother hadn't said to say hi. And tryouts were a mere formality, the floor already covered in red carpet, for Blake Casey.

"You." Coach Wilson stared at me. "Wong. Am I right?"

"Um," I said. "Okay."

"Are you stupid, or are you just avoiding your best friend down there at the end of the line?"

I stuck my head out and looked down the line. Mark White. Of course. Everyone laughed.

"Learn your alphabet, Wong," Coach Wilson said, "or you got bigger problems than making the basketball team."

Guys laughed again and shifted around uncomfortably.

The smart thing would have been to berate him for not knowing my name or not knowing how to alphabetize. The smart thing would have been to march off the court with some dignity. Instead I put my head down and dragged my ass to the end of the line.

"Fuckhead," I muttered.

Mark grunted. It sounded like some kind of acknowledgment, which at least was better than a fist in the face or a headlock. Or utter silence, which is the sound you make when someone doesn't even exist.

Mesoamericans had a religious ball game that they used to settle disputes. They played in teams in narrow, stone-walled courts, and the goal was to hit the ball off your hip and make it bounce against the walls and toward your opponent. If you weren't fast enough, or if you were afraid to bump and slide, or if you were weak or tired from long days of farming and fighting, you would lose and be sacrificed to the bloodthirsty gods. Blood was sacred; it connected life to death, and sacrifice to reward. Two men could play a ball game, and one would win and the other would die, and it was such an obvious, effective way to deal with conflict. If you stole someone's cocoa beans, you'd see him on the court. If you wanted to take over a village, you'd have to prove your strength with your hips and a rubber ball. There was no holding anything inside and letting it leak out at inappropriate times. There was no shunning or backstabbing or reneging friendship. Instead of confusion and gossip and hurt feelings, there was just a game.

High school sports should be like that. Kids could decide who they wanted on their team and what they were fighting for. They wouldn't need tryouts or coaches or cheerleaders (though the Mayans weren't against carrying around good-luck figurines). Practices would have purpose. What were we doing wasting all this precious energy? What were we all working so hard for? It was a pointless game.

Except it wasn't totally about the game. There was the sense of belonging. There was the fact that beating someone else was fun. I wanted to outsprint Charlie Burge and outshoot Blake Casey, and I wanted to squeeze that nubby piece of rubber and pivot and dodge by Mark White. I wanted to play Coach Wilson. I wanted a game against Riley. I felt savage and thirsty for blood. I wanted to see someone's lip split open, someone's leg snap in two. I boiled at some volcanic center inside myself. The lava churned and fumes escaped through the tiny holes in my mesh armor. The more it hurt, the more I wanted it to hurt.

My entire body hurt. My skin hurt. My brain hurt. I was on the brink of getting some horrible new debilitating, basketball-induced flu. When Mom asked me how everything was going, I said, "Fantastic." Then I cringed because I sounded mean and sarcastic, like every last high school kid in Liverton.

There were thirteen guys on varsity and eighteen guys trying out for JV. Of the eighteen, two had tried out for varsity and been moved down. Three hadn't played last year. You could tell who we were because we didn't know the drills and the other guys' nicknames. We weren't bad; we just looked lost.

Out of eighteen, there were ten white guys, two black guys, three Mexicans, two undetermined, and one lone Asian, which was me. The white guys shopped at Abercrombie and drove shiny, hulking trucks. The Mexican guys, all wiry and fast, did their drills together like they were in a gang. And the two black guys sauntered when they walked because they knew they'd inherited the right to play basketball and someday make the all-state team. They had ropy muscles in their forearms, and calves that bulged with five different types of calf muscles. I felt sorry for them—that they'd gotten this way because their ancestors had been bred to pick cotton and be human mules. I was also afraid to look at them, in case they wanted to kick my ass.

I was the only Asian. As Madison had pointed out before her skin got all thin, I was "confused looking." Everyone else on the court probably thought: *Go join the debate team. Go do tennis or Ping-Pong or tai chi. Basketball's not for Chinese guys. Forget your Crawford side, your Texas inheritance. Do they even know you exist?* I don't know, I wanted to say. I don't know if they or the Wongs know or even care, and it's like that if-a-tree-falls-in-the-forest question: If a family member is born and no one knows, does he actually exist?

Day four. Jump rope and weighted jump rope, cone hops, T drills, burpees, wind sprints, and suicides. I wanted to make the team. Sweat dribbled down my back, crawling over the mole on my cheek, the cheek down there, and making my crotch damp and my balls itchy.

"Hurry up, ladies!" Wilson screamed at us. "You call that running?"

Bounding and hopping and lateral leaps and change of direction. More heavy rope, T drills, wind sprints, gut busters. I wanted this. I wanted this despite the fact that it hurt. I wanted this because it hurt.

"I'm not gonna make it," I told Dad. "I'm not like everyone else out there."

"You're trying for it, and that should be all that matters," Dad said. He stood at the stove, throwing vegetables into a wok.

"That's not all that matters," I said. I dropped the plates on the table, hoping they would break. They bounced tamely on the blue place mats. I was acting like basketball was the reason I existed.

"It is if you choose it to be," Dad said.

"It's like when people say all that matters is that you're a good person," I argued. "When is that true? When do people reward you just for being a good person?"

He didn't look up from the stove.

"Seriously, Dad. In second grade it was okay just to try. Now it's like making up a big excuse. I *tried* to play basketball. I *tried* being cool and fitting in for once."

I tried being funny, but Madison had missed the point completely. Screw Madison. I was sick of trying, and I certainly wasn't going to apologize. She was the one who started the whole racist-joke thing.

"Pam, dinner!" he called into the den. "Vee, can you get out the salad mix?"

I sighed, loud enough for him to hear. I went and leaned against the fridge.

"Dad, remember Yoda? Yoda said 'Do or do not. There is no try.'"

"Yoda is a sorry caricature of a Buddhist Zen master."

"Oh," I said. "Right. Of course."

"If you don't play basketball," Dad said, "you can concentrate more on your classes. You can't get cut from your classes, can you?"

"Funny," I said. Riley would love to cut me from his class. Coach Wilson, too. Maybe all the teachers felt this way about me, and it was just their job to smile and suffer through.

The girls came in to practice after we did. Sometimes they came in early and lounged around the bleachers and distracted us. The girls who played basketball fell into two distinct categories: princesses and lesbos. The princesses were thin and smooth and gorgeous, and also bitchy. They were the ones who distracted us. The lesbos made me cower; they had wide shoulders, square jaws, solid thighs, and either flat chests or huge breasts. They didn't cut one off to shoot arrows, like the real warriors of Lesbos, but they did mush them into tight sports bras and wide-shouldered tank tops and clothes that didn't quite fit right. They were loud and rude, more like boys, and they squatted on the bleachers and gave one another shoulder rubs before practice.

Adele was there sometimes too, and she was friendly with the lesbos while remaining a bit of a princess. Often she sat a little bit apart from everyone else, like she was holding herself to higher standards. She always seemed to be quietly laughing at everyone, like she knew things that no one else did.

Sometimes after tryouts, while waiting to get picked up, I sat in the bleachers and watched the girls practice. I tried to pretend Riley wasn't there, that it was just me and the girls. He was hard to miss, though. He always wore a faded black Liverton Lions Basketball sweatshirt with COACH emblazoned in orange on the back, as if there was any doubt who the guy was who was striding up and down the floor, blowing his whistle, screaming his head off. He'd occasionally say "hey" to me in passing, like we were buddies off the court or something, but I knew he hated me. He hated how I was a brat in his class, a know-it-all, lying, rude brat. *I* hated how I was in his class, but it was his fault for being so dumb and boring and humorless.

I ignored Riley and watched the girls. I could barely withstand the barrage of pheromones bounding off the polished floor and the awesome girl-sweat slicking their legs and the shirts thrown in a pile and half the girls just in their bouncing neon sports bras. Their breasts pushed against the bright pilled cotton, and sometimes sweat collected in a darker crescent shape underneath. Sometimes one of the girls caught me watching her, and she'd smile, like I hadn't just turned her into a busty sex object. Adele smiled at me occasionally, and I wondered all over again why she'd lied to me about going to the dance, and why she'd danced with Mark, and why—if this was the way she was—she'd ever bothered to help me save face in front of him.

Coach Wilson had nicknames for the kids he liked. Hook, Steel, Q, Patsy, or Saint. He kept calling Blake by his brother's name. And he kept calling me Wong. That wasn't a nickname. Nicknames were cute and gave you a personality. What did Wong say about me? I was ridiculous. I was a joke. He didn't like me. He didn't even know my name.

By Friday, the last day of tryouts, we were so beaten down that even the easy drills felt like gut busters. When we scrimmaged four on four, nobody seemed to be able to make a basket from anywhere. Coach Wilson sat us down and screamed at us for being pussies. He didn't use that exact word; if he had, the lesbos lounging around the gym would have rushed over and torn him apart.

Pussies? they'd say. Then they'd drop-kick him into the bleachers. Who you calling pussies? Dick. Dickie. You're one to talk.

Imagining Coach Wilson in a headlock, squeezed up against a meaty breast, put me in a good mood. When we got back to playing, I made a sweet half-court pass to Mark and then pressed the crap out of Blake for the next five minutes. I imagined that the girls were watching me. In those five minutes the focus of my life shifted and narrowed and brightened. I could do archaeology when I was older, when my hair thinned and my knees got stiff and swollen. Right now I could regurgitate information and get better grades and stop giving a damn about what we were learning. I could stop worrying about Madison and whatever she was thinking about me. I could collect all that wasted energy and focus it on basketball. My chest thudded violently against Blake's shoulder. I could be patient about China and Texas and family stuff that didn't matter anyway, since none of it made a difference in my daily life. Basketball made a difference in my daily life. The girls watched me sprint up and down the court, and Mark whooped when I got down inside the post and drew a foul, and I figured I could even forgive him for being a general jackass, if we were on the same team. When five minutes were up, I sat back down and Coach Wilson said, "Way to work hard, Wong." I wanted to say: I'm just getting started, Coach. But I didn't say anything, because there was no reason to try to make a happy coach happier.

I went back in for another round, and in my first two seconds with the ball, one of the black kids came knocking for it, and it shot out of my hands, and we sprawled onto the court to wrestle for it. His elbow came flying up toward my face and something between my eyes cracked, and my hands flew away from the ball and covered my face.

The game stopped. I wasn't crying, but my eyes stung and spilled over anyway. I couldn't see for all the tearing up I was doing, but that was just some bodily reaction, because I wasn't actually crying.

"Dude," someone said.

"I've still got all my teeth," I announced from behind my hands.

"Let me see." That was Coach Wilson.

I took my hands away, and there was blood everywhere. It made me gag, and then I coughed, which caused more stinging and pseudo crying. I shielded my eyes with my bloody hands.

"Congratulations, you broke your nose," Coach Wilson said.

"He broke my nose," I said, pointing at the black kid.

"Me?" He pointed at himself and acted surprised. "Me? That wasn't me. That was Jamal." He pointed at the other black guy.

"Sorry. I can't really see," I said. I could have sworn it was the one everyone called Q. They looked almost the same, except that one had a wider face than the other.

"At least it wasn't me," Mark said. He laughed, but no one else joined in. He wasn't half as cool as he thought he was.

Someone brought me paper towels, and I held some to my face and wiped the floor with the rest. Someone else brought me ice and a cell phone to call my parents. I called Mom, then Dad, and neither answered.

"Probably in surgery," I said to the guys on the bench. Half the team was already back out on the court. I shrugged like it didn't matter. My gut muscles were shaking, though, as were my hands and legs. What did they do for a broken nose? They couldn't put it in a cast. What if they couldn't get it straightened out? What if I looked even more retarded and rearranged after this?

I sat on the bench for the rest of tryouts, which was probably only ten minutes but felt like ten lifetimes. I didn't want to be a bench sitter. I wanted to be a player. I was a player.

Players took risks and sometimes broke their noses. My bloody jersey felt like a badge, as if I'd just survived some essential rite of passage. In Amazonian tribes boys got their noses pierced as a puberty ritual. In places in the Middle East and Africa they got circumcised. And in gangs like the Bloods, guys had to slice open the cheeks of innocent strangers in order to be initiated. Comparatively, a broken nose felt like a good deal.

Just as soon as I'd talked myself out of my panic, Coach Wilson called everyone over and made nice noises about our hard work. Then he said the team list was posted on the locker room door. "I can't keep all of you," he said, "but I'm proud of all of you." He stared at the wall behind us as he said it, which made the whole touchy-feely aspect of it seem like something he'd practiced in his bathroom mirror.

We sauntered toward the locker room like it didn't matter. Some guys slapped the paper like it was asking for a stinging high five. Some did their end zone dance moves. Those of us who weren't sure hung back and waited until we could be alone with the list.

Mark's name was at the bottom. White, Mark.

That was a good sign. I scanned up the list.

Gonzales. DeWitt. Cross.

I put my finger here to mark where my name should have appeared.

Then Casey, Burge, Brown, Arnett.

I checked again, this time for Wong, but Mark's name was the last name on the list. Had Coach Wilson even given me a chance? Had he even been watching me? Did he even know who I was? I took my hand off the page and left behind bloody whorls, my fingerprints, clustered around the spot where my name was missing. My face throbbed and my eyes stung. I deserved to be on that list.

"Shit," Mark said. "Thank God." Then he looked at me and shrugged. "But I mean, he's still an ass monkey, okay?"

"That's my word," I said. "You can't use it."

He stood awkwardly next to me for a few seconds, and then he pushed through to the locker room. Good. He could take his pathetic pity, his lukewarm sympathy, and shove it up his own monkey ass.

My ice bag was leaking, creating a cold, pink puddle on the gym floor. My face felt hot. I threw the ice bag away and stood in front of the heavy orange doors. Mark was probably forcing everyone in there to give him high fives. Rah, rah, go team, that kind of crap. My nose was on fire. I could hear the ice machine whirring somewhere down the hall, and I followed the warm hum past the janitor's closet and the evil basketball office. Just before the hallway dead-ended into the carpeted team room, I found the storage closet–slash–ice machine room. The door had a brass label like it was some executive's office: ICE MACHINE. I opened the door and found Adele leaning against the open machine and eating little pellets of ice one by one out of the machine's frosty mouth.

"God," she said, "what happened?"

"Nothing," I mumbled. For the first time ever I wasn't excited to see her. "I broke my nose," I said. I felt dizzy, probably from the loss of blood, and I quickly sat down on the cold concrete. Freezing water from the mammoth machine soaked my shorts and boxers.

"You need some ice." She tore a plastic bag off a big roll and scooped up the pellets with her bare hand.

"Hah," I said. "I need more than ice. Way more. I need to do this week all over again. I wouldn't waste my time here. I wouldn't get cut. I need a new life." I was being melodramatic—I could hear the high-pitched whine in my voice—but I couldn't stop. "I need a new school and new teachers that don't suck and new friends." If Dad were here, he would start laughing about now and say: Diarrhea of the mouth, that's what you have. But Dad wasn't here. He and Mom didn't have a clue. "And a new family. I need a new fucking family."

Adele sucked the air out of the ice bag and tied the top in a knot. "God, family. I'm totally there with you. My whole life is, like, shuttling between houses, and my stepmom—I call her Medusa—is crazy and probably bipolar. She tries to force me to babysit her twin brats whenever I'm around. Like I'm slave labor." She handed me the ice bag. I held it close to my nose, but it felt too sharp and cold, so I didn't make contact.

Adele tore off another bag and began filling it. She was in her practice jersey and shorts, and I could see the goose pimples on her legs. "That's when Neil saved my ass this summer. When I wasn't talking to my mom, and then Medusa picked a fight and kicked me out of the house."

"Neil?"

"Yeah," she said, "you know, Neil Riley." It sounded so matter-of-fact, like didn't we all call our teachers by their first names?

"He let me crash on his couch for a week. He's totally cool like that."

Something turned over in my stomach. I wasn't supposed to know stuff like this.

"I know he probably wasn't supposed to, but I was desperate and homeless, and he's such a nice guy. It's like we're friends or even like he's my dad, except I never want him to seriously be like my dad. Have your parents ever kicked you out of your house?"

"Well . . ." I wanted to say yes, but I could never see them doing something like that. We didn't fight. We avoided talking about things that could cause a fight, and when we couldn't avoid those things, we laughed at them.

"Will you wrap this on my knee?" she asked.

I struggled to get up. Water from my wet boxers dripped down my legs.

"I maybe tore my meniscus last year, so I always have to ice." She handed me a roll of plastic wrap. "Do it tight." She propped her leg on the machine. I carefully put a hand under her knee and unrolled the plastic wrap around her leg and the ice bag. "Tighter," she said. I glanced up at her and caught her watching me and half smiling. "Gorgeous," she said. "You could be a student trainer."

"I want to be a basketball player," I said. I was such a whiny brat.

"You are," she said. "No one else can tell you what you can be."

"That sounds nice, but I just got cut. So that's pretty much the end of that."

She lifted her leg off the machine and cupped my cheeks with her palms. They were shockingly cold, but I didn't flinch. We were the same height. We could have been very awkwardly dancing or getting ready to kiss. "I'm so sorry," she said. "I've been completely insensitive. That's horrible. Dickie's a horrible coach. Too bad you can't play for Neil."

"That makes me feel better," I said.

"It's like he doesn't even see his players as real people. He treats you like little kids."

"It's not right," I said.

"You look like hell," she said. Her eyes were focused on my nose.

"Yeah?" I said. I wondered if she was impressed. It felt impressive, a broken nose. Something obvious that couldn't be mistaken for wimpiness and melodrama. "You think I'll survive?" I said.

She laughed and gave me a quick one-arm hug. She smelled like vanilla. I tried to think of something clever to say, something else to make her laugh and stay here with me, but she sauntered away before I could get it together. She had her team out there waiting for her, and a coach who was like a friend or a father. I couldn't compare to any of that.

13

The bruise from my nose spread under each eye in a mottled purple pattern. I'd spent the weekend staring at my face in the mirror, watching the bulging knob of my nose slowly subside and leach puddles of color under my eyes. The doctor had said it was a clean break, and all he did was give me a pack of ice and a handful of ibuprofen.

"And he gets paid for that?" I'd said to Dad.

"It takes a lot of wisdom to make a small decision," he'd said.

"Okay, Yoda. Let's go to In-N-Out."

"A very wise, very simple decision," Dad said.

The nose earned me cooing sympathy from random girls and grudging props from the guys in my PE class. For this first day back at school it was almost as if I'd made the team. Jamal and his thug friends passed by my locker and nodded at me, and Mark didn't sneer when I ended up on his badminton team for PE. No one—not Madison or Emily or Thor—asked me if I'd made the team; they all assumed, with a war wound this ugly and bloody, that I was on the roster.

At the end of a worksheet-filled history class Riley stopped by my desk and asked me to stay behind for a minute. Emily shot me a look that, if it had sound, would have been the *ooh-OOH-ooh* that means "you're busted." Had Riley discovered my cut-and-paste job, my invented family history? I was going to get kicked out of high school. I wondered about the sort of school where they sent truants and flunkees and druggies and "troubled" kids. I doubted there'd be any other Asian kids there.

I slowly packed my backpack and waited for everyone else to leave before standing up and facing Riley. He stood next to his desk, a messy stack of worksheets in one hand. Adele looked like she hadn't moved an inch since the beginning of class. It crossed my mind that she sat in on most of our classes as a sort of payment for sleeping on Riley's couch that week over the summer, even though the whole thing didn't make a lot of sense to me. I thought about how weird it would be to sleep on a teacher's couch. Had she showered there? Had she made herself breakfast? Had Riley ever seen her naked or in her pajamas? Adele seemed like a Victoria's Secret kind of girl—lace and mesh and slick, tanned skin. Who wouldn't want to catch a glimpse of that?

"Buddy," Riley said, snapping me out of my daydream. "I heard you got a tough break in basketball."

Ha. Ha, ha. *Tough break*. I got it.

But then he kept talking, and I wasn't sure he'd even caught his own joke. He asked me if I wanted to help him out.

"Okay," I said. This was obviously the answer he was looking for.

"I need a manager."

I wanted to say: You need a life. Who lets a high school girl sleep on his couch? Thinking of him seeing her seminaked made my insides squirm.

"I think you have potential," he said. "You seem organized and reliable." He paused. I had no idea what sort of expression was on my face, but he smiled, and I wondered if he was feeling sorry for me. The sad sophomore with a broken nose who wasn't good enough for the JV team. Screw him. Adele might need some sort of sugar daddy, but I didn't. I had a completely competent father.

"And I'm sure you know it counts on your transcript like a sport," he said.

"Bye-bye, PE," Adele said. Her feet waggled on the desk. "Bye-bye, Mr. Wilson." She winked at me.

Suddenly it all became clear. The proverbial clouds parted and an imaginary beam of sunlight streamed down on all of us. Adele was saving me. She had convinced Riley to make me manager to help me avoid Mr. Wilson and the unathletic losers who would populate a second-semester PE class. It meant I had to see more of Riley, but at least he knew my name. And I guessed he knew more about basketball than world history, so he wouldn't be so aggravating. And then there was Adele—more time with her, more potential ice room run-ins. So what if I was only a manager? Managers were smart. Managers could even get good scholarships. And most important, managers got time with the team. That whole "love the one you're with" thing. I'd charmed

Adele in the ice room; I could do it again. I immediately forgave her for dancing with Mark. She had, after all, helped me save face with him. Maybe she hadn't wanted to go to the dance, but she didn't have anywhere else to go—not home, not back to Riley's house. It felt daring to feel a little sorry for someone like Adele.

They were waiting for my response. I gave them a weak thumbs-up. At this point, what did I have to lose?

When I got to the gym after school, I waited for all the boys to clear out before heading in. I didn't want anyone thinking I was moping around, hoping for another chance. And I wasn't thrilled at the shift in my image—badass broken-nose guy to clipboard holder.

Inside there were so many girls, so much gleaming girl skin, that I wanted to bolt. I would never fit in, never feel comfortable around all these older girls. It had been stupid to say yes to Riley. The girls were stretching in a circle in the middle of the floor and for each stretch counting to ten in high-pitched unison. Riley saw me lurking in the shadows by the door, and he waved me over.

"I'm sure you guys know Vee," Riley said. "He's our manager now."

Now. Now that I wasn't a player anymore.

"Nice schnoz," Steffie said. Steffie was cocaptains with Adele and was also queen of the lesbos. She was built like a brick wall. "Did ya get it from b-ball?"

I nodded. Steffie was loud and brash and scary. I knew

instinctively that saying nothing was the best way to stay out of trouble around her.

"The manager?" Dad said that night. "Do you get to play?"

"On the girls' team? That'd be a little strange."

"I think it's wonderful," Mom said. "You could make some new friends." Of course she'd noticed how Madison was never around anymore. And of course, being Mom, she hadn't said anything.

Eventually, Riley did let me do more than stand around and sulk. He explained the details on the stat sheet, how to fill out the boxes from the rosters, and how to read the clock, the time-outs, the ejections, the score.

"You're our first line of defense if we disagree with the numbers up there," he said.

The first line of defense. It sounded like an advertisement. *Vitamin Vee. A hundred percent of your daily allowance of Vee.* Didn't Riley know what always happened to the first line of defense? It was the first thing to get mowed down. *Kamikaze Vee.*

"These boxes are really small, so try to be neat," he said.

Try to be neat? I'm Chinese, you retard. I can torque my body and fit into a box the size of your open palm. I can write the history of the world on a grain of rice.

Halfway through every practice I went back to the ice machine room and filled fat green bottles with ice and water from the tap.

I carried them back into the gym, and the girls fell on them like they were chocolate-covered manna from heaven.

Adele took one of the bottles and sucked on it. She smiled at me while keeping the white plastic piece between her teeth. I'd been on the job three days and hadn't fucked up yet. She had chosen me, and I had been a good choice.

"Aahh," she said. She dribbled water on her forehead and wiped it off with her sleeve. "You are a god, Vee."

"So I've heard," I said.

I waited for her, for anyone, to laugh, but no one seemed to hear me. It was a stupid, self-important thing for a manager to say. My cheeks got hot.

Steffie rolled her head side to side. I could hear her neck crack from ten feet away.

"Nasty, Steffie," one of the lesbos said.

"You're nasty," Steffie said.

"Damn straight."

"Straight, my ass."

They both laughed. I gave a nervous chuckle.

Steffie looked at me. "What?" she asked me. Her face was totally serious.

The world went hazy with my panic.

"What?" she said again, then she cracked a smile and swung an easy, arcing punch through the air in front of her. "Heh," she said, "I'm just raggin' on ya." She walked over, crouched down, and gently put her shoulder into my gut. "A little hazing for our favorite manager."

I was their only manager.

"She'll buy you out for padding her free throw stats," Caitlyn said. She was a princess, pink sports bra and all. She might as well have lined it with rhinestones.

"I'll eat you out and you'll love it," Steffie said.

That shut Caitlyn up.

Steffie didn't think before she spoke, but she never apologized for what came out. She scared me, but I was starting to like her. I wanted the thrill of her attention, which felt like a blazing spotlight. And she and Adele were captains and best friends, so the more I was in Steffie's spotlight, the closer I was to Adele.

When Riley coached, he paced and threw his hands up and pumped his fist in the air and yelled. He yelled constantly, but it was different from Coach Wilson's drill-sergeant-slash-PE-god voice. Instead of commanding, he badgered and teased the girls. He always seemed on the verge of giving up on them.

"Can you please turn your back into it?" he yelled.

"When are we going to get moving?"

"Go, go, go! You call that moving?"

"Val, get a clue! It's called awareness!"

"For God's sake, Steffie, watch the elbows!"

"What the hell was that, Caitlyn?"

"What are you doing? What were you thinking?"

The gym echoed, and his voice seemed to come from every direction. At least here he had real passion, real balls, not just the caffeine-induced pep he had while playing teacher. I wished that in history class he could just take off his silly teacher mask and be himself every once in a while. He was stupid for thinking we didn't all see right through him. At least seeing him every day on the basketball court, I was starting to sense there was something genuine underneath.

Sometimes I did mess up. I'd be watching Adele's thighs and the way she hiked her mesh shorts up when she went into a crouch, and suddenly Riley would storm over to me and chew me out in front of the girls.

For example: "I called your name twenty times! For God's sake! We're scrimmaging in five! I want you on the clock! What do you think you're doing out here?"

Then, while the girls were scrimmaging at the end of practice, Riley blew the whistle extra hard and all the girls stopped moving. I panicked as I checked the clock and the stat sheet. What had I done wrong?

"Foul!" he yelled. "Goddamnit, why foul?" He was yelling at Lily Park.

I put a pencil mark at the intersection of Lily Park and the personal foul column. Lily didn't look like a lily. She was half Korean and half ugly. Fugly.

Someone tossed Adele the ball, and she toed up on the free throw line.

"Riles, that was totally clean," Lily protested. "All ball. You didn't even see it."

"Don't mouth off to me," Riley said. "It won't get you any-where."

She mumbled something under her breath.

"What?" he asked.

"Nothing." She glared at him from under her straight black bangs.

"I'm waiting."

"I said, don't make up fouls just so other people can practice their free throws!"

He took a threatening step closer to her. "Nice mouth, Park. Get outside and run a mile. Come back when you're smarter."

Friday after practice, I sat on the cold concrete steps outside the gym to wait for Mom. The girls filtered out a few at a time. Some waved. Some ignored me. Everyone was edgy. Riley had less than two weeks to get the girls ready for their first game, and he was using that as an excuse to rip into everyone.

"Whaddup, Vee." Steffie clumped down the steps. "Ya need a ride?"

"Nah." I shrugged. "I'm getting kinda attached to this piece of concrete."

She sat down next to me. "I need a new ride. Girls are such ditzes," she said.

"Oh. Uh-huh," I said because I thought that was the right answer. Compared with Steffie, most girls were ditzes. Steffie was like an anti-Barbie: flat chested, big footed, loudmouthed, and not at all attracted to Ken.

"First of all, they don't listen to Coach. They don't genuinely listen, which is why we still suck."

I nodded.

"And then he thinks that gives him license to insult us, to treat us like bimbos. We're not bimbos."

"No, you're not."

"And Adele doesn't want to talk to him, to tell him to cool it. We need to work together. Maybe she doesn't get reamed because she's his superstar, but she's supposed to look out for the team, don't you think?"

"Yes indeed," I said. I was like the chorus in a gospel choir. Maybe next I'd bust out with *Praise the Lord!* Or *Jesus, amen!*

"I'm about ready to go without Adele and tell him to cool the ego trip and keep his big swinging dick in his pants. He knows he can't push me around."

I wanted to say: Maybe he's just trying to be motivational. Instead I shook my head. "Not you," I said.

"I wish everyone was as tough as me," she said.

I nodded.

"I mean, you're tough," she said. "You let me know when you think he's crossed the line, right?"

I wasn't sure if this was a question or a command. My butt felt fused to the cold concrete. There were a lot of lines out there; it was impossible to watch them all.

A silver Volkswagen Bug careened around the parking lot in front of us, turned, and drove straight at us.

"Shit," Steffie said.

The car shuddered to a stop ten feet from where we sat.

Adele leaned out the passenger window. "Get over here, you dumb fuck. You can't hate me forever."

Steffie shrugged and stayed next to me. She was upset that Adele wasn't more upset, but Riley didn't bother Adele; she'd even told me he was like a buddy, like a father. He never yelled at her. Maybe last summer he'd even seen her in her pajamas.

"You're such a bulldog," Adele said. "Attack, Steffie, attack. Bite. Good, Steffie."

Steffie pulled her sweatshirt hood over her face to hide a smile. She stood up slowly and ambled toward the car, then got in the car and dragged the door shut.

"All right," Adele said as they pulled away with a few clattered lurches, "hasta la pasta, Vee."

Hasta la pasta. You had to be someone like Adele to say that in public and still be cool.

14

Winter arrived the second week of the basketball season, and every day felt endlessly cold and cloudy. I was happy to have a big, bright, loud gym to go to, especially after flying solo all day at school. I was tired of not being friends with Madison. I felt dull in class and didn't even needle Emily about her new boyfriend, Chad, who played clarinet in the marching band and obsessively texted her. I spent a few awkward lunches out on the cold benches where the basketball girls congregated. I hoped Madison saw me surrounded by these loud, aggressive girls. I laughed when they laughed, and though they didn't chase me away, they didn't ever say that much to me. I missed belonging somewhere, and I didn't know how to bridge the gap that my cake and her stubbornness had created.

The weekend before Thanksgiving, Madison's grandfather died of liver cancer. I found out about it from Emily on Monday morning. Madison came to school at the end of math, which was right before lunch. I walked with her to lunch and sat with her while she ate nothing. I ate nothing too, because a grandfather dying should be more important than taco salad. We didn't talk, and we didn't eat, and we sat there together, thinking about our grandparents. I wondered if I'd ever meet the man in the fishing boat in the faded photograph, or if he'd already died, or if he was alive but completely out of reach. I wondered about my letter and for the millionth time imagined it falling out of some mail truck or slipping through the cracks in a U.S. Postal Service airplane, or sitting in an abandoned box of letters in a dusty, rural post office in China.

Madison was pale and quiet all through the afternoon, and I worried that she was sick, or that she was making herself sick with sadness. I was almost making myself sick about my own grandparents, and my sadness was mostly imagined.

After school I found her unloading her books from her locker.

"I'm sorry," I said for the ten thousandth time that day.

"I'm not mad at you."

With my arms full of heavy, useless textbooks, I opened my locker, and my Spanish notebook came sliding out. I caught it awkwardly, stuck it between my teeth, and tried to open my backpack. The zipper jammed, and I dropped it and all my books onto the floor. I looked up and caught Madison smirking at me, which at least meant her mind was off her grandfather, so I hammed up the awkwardness of the whole operation.

"Go ahead and be mad at God or at cancer," I said. It was a relief to talk about it directly. "You're entitled to that. Or if there are Chinese gods you're mad at, that's good. I'm sure they deserve it."

She continued to stare at my Spanish notebook, which had fallen out of my mouth and was now splayed open in the middle of the dirty hallway.

"I'm mad at my parents," she said. "I'm super fucking dirty mad."

I literally winced. I'd never heard her swear before, not even a "goddamn" or a "Jesus Christ." One simple "fuck" coming from her mouth was worse than someone else screaming it into the school PA system.

"They won't let me go to the funeral with them because I'd miss, like, three days of school. Three days! Like I won't get into college if I miss three stupid days of school." She took a deep breath and shifted her eyes to the ceiling. "And now there's no point in going at Christmas. I was supposed to be visiting *him*. I was going for *him*. And it's too expensive for them to go twice in one month, and I can't go by myself."

"Ouch," I said. "The renege on the birthday present."

"I hate them. My grandma is babysitting me until they get back. They actually said that, *babysitting*. I hate them!"

She didn't cry, but she slammed her locker so hard that a few in the row that hadn't been shut well sprung wide open.

My zipper magically fixed itself, and I loaded up my backpack. "Can't you just talk with them?" I asked.

"Jesus Christ, Vee, have you been listening? We're talking about my parents. My *parents*. You don't talk with my parents. You obey them. You bow down and grovel."

This monstrous image of her parents didn't fit with the

images I had of them: Mr. Chen picking us up from the movies and retelling the entire plot of the latest *Law and Order* all the way home. Mrs. Chen offering me iced tea or homemade cookies or insisting that I take the leftover noodles home. But my parents probably didn't seem stubborn and secretive in front of other people either. Everyone knew how to put on a polite, proper face for company.

Madison and I walked together in uncomfortable silence to the end of the hallway. At the door there was a moment of awkwardness when I thought about lunging in front of her so I could hold it open for her, and she hesitated because she was thinking the same thing, but then I didn't want to cut her off, and she didn't want to assume I'd be gentlemanly, so we stood there for a second and then ineptly pushed the door open together. Her grandmother was waiting, windows up and engine running, in her parents' slick silver Nissan Altima.

"Do you think your grandma can see over the wheel?" I asked.

"If we get in a car crash and die, it'll serve them right."

"Mads," I said, "melodrama doesn't suit you." Then I held my breath, because maybe I'd just blown my chances at making amends with her.

She turned her back on the line of cars, the neat, glistening line of parents and grandparents coming to collect their offspring. "I know," she said. "Sorry."

"Are you coming to the girls' basketball opener? Should be good."

She shook her head and looked down at her ballerina slippers.

A streak of hair that she'd dyed blond was starting to fade.

"Why not?" I asked. "It'll be Wednesday, and no school the next day."

"I'm being *babysat*. I won't be able to go anywhere."

"So?" I said. "Tell her it's something for school. Extra credit. A movie."

"A play."

"A *French* play."

"Ooh, that's good."

When she turned away to meet her grandmother, she was smiling. It made me feel better about everything. I even waved at her grandmother, who waved back but probably couldn't see far enough to know who I was. I'd only met her once, and we'd had a strange conversation about the Middle East and the orchid plant she'd recently bought. I wasn't good at talking with old people, since I didn't have my own grandparents to practice with, and the whole time I wondered if she was totally senile, or if she was just pretending to be loopy so she could secretly judge my manners and my character.

Later she might have said to the Chens: That Crawford-Wong boy, he's rude and can't carry on an intelligent conversation.

Or: That Crawford-Wong boy, what a delightful, scholarly young man!

Or the worst: The Crawford-Wong boy? Who is that? I don't remember a thing about him. . . .

15

The day before Thanksgiving we got out of school early, so it already felt like a holiday by the time I got to the gym. The girls, in their silky orange warm-ups, were lounging on the bleachers. Jen, one of the big-boned lesbos, was drawing a basketball in Sharpie on Steffie's thick upper arm.

"Hold still," Jen demanded.

"Doesn't Sharpie have some chemical that gets you high?" Lily asked.

"Whatever," Jen said. The basketball looked more like a cinnamon roll. Steffie flexed her arm and it quivered. "Oh yeah," she said. "Love it." Then she turned and saw me and said, "Sexy tie, manager guy." She whistled a long, low whistle. I fiddled with the knot at my throat. It was a dark blue tie with embroidered orange basketballs on it. Mom had just given it to me an hour earlier, in honor of my first big game. Dad had spent twenty minutes tying it, and it still looked goofy and crooked.

I plugged in the clock and turned on the scoreboard, then I filled the water bottles until they overflowed. When I lugged the bottles out, the girls were in action, hooting and running warm-up patterns on both sides of the gym floor. Thumping music reverberated from the announcer's table.

Once the game started, Riley had me sit next to him to keep track of field goals, free throws, and rebounds, and when he wasn't screaming, he explained why the full-court press wouldn't work against the Wilder Wildcats. His knee occasionally bumped mine. I wondered if some of the basketball guys were up in the stands; maybe they were the sweaty guys with orange-painted chests. I wondered if they could look down and see me sitting here like this, knee to knee with the coach, close to the big-time varsity action.

"Coach?" I said. "Steffie's in foul trouble."

"Damn. We need her. Let's get her out," he said, "but just for a minute. She'll have to go back in and really use her head. Shelley, go."

Let's. Like we were working on it together.

We were up by eight when Adele went up for a basket and came all the way down. And didn't get back up. Everyone stopped playing and gathered around her. She sat on the polished floor, held her knee, and gulped air.

"I'm sorry!" said a freckled girl on the other team. "I . . . we were . . . I mean, is she okay?"

Steffie had leaped off the bench with the rest of us, and now put her arm around the girl. "Hey, calm down. Stuff happens."

Riley and Steffie got on either side of Adele and put her arms around their shoulders. They put their hands under her hamstrings, lifted, and carried her off the court.

"Get some ice," Riley told me.

I sprinted to the back of the gym, got inside the ice room, and realized that I had nothing to carry the ice in. I couldn't find the roll of plastic bags. I grabbed a bottle off the shelf and packed it with ice, freezing my hands in the process, even dropping the bottle once into the bin, where it rolled to the back of the machine, and I had to crawl in there until my crotch was up against the cold metal front and my hair was salted with little ice pellets.

I returned to where Adele was sitting at the far end of the bench. The game resumed, and the crowd, which had been eerily silent the last few minutes, started up with "Here we go, Lions, here we go!"

I poured some ice into a practice jersey that I'd found at the bottom of the ball bin. I slowly pressed the dripping makeshift bag against her swollen knee. She winced. I knelt down next to her and held the bag there.

"How does it look?" she asked.

"I don't know," I said, "unless you want me to take the ice off."

She sighed. "No. That's okay." She bent her knee a bit and winced. She stretched out her hand and wiggled it, so I took it and held it. I buzzed with importance. I wondered who was watching me hold Adele's hand. I hoped Mark was in the stands. Maybe Madison, too.

The buzzer made my insides jump, and I looked up at the scoreboard. We were tied. Riley had called a time-out.

"I should go," I told Adele, nodding to the other side of the bench.

"Can you put a little more ice on it first? That feels good."

I glanced at the group of girls huddled around Riley. Adele squeezed my hand. I was shaking ice water out of the bottle and onto the jersey and the floor and all over my pressed shirt and basketball tie when Riley called my name.

"We need the stats," he called out. "I'm pretty sure they gave that last foul to Steffie instead of Shelley. Will you check?"

I felt the entire gym staring down at me. I stared at the Gatorade logo on the water bottle and put it down next to Adele's knee. As if in slow motion, as if underwater or in a bad, bad dream, I retrieved the clipboard from the bench and approached the circle of girls. I looked down at the stat sheet, which was blurred and shaking.

"Um," I said.

I looked up at Riley. He knew I didn't have the stats. He'd told me to take care of Adele. I couldn't be everywhere at once.

"Cough it up," Steffie said.

"I—I don't know," I whispered. I hadn't even seen Steffie go back in. My life would be over if I burst into tears in front of these girls and Riley and the boys in the bleachers.

"Dude," Steffie said. "Get in the game, Vee. I'm not fouling out because of some bullshit call."

"Let's deal with the situation at hand," Riley said.

"Are you kidding?" Lily said. She was looking at me.

I could lie and say I had the stats. I could go over to the desk and argue self-righteously. It was their error even more than it was mine. "It's the desk's fault," I said.

"Shut up," said Riley.

"Let me talk to the refs," Steffie said.

"Sit down," Riley said.

"I'm a captain. I'll go talk to them."

"No," Riley said. "Send Adele."

Steffie laughed angrily. "Send Adele? Did I miss something, or aren't *both* of us captains? Do you have to make it so obvious?"

"What's best for the team, Steffie—"

"No." Steffie cut him off and took two threatening steps toward him. "You don't know what's best for the team. You don't love this team like I do."

"Sit down," Riley said again. He ripped the clipboard out of my hands, and I thought he was going to chuck it at her.

"Fuck you," she said.

"Vee." Riley handed back the clipboard. The whole gym was staring at us. "Vee, mark down that Steffie's fouled out."

Steffie glared at him, then me, then clomped down to Adele, moved her leg from the bench, and sat down in the wet spot made by my makeshift ice bag. I didn't look at them for the rest of the game. I didn't want to know who was still glaring at me, or Riley, or Steffie, or who was laughing at us, or who had given up on us and gone home. I didn't look at anyone but the galloping players and the tight little squares on the incomplete sheet in front of me.

We lost by six, and I waited for the girls to collect their

warm-ups and move to the team room before carefully picking up water bottle after cold, sweating water bottle until my arms were loaded. The front of my shirt became a dark blue puddle. I emptied the bottles outside, into the gutter, as people streamed out of the gym, laughing and roughhousing and probably talking about the losing team's loser manager. It was my fault we lost; all of it was my fault. I threw the bottles in a wide wire basket and carried the basket to the ice room.

I could hear Riley talking in the team room. There was no yelling or swearing or clipboard-throwing, at least not yet.

I stacked the water bottles on the shelf and turned each one so that the Gatorade logo was facing forward. I wondered what they were talking about. I wondered if they were talking about me, if I should go in there and defend myself. I picked up a Gatorade bottle and hit it against the ice machine. It made a whooshing noise, but the voices next door didn't stop. I hit it again. The dent was a whitish crease, like a scar. The voices rose and fell and turned into rustling and laughter as the girls trickled off to the locker room. I wanted to swipe all the bottles off the shelf and crush them and chew them into little bits. I wanted to slam them against the concrete until they folded and broke into a million soft pieces, until they were ground into dust that then became the air that then became nothing. I wondered if every-one had gone, if it was safe to sit down and cry. I wanted Riley and Steffie and Adele and basketball and school and everything, everyone, to just disappear so I could start over.

"Knock, knock," someone said, and I jerked, knocking a few

of the bottles to the floor. I wiped my eyes and bent to pick them up and turned, and there was Riley, leaning against the doorjamb, watching me flub around.

"Oh," I said.

"I need to talk to you."

I looked down at the puddles on the floor.

"Vee, you've got to stay focused. I've asked you to do one thing, and that's to keep stats. Particularly during games."

"No," I said. I sniffed a loud, snotty sniff. Snot clung to my tonsils and I coughed. "No, you ask me to do a lot of things. You told me to get ice for Adele." I knew I should just keep my mouth shut. I didn't want to argue. I wanted to go home. I wanted to stop thinking about my stupid mistake and how everyone in the gym saw what an idiot I could be. What a girl-crazy, stupid, loser idiot I was.

"Look," Riley said. He took a step into the small room and fiddled with a knob on the ice machine. "I know things have been tough for you. I wanted you to have this job so you could feel some ownership of something. But you have to do this one thing, no matter what. Okay?"

He wanted me to have the job. Not Adele. Him?

"What," I said, my face burning despite the frosty air, "what, like I need your help? Like I'm a charity case? I don't need saving, thanks anyway." I kept my eyes on the floor. I knew they were sad and swollen.

"Not charity," Riley said, "just good old help. I mean, fighting, clowning around, getting suspended, not turning in your work,

I mean, all these are signs you need someone looking after you."

"Shut up," I said. "I don't need your help. I don't want to sleep on your couch, you dirty pervert." I hadn't meant to say any of this. I hadn't even realized, until the words left my mouth, that this was how I thought of him.

My words slapped him in the face, and he took a step backward, then a step forward, back to where he'd started. "Vee," he said, "stop. Just stop right there."

"Why?" I said. "I know all about it. You're not actually her father, and you can't pretend you are."

"You don't know the whole story," Riley said. "You don't get it at all. How am I the bad guy? Listen to yourself. You're telling me you don't need some guidance? You're slinging around accusations like a child. Just stop."

But I couldn't.

"I'm pretty sure you'd be in deep doo-doo if people found out what you did."

"What? Help someone? Vee, listen—"

"I'm just saying it doesn't seem right."

"You know what?" Riley said. "I'm done with you. I'm done. Fine. You don't need my help. You don't want it. I get it. I'm done." The door sighed shut behind him.

"No more Mr. Peppy Teacher Guy," I said. The ice machine had tha-dunked into a quiet hum, and my voice sounded hollow in the small room.

I'd just threatened my teacher. Threatened him and freaked him out. Because he was stupid about high school girls or world history or basketball? Because I'd made a mistake tonight? I rearranged all the Gatorade bottles, lining them up perfectly, hiding the scarred, dented one in the back. They were an army of thin green plastic, and they'd taken my abuse, and now they cowered at the very idea of me.

16

When Mom picked me up outside the gym, she asked what had taken so long. I shrugged and told her the truth: that I'd been putting away equipment, etc., etc. I also said that Riley's star player had hurt her knee.

"Riley's?" Mom asked.

"The coach. You know, my history teacher."

"I see," Mom said. But she didn't. She didn't understand that he'd tried to make me a charity case, and that I'd accused him of unmentionable things. I didn't want to think about them. Maybe he really was a pervert. I'd called him on it, and now he was scared of me.

"Is she going to be all right?" Mom asked. "The girl with the hurt knee?"

"I don't know," I said.

"Oh dear." Mom reached over to pat my knee, as if I were the one physically bruised and broken.

We took a wrong turn, and as I cleared my throat to say something, Mom smiled and mentioned that Dad was meeting us at

Tom Fat's to celebrate the Thanksgiving weekend and my first game. I wanted to tell her that it didn't count as "my game," since I didn't and couldn't play in it, but Mom still clung to the grade-school philosophy that just being on a team was cause for celebration. It was a lot like Dad's idea that trying was all that mattered. How did these people who'd brought me into this hugely complicated world manage to survive with such immature views?

I tried to act excited about fast-food Chinese, but all I could think about was how I was about to get fired from the only job I'd ever had. How I couldn't even cut it on the girls' team.

Tom Fat's restaurant was called Golden Dragon. The glowing red sign had three yellow Chinese characters next to the English name. When I was little, I used to think that by looking at them, I was learning Chinese. There were two squat figures with thick lines, one like a house and one like a cat. The third character was lighter and seemed to dance. It was my favorite. I used to name the characters: Dad, Mom, Vee. But today they looked like gashes, like raw, open wounds.

We sat in a sticky booth and ordered prawns in sweet-and-sour slime, kung pao chicken, and oily chow mein. Mom and Dad asked about the basketball game, and I tried to remember the parts that didn't include me or Adele or Riley. I was amazed they couldn't see right through me. They didn't sense that things were horribly wrong. At least I knew that their lives were a complicated, secretive mess. They didn't know anything about me, and they were stupid enough to believe me whenever I told them that things were just fine.

Tom Fat came over midmeal to chat with Dad and to let us compliment him. I told him that everything was wonderful, and I tried to sound sincere, since my mess wasn't his fault and his grease-pan cooking style wasn't mine. I wondered if Madison's family ever came here. They probably gagged at the idea of beef and broccoli or sweet-and-sour pork. They probably thought that Tom Fat was an embarrassment to Chinese culture, that he was an antiambassador of the beloved homeland. His restaurant was filled with big white people and Asians who spoke English at the dinner table. I liked him, though. He reminded me of Santa, if Santa were loud and Chinese and had bad skin. We always got something free or discounted or pushed on us, like the egg flower soup that Mrs. Fat made or the shrink-wrapped almond cookies that sat in an Easter basket next to the cash register.

"Smart boy," Tom Fat said every time he saw me. Tonight was no different. He pointed a meaty finger at me and nodded while saying, "You do well in school." It was meant to be a question, but he didn't understand how to put that inflection in his voice.

"Of course," Dad said. "Of course."

Of course, my ass. Why did we have to lie to everyone, including Mr. Santee Claus, about how great I was? What face were we saving? Would anyone like or respect Mom and Dad any less if I were a total fuckup? If they were failing their latest parenting test?

"You do basketball," Tom Fat asked, "and go play basketball at Harvard, okay." This cracked him up, and he and Dad clucked away in Mandarin for a few minutes while I thought about how useless it would be to play basketball at Harvard. Smart kids didn't play basketball. Smart kids didn't play sports at all except maybe tennis or badminton, and they certainly weren't beating down the admissions office doors of Georgia Tech or Oklahoma State. Play basketball at Harvard? Why waste your time? They hadn't gotten into the NCAA tournament in the last millennium. March Madness at Harvard was probably some midterms-driven, stress-based illness that afflicted former high school valedictorians.

After we'd eaten all the greasy Chinese we could stomach, and Dad had scooped the leftovers into leakproof boxes, and we'd said good-bye to almost everyone in the restaurant, I drove home with Mom. I fiddled with the glove compartment and my seat belt until, finally, Mom asked what was wrong.

"I think I might quit," I told her. "The basketball thing. I'm not really enjoying it."

"You can't do that. You just started."

"The coach is kind of an asshole," I said.

She didn't even tell me to watch my language. "You made a commitment. You can't go around breaking commitments because they're tougher than you expected."

"This is more of a conscience-driven decision," I said. I stared out the window and waited for her to ask me what I meant, and when she did, I said, "I don't approve of the way he treats his players."

"You don't approve, do you?" She was laughing at me. Her

voice was laughing. Clearly, to her, this was ridiculous logic. Back in the good old days, when everyone was tougher, it didn't matter if students approved of their teachers. It didn't matter that a coach might have some fishy interest in his hot eighteen-year-old athlete.

I picked at a grease stain near my knee. If I told her what I knew about Riley and Adele, they'd get in trouble, and I didn't know what kind of trouble, how big or irreversible. And then Adele would never talk to me again. Plus, I had no idea how to talk about perverted stuff with my mom.

"Forget it," I said.

"Do you need more time to do your homework?" Mom asked. "Is that it?"

I'd promised to raise my GPA to a 3.7 by the end of the semester. I hadn't done the math on whether this was feasible or not, but they hadn't left me many options that didn't include tutors, summer school, or permanent grounding. Here Mom was giving me an easy excuse to drop basketball, but then she'd expect me to be in the library every day after school, and I didn't want that.

"I'm good," I said. "If I needed more time for homework, I'd tell you. Why would I lie about that?"

"I don't know," Mom said. She glanced at me and then back out at the dark street. "I don't know about a lot of things, Vee."

By that she meant me. Now was not the time to tell her that I didn't understand myself most of the time anymore either.

• • •

So what if Mr. Riley seemed weird and wrong to me? So what if he freaked out when I told him he was a pervert? Lots of things seemed wrong and weird. I had an endless, random list of things I didn't understand. In no particular order:

1. The Aztec alphabet
2. Spanish past perfect verbs
3. Chinese
4. The absolute absence of any mail from China
5. Silent grandparents
6. Brawling NBA players
7. Everything in the news
8. Silent parents
9. The Chens' absurd expectations of Madison
10. Adele
11. High school sports
12. High school in general

And now, Ladies and Gentlemen, wearing lucky number thirteen is none other than the trash-talking, the ego-crushing, the one, the only, the infamous MR. RILEY! (The crowd goes wild. They want to know who his next charity case will be. They want to know his IQ. They want to know who he'll offer his couch to next. They're waiting . . . the anticipation is killing them. . . .)

● ● ●

I dreaded the return to school and history class on Monday. I dreaded seeing Adele. I kept replaying in my mind the way I'd held her hand and messed up the stats. More than anything, though, I dreaded seeing Mr. Riley. He'd said he was done with me, but I didn't know what that would look like.

The Thanksgiving weekend was endless, and everything reminded me of disaster. We had a gigantic, all-American meal for just the three of us, a sad parody of the happy Pilgrim families gathering en masse with all their red-skinned buddies. Mom and Dad did that obvious *We're being parents right now* thing and asked me what I was thankful for. It was so much easier to come up with what made me feel angry or inadequate. The fact that they thought a holiday meal was fun with just the three of us. The fact that they thought our whole lives were okay that way. I hadn't heard back from China. I was never going to know my family in Texas. I had no brothers and sisters or aunts and uncles or even a pet goldfish. I was all alone.

"Huh," I said. I hated that they even felt like they could ask the question. What were they thankful for? Their dysfunctional family relationships? Their fubar son? "Family and friends, I guess," I said. Sarcasm. Lies. But we toasted to it anyway, Mom and Dad smiling away, and ate until we felt ill.

Then Dad and I saved Madison from her senile grandmother by taking her to the movies. The whole time, sitting there in the dark, I couldn't bring myself to tell Madison what a dumb-ass

I'd been just the night before. I didn't even know if she'd gone to the game or if she'd seen my disaster. I couldn't bring up what I knew about Adele because Madison was always a little harsh on her, as nerdy Asian girls tend to be toward tall, hot, athletic, popular upperclassmen. And I couldn't say anything about my confrontation with Riley because he was her teacher. In order to love school as much as she did, she had to believe that her teachers were faultless fountains of knowledge, not stupid pedophiles. I couldn't destroy her world like that, especially since I didn't know all the details. Even though I was still stuffed with turkey and pie, I sat in the dark and ate a whole bucket of popcorn just to distract myself from thinking. Not that it helped. I couldn't turn off my stupid brain.

The next day we rescued Madison again and went to the Oakland Museum to check out an exhibit on earthquakes. The exhibit was sprinkled throughout a few dark rooms, and I wondered if we should have done something happier, like go to Six Flags.

"Number one on the list of most deadly earthquakes," Madison said, reading a placard, "a magnitude eight in central China in 1556 that killed over eight hundred thirty thousand people. How is that even possible?"

But it didn't depress her; she didn't connect these natural disasters with the recent disaster in her own family. In fact, she studied each picture and placard like there'd be a test on it later. She waved me over to an exhibit about the 1906 San Francisco quake and said that her mom's side of the family was able to get into America because of it. She pointed to a diorama of an Angel Island interrogation cell and the placard beneath it.

> *After immigration records were destroyed in the fires, many Chinese residents claimed citizenship and forged and sold immigration papers to men who posed as their sons. These men were known as paper sons and became dynamic, contributing members of a vibrant Chinese culture in the San Francisco Bay Area.*

"My great-great-grandparents were paper people," Madison said. "Vee, take a picture."

"Take a picture? Of the kumbaya historical summary?"

Madison tilted her head to the side. "Would you rather have it racist and anti-Chinese? Maybe that'd be better, more authentic, since that's how people felt at the time."

I had to hand it to her. The girl could debate.

She said, "Did you know they made immigrants name everyone in their village, and every little detail about their neighbors, to prove they were who they claimed to be? Can you imagine how stressful and humiliating that would be? How much you would feel disliked by this country you wanted to be a part of?"

She was trying to win the sympathy argument, but compared with real torture tactics like waterboarding and sleep deprivation, having questions thrown at you didn't seem like a big deal.

"You do whatever you have to do to get here," Dad said. "There's no shame in that."

Without a second of hesitation Madison asked Dad how he'd gotten here. Dad continued walking like he hadn't heard her, and Madison looked at me. I shrugged as if to say, *I told you so.*

We followed Dad into the next room of the exhibit, and Madison continued commenting on the Angel Island prisoners as if she'd never asked a question. This room had the same black draperies, but someone had built a stone wall and then had knocked it down. The jagged remainder of the wall stood precariously to my right, and large, soft-looking pieces of sandstone were sprinkled around the room. To my left, a blown-up, colorized photograph of a burning city lit up the entire wall. An audiotape of people screaming and sirens blaring played on repeat. It was a genuine Disney experience.

Dad leaned against the crumbling wall, which he probably wasn't supposed to do, and said, "I took a bus to Beijing, then a train to Shanghai, where a friend said they gave out more visas. Then I stayed for almost two years, then got accepted into school here, then took a plane the whole way to San Francisco. And that's the end of the story."

"You had to wait two years to get a visa?" Madison asked.

"I had to study and wait for Chairman Mao to die."

Madison stared at him, her mouth opening and closing and opening again. I'd never seen Madison speechless before. Fortunately, she recovered quickly. "You actually thought that? Couldn't you have gotten killed for even thinking that?"

Dad rubbed his hands over the top of the broken wall. "I guess I did not actually think that. I only knew that things were changing, and at the edge of that change I would be able to come to America. I was waiting for my happiness." He looked around the disaster-ridden room and rubbed his hands together. "And here it is!" he said.

"And that's why you say you're from Yangzhou when you're actually not," I said.

"I was from Yangzhou at the time."

He wasn't going to admit to lying to me my whole life while Madison was standing by as a witness.

This whole time I'd wondered in the back of my mind if he'd sneaked into America by hiding in some cramped cargo hold for months on end, or by bribing a high-level official, or by drifting, the way the Cubans do, in a boat the size of a bathtub. Madison's family, with their false papers and grueling interrogations, were more interesting than Dad's immigration. His trip sounded about as exciting and difficult as an excursion to 7-Eleven.

"Yes," Dad said out of nowhere, like he'd been talking to himself, "I don't know now if it was necessary, but the recommendation at the time was to use a Yangzhou address and name. I think we were scared and wanting to be invisible to the government."

"You gave them a fake name? Like an alias? What was it?" I asked. I could see him putting down something like Hu Flung Pu or Wun Fat Gai and getting a good laugh out of it.

"Wong."

"No, your other name."

"Before Wong?"

"You had a name before Wong?" I asked.

"I just explained that we invented new ones."

"Ohmigod, that's cool," Madison said. "That's like something out of a spy novel. You changed your name to foil the government. Like going undercover. That's awesome."

"I'm sure it made no difference," Dad said. "But we were young and we thought it did. At the same time, remember, people in Berkeley were changing their names to Sunflower and Peace Blossom and such. There was this belief that we could change who we were and not be tied to mistakes of the past, and it was not just a hippie American movement."

"Dad. Dad. Wait. Back up. We're not really Wongs?"

"No."

"What the hell are we?" My voice was rising, and an Indian couple that had drifted into the Disney diorama eyed me suspiciously.

"In Mandarin our name is closer to Wang."

"You only changed one letter?" This seemed unimaginative and pointless.

"In English, yes, it is only one letter. But Wong seemed like someone more American, someone from a city like Yangzhou, but something I could still remember to answer to."

"Well, of course a letter hasn't come back from China," I said. "The friggin' mailman is looking for people who don't exist!"

"You sent a letter to China?" Madison struck one of those

hands-on-hips, eyebrows-raised, bitchy-girl poses. "And you didn't tell me about it?"

We'd written the letter during the Twinkie disaster, and it had seemed insensitive to bring it up after I found out about her grandfather.

"I have family in China too, you know," I said.

"You *do*?"

"I made it right by the characters," Dad said. "You wrote 'Wong,' and I wrote 'Wang.'"

"So basically everything I did was gibberish."

Dad looked at me and tilted his head sideways like a curious dog. "But you knew that. You're like that saying: 'It's all Chinese to me.'" He and Madison looked at each other and laughed. Side by side, they looked like father and daughter. I stepped up on one of the sandstone pieces in the middle of the room, teetered, and then jumped off dramatically.

"Sure, go ahead and pick on the American," I said.

Madison rolled her eyes. "We're all American, Vee."

"I mean the guy who never went to Chinese school."

"You never needed to go to Chinese school," Dad said.

"I never needed to be on the debate team in junior high, either, but that didn't seem to matter. It's easy for you guys to take it for granted. It's obvious what you are." I walked over to the photograph of the burning street. From this close it was grainy and indecipherable, a random mosaic of black, white, and crimson dots.

Madison and Dad were both leaning against the broken wall

now, and he was getting out a pen to draw our family name for her, and she was nodding and copying it, and it was a great bonding experience. For them. I had no choice but to sulk and hope they wouldn't spend the rest of the day clacking away in Mandarin. I could see that happening, though, since they didn't seem to be aware that I'd been left out of so much already.

When we got back from the museum, I checked the mail. Nothing important. I stood on the sidewalk in the light rain, and the skin on my face felt hot and tight. I knew I'd never get a letter back. I dropped the junk mail on the kitchen table and watched it separate and scatter: JIFFY LUBE HOLIDAY SPECIAL. IPODS FOR EVERYONE YOU LOVE. AT&T FAMILIES-TALK-FREE PLAN.

Dad stopped whistling and appeared at the base of the stairs with the pile of junk mail in his hands. "Look at all this waste," he said.

"You mean I should return the stuff I got you?" I said. "The car maintenance coupons and rolls of flowery return labels?"

"No way!" he said, and laughed. "I love American junk."

I was drifting up the stairs backward, one step at a time.

"I'm still sort of hoping for something from China," I said. "It's been a month."

"From China?" Dad said. "I told you not to expect anything."

"Because you changed your name? Because they're mad you left?" I said. "You could go back. We could go back together, to visit." I thought about Madison and how her parents had denied her the chance to say good-bye to her grandfather. "Before it's too late, I mean. We could try to find them. Your parents." I realized that this was what I wanted. That anything less than seeing them in China was going to be anticlimactic.

"We could just go to Chinatown. That's a lot closer."

"Thanks, Dad." I'd reached the top step. "Great time for a joke." I thought he'd cared about the letter too and wanted to be welcomed back into the family with his only son by his side. But he'd just been humoring me. He'd known all along that they wouldn't respond, that they'd drop my letter in the mud or tear it up and fling it into the river. He'd known they wouldn't read it and they certainly wouldn't write back. Why would you send a letter to someone who was dead to you?

I couldn't explain to him why I was so mad. He wouldn't get it. My grandparents were as good as dead, and I was never going to go to China to meet them. Like Madison, I'd been screwed over by my parents.

Maybe. Unlike Madison, my grandparents weren't certifiably dead. Maybe I could finagle to get something I wanted. I took the phone up to my room and punched in Madison's number.

"I have a plan," I told Madison. "I have a plan that will fix all our troubles."

"I already don't like it," she said.

"Where's the love? Where's the trust?"

"Our troubles are different," she said.

"Not really."

"Oh yes they are. You don't have parents who won't take you to your grandfather's funeral. They called while we were out. They're having a good time. Literally, that's what they said. Ohmigod, I hate them."

"That's horrible," I said. Even if they were actually having a good time, they were there for a funeral. They shouldn't have said that. "At least you knew him. I don't have grandparents at all."

The line hummed. "You have them," she said.

"Right. Technically. What if I told you there was a way for both of us to get what we want?"

"Your plan. I told you I already don't like it."

"You're going to write the letter, Mads."

"What letter?"

"You're going to write a letter as if you're my grandparents. You're going to ask us to visit you in China."

"No way. No."

I had expected this. Madison was a better person than I was.

"Yes," I said. "We'll talk more later."

"No, Vee. That's wrong."

"See?" I smiled into the receiver. "You're already tempted."

17

Madison wanted to do homework for the rest of the weekend, and I was busy watching Comedy Central, and then before I knew it, it was already Monday morning. Time to face Riley and everything I didn't want to know or think about him. Just the idea of history class made my stomach churn like a Lava Lamp. I tried approaching the classroom from three different angles, but each time I chickened out before I got there. Then the tardy bell rang, and I ducked into the bathroom and locked myself in a stall. My heart was racing. I'd never cut class before. I wondered what they were doing in there—if Riley was taking roll and wondering if I would ever come back, if Adele was on crutches, if Madison and Emily wished I were there to make things less boring.

I didn't want to deal with Riley. I just didn't want to deal with him at all. He didn't know how to help me, just as Steffie didn't know how to help the team, and I didn't know how to help my parents, and Adele didn't know how to help herself. The world was full of people who stumbled around and tried to be good but didn't know how to make the right decisions. I actually felt sorry for Riley; he was a grown-up and still so clueless. I promised myself right there, in the handicap stall of the skuzzy gym bathroom, that in ten years, if I reminded myself of him, I'd do something drastic like shoot myself or crawl into a hole and die.

From my hideout I heard the familiar thumping of a basketball. I put my hand on the cracked tile and felt the reverberations—small, erratic heartbeats—against my fingertips. I worked up the nerve to walk out of the bathroom, around the corner, and into the gym. Steffie was shooting free throws in the dark. I could only tell it was her because of a few dusty rays of light filtering through the high, grimy windows.

"They don't have lights in here?" I asked.

"Vee-Man," she said when the ball sailed through the air. "Aren't you supposed to be in class?"

"Aren't you?" I asked.

She snorted. "Well, aren't we a lot alike." She passed me the ball, and I caught it, though barely, and dropped my backpack and dribbled out toward the top of the key. She came toward me, and I head-faked and spun and decided I'd rather miss a three-pointer than get the ball stripped from me on a drive, so I stopped and shot. The ball swooshed effortlessly through the net.

"Holy shit," Steffie said.

"That never happens to me," I said.

"I wouldn't be too honest," Steffie said. "Take the credit, man.

Act like you could do it again." She tossed the ball back to me. "Though I bet you can't."

I turned the ball in my hands. Steffie slapped it away and dribbled down the court and finished with a graceful layup.

"Seriously, why aren't you in class?" she asked from across the gym. She was slowly dribbling her way back.

"I've got Riley for history," I said. "I just couldn't do it. Not after the, you know, the game."

Steffie put her arm around me. She smelled like baby powder, which I would never have guessed. "Don't worry, man," she said. "He blows up and then it's over. And I said something to him anyway."

"You did?"

"Yeah." She tried spinning the ball on her finger.

"But it was your foul I fucked up."

"Yeah, and next time he's gonna let me talk to the damn refs. Captain's gotta have privileges, right? Adele may kiss his ass, but I want it straight."

She wasn't even talking about me. My mistake hadn't even registered as a mistake. It was all about power—how much she had, how much Riley would concede to her. I was relieved and also the tiniest bit irritated.

"How's her knee?" I asked.

Steffie dribbled the ball back and forth between her legs. "Meh. With her, it's always something."

"Huh," I said. She hadn't answered the question. Adele could be in surgery right now, her leg getting sliced open. I imagined myself by her bedside, holding her hand, feeding her sips of Gatorade through a straw.

"Coach knows if I complain to the right people, he's dead," Steffie said.

"About what?" I asked. "You'd just make something up?" Did Steffie know what I knew? What I'd already said? She could accuse him of rape or sexual harassment, but I'd pretty much beaten her to it. I hadn't used those terms, but the word "pervert" was a strong one, and he hadn't liked hearing it.

She head-faked me, then dribbled down and sank a jump shot.

"No, dude," she said. "It's all right there. Boosters don't want a male coach being too harsh on a bunch of girls."

Or inviting them to his house for a sleepover.

"A few things he's said or done, out of context, with a different tone . . . that's it for him."

"You said that to him?" I asked.

"Sure I did." She shrugged. She had no qualms pushing him around. My only question was this: Did she know how he'd helped Adele, and did she know how defensive he was about it? This was what bothered me the most, aside from the fact that I'd become a disrespectful little snot. He wouldn't have been so defensive if I hadn't hit some nerve. Some sort of truth. People always wigged out about the truth.

A few guys came into the gym. These guys weren't the basketball team; they were a ragged posse of stoners, guys too lazy to have a first- or second-period class. All of them had shaggy hair and low-slung jeans. They looked at us coldly.

"Nursery school's over, kids," one of them said. "It's time to clear the floor."

I started scooting toward my backpack, but Steffie put her hand on her hip and smirked. "You're telling me to move?" she said. "You want *us* to get off the court for *you*?"

The lead stoner was visibly taken aback.

"Just so you know, I've got clearance to be in here, and *just so you know*, I've got more basketball talent in my left nipple than you do in your whole life."

I coughed to cover my laugh.

The stoners wavered.

"You don't want to duke it out with me, though I'd be more than obliged," Steffie said.

The stoners shrugged, as if caring too much about anything would ruin their image, and broke apart from one another and drifted off, probably back to their smoky cars.

"Well," she said, "that was fun." She returned to the free throw line and lined herself up for a shot.

It was no wonder Adele called Steffie a bulldog. Steffie was a doer, a go-getter. She was willing to use her fists to make things happen. Fighters were the ones who survived, the ones people listened to. Mark had learned that I was a fighter, and pretty much left me alone now. Genghis Khan and Napoléon and Teddy Roosevelt and the 9/11 terrorists all figured it out too. Violence worked, which was why world peace was nothing more than a bumper sticker: WHIRLED PEAS.

• • •

Madison (*holding up a Twizzler for emphasis*): He asked where you were. Where were you?

Me (*mouth full of pizza*): I just can't handle him anymore, and my mom won't let me quit basketball. You ladies (*gesturing with pizza crust to Madison and Emily*) don't get it. He doesn't pick on you.

Emily: God, I thought being the manager would make you his BFF or something.

Madison (*smirking*): Mark did suggest that you'd gone back to China.

Me: Racist prick.

You couldn't ever undo your reputation. Even though we'd invented Mark's racism, once that was established in our minds, everything else seemed to fit. He'd actually become a racist prick—maybe because he'd always been, and now we just saw it more clearly, or maybe because we only ever saw what we wanted in other people.

The same went for Riley. He didn't want me knowing things about him and Adele—that was clear by the way he'd freaked out on me when I called him a pervert. Either he was a pervert, or he was afraid of me telling people he was, but either way he didn't like this power I now had over him. The funny thing was I hadn't asked for it. I hadn't meant to say anything to him. But I had, and I couldn't take it back, and as much as I wanted to, I knew I couldn't avoid him forever.

• • •

I had nowhere else to go after school, so I dragged my feet all the way to the gym. When I stepped inside, I was gritting my teeth so hard that I could feel them turning into chalky dust. The girls were sitting around the bleachers. Lily was chewing on her nails, and Adele was giving Valerie a neck rub. I glanced at Adele's knee, but it was hidden under her sweatpants. She didn't look in pain. She looked bored, which was her usual expression.

"Yo," Steffie said. "Chalk talk. Pop a squat."

Riley appeared, walking backward and struggling to pull a rickety rolling chalkboard onto the gym floor.

"Oh, hi, Vee," he said. "Mind giving me a hand with this?"

I stood up. So this was how it would be. As Steffie'd said, we'd had our blowup and now it was over. I could almost believe he'd forgotten our conversation. Okay. I'd pretend that I didn't know certain things about him, that I didn't have some weird power over him now. I was good at this game of pretending everything was normal. With my family, I'd had a lot of practice.

"What we're doing isn't working," Riley told the team.

"True dat," Steffie said. Her hair was in a tight little ponytail, and the skin around her face seemed painfully stretched.

"Just listen," Adele said. Her fingers dug into Valerie's shoulders, and Valerie slowly collapsed under the pressure.

"I'm throwing my support behind Coach's new strategy," Steffie said. She stood up and shook imaginary crumbs off her cargo pants.

"Shh," Adele said.

"What? I love this team," Steffie said.

"Sure you do," Riley said. "You're just a little fierce some-times."

Girls laughed, and Steffie laughed along with them, but I couldn't tell if, underneath, she was boiling. She wasn't swearing at him anymore, but now she knew that she could—and could get away with it. Was that enough of a victory for her, or did she want more? Did she want everyone to think that she ran the show? Because right now, her teammates were laughing at her intensity, as if they couldn't remember all those days when Riley had cut them down. She seemed like a cartoon bulldog, a college mascot, all bark and no bite.

The girls ran warm-up laps around the gym, and Riley stud-ied his clipboard, then the girls. Lily ran by. She was wearing a purple shirt with the words MATH FRIDAYS stenciled on it.

"Our resident nerd," he said. "Helping with team GPA."

Lily was in the math club. Why was he always ripping on the girls, as if he were the ambassador of cool? As if the math club could never be cool?

"Dude," I said, without looking at him. "Just because she's Asian?"

"What do you mean?" he asked. "That's a fact. We need peo-ple to help with our GPA. Steffie and Adele aren't doing much for it. We don't want to be a team of dumb jocks. Or if we are, at least let's start winning."

People did divide athletes into categories of smart and dumb. Smart kids were golfers, swimmers, tennis players. Dumb jocks were football players and wrestlers. Basketball was on the fence. Riley had a point, but his point was all wrapped up in his snarky comment about Lily's shirt. Why did he have to be snarky? This was Steffie's point exactly.

"Yay, math club," I said in Lily's general vicinity after the girls had stopped to stretch in their warm-up circle. "Yay for keeping up the team GPA."

She looked up and gave me a fake, sugary smile. "If you like math so much, maybe you should practice your counting."

I sighed and focused on the scuffed, waxy floor. I'd just meant to flush out Riley's side comments, put it all out in the open. I hadn't thought it through enough before opening my big mouth.

"Lily," Steffie said. "Cool it. That's not being positive."

Lily rolled her eyes and dramatically took off her shirt, turned it inside out, and put it back on. "Better?" she asked.

"I don't think he was being sarcastic," Steffie said. "Were you, Vee?"

"Oh, no," I said quickly. This wasn't supposed to be about Lily and her stupid shirt. "I do love math. I mean"—I gave a little chuckle—"I'm Chinese."

Only Lily laughed.

"Okay," Riley said brightly. "Moving on."

I desperately wanted to defend myself. Those weren't my words. Riley was looking at me, though, with a steady, almost stern expression. And the girls already knew what he was like. I tightened my mouth and swallowed the words. I wouldn't say anything ever again, and I would turn my back on Riley next time he made a mean, funny comment. Steffie was right. Riley needed someone to bully him into submission.

Adele began counting out the next stretch as if my interruption had never happened.

I kept my mouth shut the rest of practice and hopped to whenever Riley or the girls asked me to do something. Riley was polite and professional. Adele was cool and untouchable. Steffie sulked. I cowered. Everything we weren't saying continued to glimmer just under the surface.

18

The Chinese during the Shang Dynasty invented writing so they could predict the future. They carved characters onto turtle shells and burned them until they cracked. The weaknesses in these oracle bones, the patterns of the heat-induced cracks, told the Shang what they wanted to know.

The Shang had something more than a Magic 8 Ball or a Ouija board; the oracle bones weren't a trick for them. They had figured out how to turn their thoughts into language that could be seen and burned. They agreed that this was how their world was ordered. They agreed that the ash-filled cracks were purposeful and true.

I didn't know who to turn to who would understand how my life was ordered. I didn't even know myself, and I wanted something like my own tortoise shell and fire. I wanted ancestors to worship and ask for help. I was filled with restless anxiety about Riley, Adele, Steffie, Madison, my parents, my grandparents, and all of it somehow about me, too. I mentioned the forged letter idea to Madison a few times, but she always turned her head away or whispered, "Not now." She didn't understand that now was the perfect time. My answer to not knowing something was to invent it—it's what I'd done with my history essay and with my guesses about Riley's relationship with Adele. Invent and forge ahead. This was my new motto.

But the two weeks leading up to winter break felt like a holding pattern. We circled and hovered and looped back to where we'd started, and every conversation felt dingy and recycled. I was not inventing. I was not forging ahead.

A few days before winter break Mom and Dad sat me down and surprised me with an early Christmas present.

"We e-mailed some of your teachers," Mom said, "about your grades."

I went into temporary cardiac arrest. When my heart started up again, it rushed all the blood in my body directly to my face. How could I be embarrassed in front of my own parents? Wasn't it their problem if I was retarded, and my teachers sucked, and I couldn't get that precious 4.0?

Dad told me I needed to take some responsibility for my learning. "Choose your own success," he said.

"I thought the saying was 'Choose your own happiness.'"

"The saying just changed," he said.

"You promised us all A's," Mom said. "That's what you said you were capable of."

"Huh," I said, like I'd forgotten. "At least I'm confident?"

Dad laughed but then remembered he was supposed to be disciplining me.

"Are we supposed to take away driving privileges?" Mom asked. I'd gotten my learner's permit, and she'd promised me a few driving lessons over the break.

I shrugged. Technically, I didn't have any privileges yet.

"I see," she said. "Well, maybe you'll like this."

She announced that I'd won the grand prize of ten days of SAT prep classes. Ten days of sitting in a stuffy, overheated classroom with a bunch of retards and Asian Nation kids, learning to sit still for four hours and identify antonyms for words like "lackadaisical" and "obsequious."

Complete the following sentence:

If you wish _____, then why ____?

   a. your parents would leave you alone . . . are you trying to meet your grandparents

   b. your history teacher would forget what you called him . . . do you feel guilty when he does

   c. that hot senior girl would pay attention to you again . . . are you afraid to talk to her

   d. to really get to know your grandparents . . . don't you resort to more desperate measures

   e. all of the above

Vacation began, and I suffered through overblown vocabulary lists and perimeters of triangles and values of x and m. After SAT class each morning I'd eat my bagged lunch by myself near the curb and wait for Mom to pick me up and take me to basketball. Every day I hoped she'd slide out of the driver's seat and say, "Here, Vee, honey, why don't you drive." But she didn't.

Aside from his reputation as a crappy teacher and my suspicions of him as a pervert, Riley ran winter break practices with calm efficiency. Maybe Steffie really had put his back up against the wall, or maybe he was relieved he didn't have to teach every day, or maybe his good mood had nothing to do with us.

It had somehow become my job to Saran-wrap ice on people's various body parts after practice. Jen's elbow, Lily's shoulder, Adele's knee. Adele's knee and smooth calf and red toenails and long, tanned thigh distracted me. Then imagining that Riley had maybe gawked at her in the same way distracted me further. It took me eons to wrap her knee, but she never seemed to notice how I bumbled. She told me endless, meandering stories about her crazy stepmom and her alcoholic aunts and uncles. Finally, one day, after a long story about her uncle who had molested his babysitter, I worked up the nerve to open my mouth.

"Hey," I said. "Wow."

"I know, right?" Adele said.

"Right. So how long did you have to camp out on Riley's couch, anyway?" Maybe my timing was bad. She'd just been talking about a molester uncle, and I wanted to know if Riley was like that, but I didn't want to be too obvious. Though Adele seemed to like talking about everything perverted and juicy, it wasn't likely she'd go that far.

"Just until I figured some shit out," she said. Her cheeks were flushed from practice and the cold, and her lips were chapped and cherry red.

"Was that weird?"

"Weird is your lunatic stepmom on a power trip."

She wasn't answering my question.

"Couldn't he get in trouble for that?"

She laughed. "That's ridiculous. He was just being nice."

"Does Steffie know all this?" It made sense that Steffie, with all her Riley issues, was in on this. And maybe, like me, she just wasn't saying anything. I carefully ripped the Saran wrap and helped Adele lower her leg and didn't look her in the eye.

"Oh, Vee," she said, "it's all so complicated that I can't even talk about it right now. I don't think I should say anything, you know?" She smiled at me as she limped out of the ice room.

I nodded. She hadn't answered my question. And I couldn't tell if she'd just invited me in closer or had given me the royal, melodramatic brush-off.

19

Two days before Christmas, I did get a letter. Technically, it wasn't for me, but I knew what it was, and I figured at the very least I could hide it so it wouldn't make Mom cry. This year it wouldn't get magnetically suctioned to the fridge for each of us to study every time we wanted a glass of juice or a bowl of leftovers. Everyone pretending, after the initial disaster, that it was as sweet and purposeless as the cards we got from our neighbors or our dentist.

I sneaked it up to my room and studied it. It was addressed to Mom, and the stamp, an ugly medieval portrait of the Virgin Mary, was obscured by the big postmark that read "Ding Dong, TX." Ding Dong. My grandparents lived in Ding Dong. I wanted to laugh because it seemed impossibly funny. In my mind they were like cartoon people—larger than life, only vaguely human, and now living in a place called Ding Dong.

Inside, the big, stiff card had a picture of the generic trio: Joseph, Mary, sleeping little Jesus. The Brady Bunch of Jerusalem.

And then some scripture about Mary conceiving the Lord. Then, in spidery script: "Love, Mae and Wayne."

Love?

I used to think that everyone with faraway grandparents only heard from them once a year. I used to think that the world was so big, so impossible to navigate, that this communication represented everyone's best effort. That this once-a-year card could actually mean love.

I couldn't piece it together. Who were these monsters who spawned my mother? Were they mentally ill? Were they brainwashed and part of some child-free cult? They obviously weren't in jail, unless their jail had a gift shop where you could buy schmaltzy Jesus cards. Maybe they were just awful people. Not proactively evil like Hitler or Ivan the Terrible or Chairman Mao, but just bad. Selfish. Unloving. Maybe Mom kept hoping that Mae and Wayne would love her, but they never did. Or maybe they thought they were loving her and just didn't know how.

I thought about the letter I wanted to write to Dad, pretending to be his parents, begging us to come to China to visit them before they died. It was a crazy idea—Madison reminded me of this every time I brought it up—but at least it allowed the conversation to continue. Mae and Wayne had been having the same nonconversation with my mom since probably before I was born. I could start one. I could ask them to visit. I could sleuth out some of the secrets that had kept them in Ding Dong all these years.

I got out a piece of paper and wrote:

Dearest Grandma and Grandpa Crawford,

*Merriest of holy Christmases to you. I always cherish your
loving Christmas holiday cards and I especially loved this
year's one. I feel so glad that you wish us all an abundance
of blessings, because we all—me and my mother, Pamela
Marie, and my father, Ken-zhi—do the same, but to you.
With your loving family support, I am learning to achieve
in school and am learning about my past and letting it lead
me to my bright future.*

*So much love and kisses. May Jesus and the Force be with
you.*

LOVE,
Vee Ken-zhi Crawford-Wong

I wasn't sure they'd get this. It sounded too nice and fluffy,
like maybe underneath I didn't want to say anything important
at all.

I tried again:

Dear Mr. and Mrs. Crawford,

*You don't know me, but I am the son of your daughter,
Pamela Marie. I am writing to tell you about me since I
don't know if you know I even exist, but I have always*

known that my mom is very upset to not have a nicer
relationship with you. Please pursue this, since it would
mean the whole entire world to her (and me).

Love (I mean this sincerely, too),
Vee Crawford-Wong

It felt like groveling. If they really did hate us, they'd laugh and laugh and pin this up on their fridge so they could laugh some more. I'd do better tricking them into showing they cared. I could tell them we'd won the lottery but were only sharing it with people who loved us. Or that we were onto their deepest, most horrible secrets and they'd better confess before we went to the press with it. I had a thousand other bad ideas too, but I needed something that would dare them to ignore us. Something that would terrify them or make them mad. I didn't want to be a polite Chinese kid. I wanted to be that punk American kid who did exactly what he wanted without thinking about anyone else. I was a conqueror. I took no prisoners. This was my crusade, and you could convert or you could be dead to me. Those were your choices.

I snapped the fresh paper in the air above my desk.

Grandma and Grandpa,

I am your long-lost grandson, the only offspring of the
woman who was once your daughter, Pamela Marie. I want

to let you know that she just died, that she killed herself at
the young age of 44 over grief. She left a note that stated
that her biggest regret in life was having parents who didn't
love her and who rejected her and her entire family. If you
care at all about this news, please contact me immediately.

Sincerely,
Vee Crawford-Wong

When sealing the envelope, I gave it a few extra-big licks for good luck. See how easy it is to ignore us now. See if one measly card once a year is enough to lift this guilt off your back, this monkey, this slap in the face, this insult, this silence.

Christmas was a big hurrah, with a tree and presents (new Nike Air Jordans, a Cal Basketball sweatshirt, a book on American archaeology, an iTunes gift card) and a ham with sweet potatoes and pecan pie. We did up American holidays so that Mom could remember her childhood and Dad could revel in traditional American excesses; at least, this was what I guessed. We'd always barbecued on the Fourth of July and on New Year's—which was never great barbecuing weather anywhere except for maybe Texas—and at Christmas we filled the gap under the tree with things that never needed to be presents, like socks and highlighters and shirts Mom would have bought for Dad anyway.

Madison's parents were Buddhist, but they celebrated Christmas the same way. The only difference was that their house teemed with aunts and uncles and second cousins and in-laws and third cousins twice removed. Madison got some seri-ous loot, and the chaos at their house was as festive as it was exhausting. Madison always told me about it with a weariness that I envied. She'd even invited me to her house last year, but it had felt wrong to leave my parents alone, and I hadn't been sure if they'd been invited, so I'd turned her down. I hadn't gotten an invitation this year. I didn't take it personally—the Chens had been back from China for only a few weeks, and Madison was still raging mad at them.

The next morning I called to invite them all to our New Year's party.

"Thanks," Madison said. "Let me ask." I waited and watched Dad squint at the instructions on a box of frozen Jimmy Dean sausages.

"Okay," Madison finally said, "but we probably have to leave early."

"But it's *New Year's.* The whole point is to stay up past mid-night."

"The whole point is to measure the earth's trip around the sun. We're just celebrating some arbitrary point in our orbit that the Romans decided on."

"Same with Chinese New Year," I said.

I heard muffled talking in the background, then Madison back on the line saying, "Of course we appreciate the invitation and would love to attend." Her voice was clipped, and I imag-ined her standing in her kitchen next to her mother and being prodded to be more polite. How could her mother continue to see an innocent little girl when Madison could bust out with such sophisticated, articulate, scientific shit? I knew I was smart, but she had the skills to talk me right under the table. Madison's parents treated her like a child. At least my parents had fun with me—or at least Dad did, anyway, and Mom was goofy in her own way. They didn't teach me any social skills, but at least they didn't take back what they'd given me. Madison was like a princess locked in a tower, but that tower was built of her own straight A's and the way she kowtowed to all of her parents' expectations.

On New Year's Eve, when the random collection of my parents' friends were milling around with their champagne and eggnog and spinach dip (my culinary contribution to the evening), I dragged Madison up to my room for a serious talk about the letter.

"Cool," she said, looking around. She sat on the edge of my bed, her feet dangling over the side. She'd taken off her sneakers at the front door, and her socks had frogs on them. I was suddenly embarrassed that I didn't have a place for her to sit. I didn't usually have other people in my room. I was too old for sleepovers, and I didn't have guy friends who came over and moped around with me. In seventh grade all my guy friends turned into dumb pricks, and since then, it had been easier being friends with girls like Madison—people who understood my sarcasm and didn't try to one-up me all the time.

"I want to go to China," I said. "I want *us* to go to China."

She looked at me sideways. The frogs waggled at me. "Not the letter idea again."

"Just listen," I said. "Your parents are fine with you going to China, right? They just don't want you to miss school and don't want to take another trip themselves."

"All true," she said. "So?"

"Once Dad agrees to take me to China, why wouldn't he agree to take you, too?"

"Your dad would take me to China?"

"He'd probably enjoy that more than taking me." It was true. I'd tag around after them and look like a mute, adopted mutt.

"Okay, I have a solution," she said. "How about you just ask your parents for a vacation to China, the way I did with mine?"

"How about you have no clue as to how my family works."

She narrowed her eyes at me. "Just tell your dad the truth," Madison said. "Tell him you want to go to China and meet your grandparents before it's too late."

"He told me that he doesn't expect anything from them," I said. "He said he'd take me to Chinatown instead."

Madison stared at my posters of Dwyane Wade and LeBron James.

"It's like he's built this wall around himself," I said, "like a castle, and knocking nicely on the drawbridge door isn't even going to register. We need to lay siege here. We need impersonation and espionage."

"Espionage?"

"I just like that word."

She laughed and stretched out on her stomach. "Okay. So what if this does work? We'll show up at this little hut by the river, and what? What if there's no one there? Or another family lives there now?"

"And what if they are there, and they see my dad for the first time in almost forty years? Think about it."

She tugged on a piece of her hair and studied the carpet. "Okay. Let me think about it."

I high-fived LeBron, who was permanently frozen middunk.

We went downstairs and joined the party, and at midnight ran our sparklers down the street like giddy three-year-olds. I wrote "Happy New Year" in the air with my fiery pen. Madison spelled out "*Gung he fat choy*," first in regular letters, then in Chinese characters. The adults chatted and drank cider, and the little kids chased after us or held their own sparklers and cried with fright. I felt fearless and invincible. I flew down the cold, dark street, my sparkler held high like an Olympic torch, fireworks popping around me, the wind and the confusion of the previous year finally rushing past and behind me.

20

Monday was our first day back to school. We were all driving to school together this morning, the happy Crawford-Wong family, because Fannie was in the shop again.

I tried acting normal in the car, but the more normal I tried to act, the more I wanted to hyperventilate. I hated school. I hated sitting still and stupid, pointless rules and classes that made my brain go mushy and numb. I couldn't cut class anymore; I'd somehow gotten away with it once, but I knew my luck wouldn't hold.

Mom and Dad listened to the news on the radio, and then Mom glanced back at me from the passenger seat. "Are you worried about something?" she asked.

"Um," I said. "No."

"You've always loved school," she said. "Just work hard and enjoy your friends. You're so smart, honey; I know you'll do fine."

Did she know me at all? She was just an old lady who had a dead relationship with her own parents. Then I instantly felt bad for thinking that. It was Mae and Wayne's fault. There was something wrong with them, I just didn't know what. Yet.

I rolled the window down to let in the drizzle, and I leaned as far out the window as I could. I felt my hair, which had been gelled into spiky bangs off my forehead, begin to droop and drip.

"I enjoyed talking with Mr. Chen at our party," Dad said. "Roll up the window."

"What did you talk about?" I asked.

"Secret Chinese things," he said.

"Everything Chinese is a secret to me," I said.

"Do you know that his family came from Hebei Province?"

Why was Dad always happy to talk about other people's families in China? Why was everything a safe topic except for the one that mattered? I had to push and push for every little piece of information about our families and our own lives.

"Is that near Yangzhou?" Dad's invented home and the invented home of world-famous fried rice.

He glanced at me in the rearview mirror.

"I don't know!" I protested. "I don't know anything."

"Not Yangzhou," he said. "Nowhere even near there."

I sat around the library during my free first period, and then I met up with Madison and Emily and sauntered to history like I didn't have a care in the world. Pretend, pretend, pretend. That's all I was good at. Pretending that my life wasn't all up in the air, my family all invented or dead or mysteriously silent.

Adele was absent—probably sleeping in or actually going to her own classes. Riley had on a new bruise-colored shirt, no doubt a Christmas present, and he sat on a stool at the front of the room and asked a few kids how their break was. He didn't ask me. He knew what I'd been doing.

"So I'd like to start this semester with an overview of history as a concept," he said.

Were we pretending that last semester never happened? I'd rather someone shoot me than have to go through Mesopotamia, Greece, and medieval Europe again.

He wrote:

History, a distillation of Rumour.
—Thomas Carlyle, Scottish historian

Oh, God. The story-in-history lesson again. What did they do, ship everyone to a history teachers' concentration camp and brainwash them so they'd keep giving us the same dull formula over and over?

"What does this mean?" he asked.

My hand raised itself.

"Mr. Crawford-Wong," Riley said.

"Well, it means that within every history there is a multiplicity of stories. And what's ironic is that the word 'story' is actually in the word 'history,' believe it or not."

I might have been okay if I hadn't tacked on the "believe it or not," but a few people snickered. So much for turning over a new leaf. He just smiled uncomfortably, like that was the answer he'd been hoping for. Wimp. Pussy. I couldn't believe he was letting me push him around.

"How many of you," he asked, "have ever heard and passed on a rumor?"

A bunch of hands went up. Madison's was kind of up, like she just had to itch her ear and decided to wave around her fingers while going at it.

He talked about the importance of knowing your sources and understanding who controlled the information channels. He didn't say anything about Iraq or Afghanistan—teachers generally pretended they didn't have their own opinions so that kids could make up their own minds—but I could tell he was thinking about how information was always being spun by the White House and the news channels.

When he was done with his pep talk, he handed out thick packets of reading material.

"Are we going to need our book, too?" Emily asked.

"No," Riley said. "We're going to shake things up. Go right to the primary sources."

Real history. Finally. Hopefully. I wanted to give him a high five or congratulate him for growing a spine or some balls or something.

At the end of class he handed back our finals, and I got a 163 out of 187, which meant nothing until I realized it was a B+.

"Pretty good for barely studying," I said when Emily leaned back to look at my score. As soon as I said it, I felt stupid for being so obviously defensive.

• • •

Madison finally caved in, saying we could always fess up if my dad's feelings were hurt—though I assured her he didn't have feelings anymore about China or his parents. We forged my grandparents' letter at lunch during our first week back at school. We didn't want to tell Emily what we were doing, but as it turned out, we didn't have to. She had started to hang out more with Chad's friends, who all congregated in the band room at lunch and after school. I didn't want to tell Madison, but it made me feel like a bit of a loser that we'd even lost the company of our dorky, pseudonerdy sidekick.

Once we got started on the letter, Madison was more than a hundred percent into it, brainstorming idioms that would sound like an old Chinese couple, and bringing in calligraphy paper and stamps she'd gotten from a pen pal. She smudged the stamps a bit and stenciled in marks that made it look like it had gone through the mail. The scheme turned into a game; it proved to us that we were special, that we were more than just a few Asian nerds geeking it out over homework and SAT classes.

On Friday, when we finished it, I asked her to read it to me.

"In Chinese?" she said.

"No. I prefer French."

"You don't know Chinese."

"I know what it says," I reminded her. "I just want to hear it."

It said that they'd received our letter on an auspicious day and had taken it as a sign that it was time to extend forgiveness to their only son. It said they were happy and healthy except for An-wen's persistent coughing. (I hadn't wanted my grandparents to be sick, but Madison had argued that it would create more of an incentive for us to travel.) They wanted us to visit: Ken-zhi and his wife and son and anyone else who was important to us. They wanted to know about our lives and our work, and they missed us (Dad) and loved us already (me and Mom) and were proud to be our family.

When Madison read it aloud, the words sounded sharp and cold.

"It's gorgeous," she said when she was done. "Just gorgeous. This is my *pièce de résistance*."

"Wuh-honh-honh-honh," I said in my best nasally French-guy accent.

She sealed it and said, "It's going in the mailbox today. I'll tell my mom I'm going home with Emily, and I'll take the bus by your house and then get my mom to pick me up near Emily's dad's office. Which is near your house."

"Could you make it more complicated?" I asked.

"I can't just give it to you. Your parents have to find it in the mail."

"Today?" I said. "Are you sure?"

"Are you chicken?" she said. "Don't you want to go to China? To meet them?"

"Come on, Mads. We both know they don't exist. Or we don't exist to them."

"Don't say that," she said. "We need this. You need this."

I couldn't argue. I did need this or something like this, something special that meant the Crawford-Wongs weren't completely alone in the universe. It was like my invented history essay and my convoluted family tree—even though I knew I was just making things up to make myself feel better, it still worked.

Mom picked me up in Fanny, who now had a new oxygen sensor and timing belt. I wanted to ask if she'd seen that greasy guy, Sal, who'd thought Dad was dead.

"Wow," I said instead, "you really deserve a new car, Mom."

"Nice try, Vee," she said, laughing softly and turning the radio to an annoying light rock station.

"What?" I said.

"You're not getting your hands on my Fannie," she said.

"Ha, ha." This was Dad's joke. Mom was a horrible joke recycler; she was goofy in her own way, but she was too sweet and sincere—she couldn't ever pull off sarcastic or inappropriate.

"You can drive when you get your grades up. We've already discussed this."

I sighed dramatically. "God, you're such an Asian mom."

She smiled mildly and kept her eyes on the road. "I'm Asian by association, honey."

I laughed. "Wow. Mom. That was actually funny."

"How was basketball?" she asked.

"Not funny."

"What do you mean?"

"I don't know," I said. She seemed surprised that I didn't tell her everything about basketball, though back when I'd tried to, she'd shut me down. Told me to mind my responsibilities. So

I'd resolved not to tell her anything more. That was her punishment: to not know anything.

"Aren't the girls doing better?" she asked.

We'd won our last two games, which had mellowed out Steffie some. Adele was playing as long as she had complicated strips of bright tape all over her knee. And Riley was all business—no joking around, no pats on my shoulder, no "thank you for not messing up." He didn't seem unhappy with me or with the team, and I wondered if the threats from me and Steffie had started to lose their punch. If he'd forgotten that I wondered about him with Adele, that I watched him closely while he was coaching her. He never touched her, but maybe watching her was enough of an offense? She was so hot, how could he not think about her in all those ways he wasn't supposed to?

I left Mom's question unanswered. I couldn't talk about any of this with her, with Dad, not even with Madison. Hot girls, bully girls, and maybe a perverted coach. They were my problem alone.

When we got home, Dad was in the kitchen humming something that sounded like the *Top Gun* soundtrack. The house smelled like an Italian restaurant. Dad always made pizza crust by hand, and once he'd even tried to make the cheese-stuffed crust like they had at Pizza Hut. Tonight the spongy dough was piled high with pepperoni, mushrooms, sausage, black olives, and cheese. He'd put out a bowl of pickled jalapeños just for him and me, since Mom didn't think they went with pizza.

"Mmm," I said. "This looks like S.O.P." S.O.P. stood for

"special-occasion pizza." Normal pizza was cheese and pepperoni. S.O.P. was whatever we could envision. Once, I'd wanted strawberries on my pizza, and Mom and Dad still laughed about how excited I'd been—and how I'd been so disappointed with the results that I'd cried and refused to eat any of theirs.

"Friday is always a special occasion," Dad said. "We celebrate no one losing an eye this week." He laughed heartily at himself. This was another one of his jokes. Since he was an ophthalmologist, he liked to say things like "It is all fun and games until someone loses an eye. Then he comes to see me." Or "It is all fun and games for me when someone loses an eye."

"Cheers," I said, raising my pizza slice. A piece of jalapeño rolled off it and splashed into my water glass. We all laughed, and I tried to forget about how sad my parents' lives must have been before they'd met each other and had me.

"Cheers," Dad said. "Miracle of miracles, we got a letter from China today."

I'd completely forgotten about the letter. I tried not to choke on the bite of pizza that was halfway down my throat. I made a soft wheezing noise and forced out a "Really?" He and Mom looked at me, and I couldn't prevent the heat from washing over my face. "What is it?" I asked in a squeezed voice. I had to act normal. I was on thin ice. Dad got up and brought the letter to the table. He turned it over a few times, then handed it to me. I wanted to rip it up and make it a joke. I felt like we were all just pretending we didn't know what was going on.

"Open it," Dad said, and I tore into the envelope with

nervousness that I hoped looked like excitement.

"Can you read it?" I asked Dad, holding out the paper and waving it under his chin.

"Let me hold it, please," he said.

He read it silently. At any moment he'd figure it out and look up at me and laugh. Or look up and be boiling mad.

"This is very curious," Dad said. "My father loved to write with such style, but here he is so shaky and formal. Maybe this coughing disease makes him more sick than he says. Or maybe . . ."

Mom and I waited. Dad shook his head.

"They must be very old now. I never thought they would write. I don't know what to think." Then he said some things that weren't in English. His face scrunched up like he was crying, but without tears, and I couldn't watch.

How could I have done this to him? What kind of person was I that I could reinvent the people he loved just so I could have a stupid vacation?

I didn't say anything, and I picked at my pizza. My breathing and chewing sounded rough and loud. It wouldn't just be a stupid vacation. It would link me to Dad, to his dad, and to an entire civilization that had gotten us to this point in time. I imagined eating dinner with his parents: everyone sitting cross-legged on a dirt floor, and little bowls of pickled things and sticky rice and egg noodles spread out before them on a low, lacquered table. I wondered if they instinctively hunkered down into themselves, each of them safe in their own little pocket of silence. I wondered what in the world we could talk about.

Dad put the letter in the middle of the table, and we stared at it as we ate. It was a mesmerizing centerpiece. I knew I should jump in now and push for the trip to China, wheedle and plead and argue while the letter was still believable and new, but I didn't want to break Dad's strange and fragile happiness. I didn't want him to discover the truth or think too much about the limitations of this postal reunion. How much weight could a polite letter throw around? How much good could come from a single trip to a vast, swarming continent?

I glanced at Mom. She was masticating (rah, rah! Ten points for using an SAT word!) and rubbing an imaginary spot off the base of her wineglass. I suddenly understood why she worked so hard to make everyone happy, to make everything seem just right: no spots on the wineglasses, ten kinds of meat to grill at every barbecue, clean scrubs with rainbows and teddy bears. That was her kind of therapy. She was scrubbing off the stains of her parents' absence in her life and her failed first marriage, feeding us to make up for that loss and neglect, acting bubbly and joyous because that's how she wanted to be. If I thought too much about it, it could make me crazy with a sadness that wasn't even mine.

I didn't know these people, my parents. I knew them better when they only existed in real time, and not also in some sad place in the past. I wished they really had come from nowhere. I wished I'd never asked about their families, and we could go back to cracking jokes and living only in this moment. I'd reached out into the world and pulled them into places they wanted to forget, but that I wanted to excavate and understand. I didn't know how to say this, how to apologize for doing this, and I could tell by the way they concentrated on their pizza and their wine that right now wasn't the right time for me to start talking.

21

I felt all mixed up with Dad's genuine reaction to the letter, and China began to seem more like a chore than a prize. Madison kept pestering me for details until I admitted, a week after Madison had delivered the letter, that I hadn't actually asked for a trip. Not directly. Not to Dad's face.

"You have to do this," Madison said. "You have to ask." We were on our way to biology, and she stopped short, turned around, and pointed at me. We were in the middle of the football field, and someone was playing the tuba, badly, in the far end zone.

"Promise me," she said.

"Okay," I said.

"No, say it."

"I promise you. I'll ask to go to China. I'll ask for both of us."

"Good," she said. "You're not like my parents. You're good for your word."

I smiled. Spontaneously, I put my arm around her neck and squeezed, and she elbowed me hard in the ribs.

In biology we had a lab that entailed dipping a goldfish into warmer and then cooler water and measuring its breathing rate. Madison and I were in the same lab group (hooray for alphabetical lists and teachers with no imagination).

"Ooh, la," I said, imitating Mrs. McKinley, "such a smart lab group!"

Tyler, the third musketeer, went to get beakers and a stopwatch. Madison tapped the side of the fishbowl, and our goldfish listed toward her fingers.

Madison said, "I looked on Google Maps, and Yihuangkou is only, like, a hundred miles from where my *yeye*'s buried."

"Yihuangkou?"

"Where your grandparents are," she said.

"Right. I forgot. Well, yours are near Beijing, which is right near Peking man. That's pretty cool."

"Are you serious?"

"Relatively."

"Who's Peking man?"

I rolled my eyes. "Only the second *Homo erectus* fossil ever discovered."

"Fantastic," Madison said, sharpening her pencil. "We can visit him, too."

"Actually, no," I said. "All the important bones disappeared after the Japanese invasion."

"How do important bones just disappear?"

"During the occupation they tried to ship the bones to America, but the crates got lost or the ship got sunk; they don't really know. It's a big mystery."

"So let's not go."

"I still want to," I said.

"What's the point of that?"

I couldn't explain it. It wasn't so much about seeing bones—even archaeologists, without all their high-tech research equipment, couldn't always tell old bones from new ones, the ordinary from the ones that made them famous. It was more about being where they'd been—the archaeologists, and the prehumans. It was about standing on the ground that man—or something like him—had shuffled around on half a million years ago.

I kept getting distracted, and finally my group got fed up and fired me, and while getting the cold and warm water to pour into the bowl, I started to worry about our fish dying. Why did we have to torture animals and call it science? There was plenty of already-dead stuff to learn from out there. I kept ruining the experiment by using lukewarm water.

Tyler asked me if I could do anything right.

"Nope," I said.

"Then at least write down what we tell you to write down."

"Yes, sir," I said. "Midas and I are at your beck and call."

"Who's Midas?"

I waved at the fishbowl. "Who's Midas? You're joking. Doesn't he look like a Midas?"

"Great. You've named our fish. Way to stay scientific."

"I'm taking the psychological approach," I said, "in case you weren't able to pick up on that. Midas has a lot of anxiety. He has a difficult time opening up to others."

"Just write down 'forty-two,'" he said.

"Perfect. That's his lucky number."

"Where's the hot water?" Tyler asked Madison, who had been reassigned to water duty. Tyler was going to be a scientist when he grew up. He had that *I feel good in lab goggles* look.

"What do you think they do with him after we torture him?" I asked.

"They'll give him back to the pet shop, Vee," Madison said. "And it's not torture."

"Who cares?" Tyler said.

"Who cares?" I said. "Who cares? I'm having a lot of anxiety."

"Shut up, Vee," Tyler said.

Madison laughed at both of us.

"Midas doesn't like harsh language," I said. "Watch your mouth or you'll mess up our whole experiment." I watched Midas drift around in his beaker, and I thought about asking if I could take him home, but I couldn't take all the Midases home, and taking them home wouldn't necessarily make their lives better anyway. What did they exist for except to serve us? They were like mice in a lab. They were like people in Korea or Mexico, and we were clothing manufacturers and fast-food companies and greedy Americans. I steeled myself and mercilessly iced down Midas and watched him swim lethargically and lugubriously, and I thought about showing off my SAT vocabulary, but I couldn't be sure my lab partners would fully appreciate what I had to say.

• • •

We had a basketball game that afternoon, which meant we were kicking the JV boys out of the gym early. I usually tried to get to practice right on time, after the boys and Coach Wilson had cleared out, but with a game there was too much to set up in advance. I kept my head down as I ran the electrical cords from the desk and from the shot clock to the wall. There was no shame in being a manager—most managers weren't charity cases who couldn't cut it as athletes—but I still didn't want to remind everyone of what could have been. To the boys I was that Asian kid who broke his nose playing basketball. To the girls, I was that goofy Asian manager. They liked me, but I was their friend, practically their pet. And people didn't date their friends. Or their pets. My strategy of just being around was backfiring.

I listened to Coach Wilson bark incessantly at the guys, and compared with him, Riley seemed tame. I wondered why no one was threatening Coach Wilson—probably because it was okay to verbally abuse guys. It made them tougher, which made them angrier, which made them play harder. I was sort of relieved that I hadn't made the cut. I'd probably wilt if someone railed on me all the time.

I was rounding the corner with the water cooler to set up for the opposing team just as the girls were filing into the gym and just as the JV boys were heading toward the locker room. It created a sort of traffic jam in the hallway, with me and the big orange tub as a kind of roadblock. So much for keeping a low profile. A few guys nodded at me. A few ignored me, as if they didn't know who I was. Jackasses.

Caitlyn and Adele sauntered through, arm in arm.

"Hi, wonderful manager man," Caitlyn said in her flirtiest voice. She was flirting with the basketball guys—Jamal, Mark, Blake—through me.

"Can you tape me up?" Adele asked. She had on her flirty voice too, but that was sort of her normal voice.

"You bet," I said.

"Kinky," Jamal said.

"You bet," I said to him, to the cooler, to the hallway, to anyone who was listening. I pleaded silently with Adele to let me have this one moment, to not spoil it by calling me on my smartass, inappropriate response.

Adele looked at me for a second, then glanced over at the guys, then threw me one of her rolls of bright pink tape. I casually snatched it out of the air, like we did this every day.

"Oh, boys," she said. "You have no idea." Then she winked at me and backed up a few steps, pivoted, and disappeared into the gym.

Jamal literally had his mouth open. Mark gawked at the gym door. I raised my eyebrows at them, then turned my back on them. I lost some of my cool as I had to steer the rickety cart with the cooler on it, but still, it was one of those moments I knew I'd file away and replay in my mind when I was feeling low.

Mom picked me up after basketball, which was unusual. Mostly Dad was my personal chauffeur because his office was closer to school than Mom's, and I actually looked forward to the ten quiet minutes in the car on the way home. Neither of us were talkers by that time of day, and both of us found radio stations annoying, and we wouldn't have agreed upon any music anyway. Silence was our best option, and it had turned into our routine.

Mom was a chatterbox. How was your day? Lots of home-work? How's Madison? What did you do at practice? Oh, you had a game! Why don't you tell me these things? I'd love to come see you, um, manage.

I wanted to sit in the quiet dark and remember Adele's wink, her flirtiness, the smooth skin of her calf as I taped up her knee, and later wrapped ice on her knee, and her grateful hug as she and Steffie headed toward the locker room.

Mom fiddled with the radio and found a song she could sing along with.

"Ack, shoot me," I groaned.

"You don't like Chicago?" She loved the oldies station: the Beatles and the Beach Boys and the Mamas and the Papas.

"Not Chicago plus Mom."

She was quiet, and I felt bad for having said anything. With her, I never felt like I could just be myself. I had to be more sen-sitive because she was more sensitive, and I always felt guilty if I disappointed her or acted like a jerk. The worst thing was that if I upset her, she wouldn't call me on it, and I was left to guess what I'd done wrong and deal with the guilt on my own. Like singing to the radio—it was annoying, but her silence now was even more annoying because I wondered if I'd made her sad.

We turned down our street, the streetlights and porch lights fuzzy in the darkening mist. Mailboxes shone like obsidian. We passed our house and kept going down the street.

"Mom?" I asked. Maybe I'd really pissed her off.

"I got a phone call today," she said. "People I haven't heard from in a long time."

I swallowed. There was no sense in pretending I didn't know. "Mae and Wayne," I said. It had taken them three weeks to pick up the phone. Three weeks. If Mom had been dead, her skin would be shriveled and her body cavity would already have burst open. Slimy, blind things would be crawling around inside her and eating her up. They were bad, bad people.

"There are things you don't understand, Vee—"

"I know."

"—and it's not your fault you don't know. But it's clear to me that I should try explaining things now."

Her voice wasn't wavering at all, and she didn't touch the dusty Kleenex box that was wedged between the parking brake and the gearshift.

"My parents are good people. I believe that. I have to believe that. But I don't see the world the way they do, and sometimes that's difficult."

"Okay," I said, even though I didn't get it. No matter how difficult they were, they were still ours. We were still theirs. Their blood was in my blood.

"My parents don't love each other," she said.

I didn't want to go down this road. I pressed my head against the window. I should never have written the letter. I should have let Mae and Wayne remain an endless mystery.

Mom sighed. "It wasn't an easy house to grow up in. I don't think you want to hear all the details."

I didn't. I felt angry and sick at the idea of Mom lying in her room with the covers pulled over her head, listening to Mae and Wayne fighting and throwing things and swearing. Maybe even hitting each other. Maybe even hitting Mom or yelling at her. I felt her loneliness, and it sat in the pit of my belly and brewed like a stomach virus.

"It's why I got married too young. And then when that didn't work out, it's why I didn't try to hold it together." She tucked her hair behind her ear again and again, which meant she was nervous.

"I think they felt guilty all the time. About their unhappiness and their stubbornness. And their neglect. But appearances were important to them. They wanted us to look like a family, even though we weren't in any real sense of the word."

I thought about all the Jesus-filled Christmas cards and if that was what chained them to each other. We turned left and began cruising up Maplewood. Mom barely had her foot on the gas. We coasted quietly past houses where we could see families having dinner, their TVs flickering, their baked-chicken-and-potatoes smell creeping through the cracks in our car.

Mom took both her hands off the wheel to tuck her hair behind her ears. "I've tried, Vee. I really have. So many times." She cleared her throat. "At some point, I guess, I decided it just wasn't worth it. I couldn't do it anymore."

We coasted past our house for the third time. I was exhausted.

"They're stupid," I said.

"I've tried, Vee. Please believe me on this."

My throat was tight. I hadn't meant to make her feel bad. It had taken them three weeks to call, those religious-freak bastards.

"I believe you," I said. "I just wanted to do something."

She accelerated down our street. "Oh, Vee, honey, I know. I did want you to know them. I dreamed about showing up with you in my arms, and them taking you to Disneyland, and all that. But they didn't want to meet me halfway."

We were going faster now. Mom was going too fast. We wouldn't make the sharp turn onto Maplewood. We stayed on Meadow. We almost caught air as we went through the bumpy intersection.

"They can't accept that I did what they couldn't and have put my life back together. That I have something with you and your father that they were too scared to try and find."

We blew through the next stop sign, and suddenly I was scared. Mom was going to kill us. She was going to drive us into an oncoming car and we'd explode. I knew my letter couldn't change decades of hurt. I knew it had barely made sense, coming out of the blue, all that anger puked up on the page.

"I answered the phone, and they thought I was dead." Her laugh sounded like a choked hiccup.

"I just wanted to help," I said. "I'm sorry. Mom, I'm sorry."

Mom passed me the Kleenex box and wiped at her own eyes

with the back of her hand. "I know," she said over and over again. "I know, honey, I know."

We kept making right turns until we were back on Meadow, heading toward our house. I didn't totally understand why we couldn't meet them in Texas or go to Disneyland. I didn't think Mom wanted to talk about the bad details, whatever they were, of her childhood and divorce and all the times she'd tried to make Mae and Wayne understand her. I didn't quite believe that silence was the only answer, but I'd been listening. Mom was done trying. I hadn't changed anything. Like Dad, she'd washed her hands of her parents, her history, and she seemed totally unconcerned that that's not what I wanted.

22

A few days later Dad took me to a Cal basketball game. All season the team had been playing horribly—losing leads, air-balling free throws, and injuring themselves in the process—and was ranked last in the conference. The gym was far from packed, and while Dad went to get hot dogs and sodas, I watched the student section fill up. I wondered what it'd be like to live with other people and only call home once a week. How often did college students think about their parents? How often did any-one think about their parents and scheme about ways to deceive them? I knew some kids who lied about things like drinking and smoking pot and cheating on tests, and I'd heard about so-and-so being a shoplifter or a slut or a pusher, and of course those were appropriate things to lie to your parents about, if anything because you loved them and didn't want to see them disap-pointed in you. But I was lying to them about their own lives. I was lying about grandparents and Christmas cards and a few sad, mangled stories. What was wrong with me? Why couldn't I be like everyone else?

I didn't have too long to think and feel sorry for myself because Dad came back with food, and the game started, and we didn't totally suck. I cheered and hissed and heckled along with the student section, which made me feel better.

"Maybe you could manage a team in college," Dad said. "That seems exciting."

I nodded and took a long pull on my soda.

"That's something to ask Mr. Riley. It could help you get into college."

"Sure," I said. I knew I couldn't ask Riley anything. The guy hated me. I hated him. I didn't just lie; I lied compulsively. What was wrong with me?

Dad sucked air through his teeth and opened a bag of Fritos.

"Frito Bandito, baby!" I said in my best Dick Vitale voice.

"Olé!" Dad said.

The cheerleaders were gyrating on the floor during a time-out. I thought about getting up to go to the bathroom so I could watch them without the general embarrassment of Dad's comments (usually something like, "That Asian girl dances the best," or even worse, "Which one do you like?"). I scooted to the edge of my seat, and just then Dad said, "How are you dealing with what your mother told you?"

I slid back into my seat. I shrugged and stared at the whirling pom-poms out on the floor.

"I'm sad for her, I guess," I finally said.

"We all have difficulties behind us," he said, "but that's how you learn who you want to be in life. You cannot divorce your past, and I don't think you want to."

"Thank you, Buddha," I said.

"We forget how old you are sometimes. She was going to tell you everything someday, when you were older. But we forget that you're older already. You're old enough to know the complexities of our lives and see us as people and not just your parents."

"When would 'someday' have happened?"

Dad sucked on his straw.

"If I hadn't asked for anything?"

The soda burbled in the bottom of his cup.

"If your parents hadn't written back?" I asked.

He stared at the court. "What do you think they want?"

"Maybe," I said carefully, "maybe they want us to visit them."

"Is that what you wanted when we wrote to them?"

I had to think about the question. Was it a trick question? Did he know? I said, "I'd like to meet them. But I wasn't sure what would happen when we wrote the letter." That actually was the truth.

"They don't want to see me for forty years. I send them letters and get no replies, and I wonder if they've moved or died," Dad said.

"I didn't know that."

"I didn't want you to bear this disappointment too, so I was reluctant to write that letter. But it's curious now to know they're alive and want what you, what we, want." The players were thundering up and down the court again, but I watched Dad chew a handful of Fritos and wash them down with soda. "It fits together perfectly, and something that was broken feels healed. They've changed. Maybe I've changed too."

I clung to my sweaty soda cup; waxy pieces jabbed under my fingernails.

"Let's go to China," Dad said. "A Wong family trip."

"Promise?" I asked, holding my breath.

Dad held out his salt-dusted fingers and we shook on it. The crowd roared around us. I watched the rest of the game without really watching it, and on the way home all I could think about was what it would be like to be in a Chinatown that was more than a few blocks long and wasn't crowded with gawking tourists buying T-shirts and miniature plastic cable cars. A Chinatown that stretched to the horizon. A Chinatown that was three thousand miles wide and six thousand years old. Even for someone like me, who understood the vastness of ancient history, I still couldn't get my mind to wrap around it.

Madison and I threw our parents together as much as we possibly could. We pretended to have group homework projects, and we casually dropped hints about how much the other parents liked ours and wanted to have them over sometime. This sparked a sort of competitive politeness, where everyone wanted to be the first to extend an invitation. My parents practically ran to the phone to ask the Chens to dinner.

The Chens came over the following Friday, and Dad made Yangzhou fried rice. Mrs. Chen asked for the recipe.

"It's not a family recipe. It's not even from Yangzhou," Dad warned her. "I found it in some cookbook from Berkeley." For some reason we were all camped in the kitchen, watching Dad cook. Mrs. Chen insisted that she wanted it anyway.

While I tried to carry on a polite conversation with Mr. Chen about how much I enjoyed biology, Madison stood at the kitchen counter helping Dad and asking him about China. She asked about our trip and where we'd go, and she mentioned that stuff about her people being close to our people. She buttered him up while dicing pork into microscopic pieces. Then they both wiped their hands and hurried into the den. I wanted to run after them, but I was stuck hearing about the wonders of adhesive dentistry.

Mom came into the kitchen to grab chopsticks for the table and asked, "Where's your father?"

"He ran off with Madison," I said. I cringed. I never meant to mention people running away or getting divorced or leaving each other, but somehow I always said the wrong thing around Mom. Everything reminded me of her past life.

Later, just before we dug into our steaming, salty bowls, Dad lifted his beer and proposed a toast. Madison and I lifted our water glasses, and Mom and the Chens lifted small, squat cups of tea.

"To friendship," Dad said. "And to the Chens for being such wonderful people."

We murmured and clinked and sipped our drinks. Dad still held his beer in the air.

"And I'd like to propose bringing Madison with us to China." He looked at Madison's parents. I choked on the ice cube I was chewing. "You do not need to answer now, but it makes perfect sense, since we're already going and we all come from the same small area of the world."

I looked at Mom, who was smiling politely. She didn't look like the odd man out, though she was. The only person whose DNA didn't go back to someplace near Beijing.

The table was filled with noise, with thank you, and thank you, and what an offer, and of course they couldn't, and how amazing, how generous, and of course they'd think about it. No one asked Madison to respond, so I guessed she'd already prepped everyone for this moment. I couldn't believe that our harebrained plan was actually coming together. Harebrained plans never came together.

Dinner conversation was dominated by China. Dad said he thought we'd go at spring break. Spring break was a good time to travel. He said people liked to have their LASIKs and canaloplasties over the summer.

"And we would not miss any instructional days," I said. I didn't know why I'd started talking to the Chens like I had starch up my ass. Like if I impressed them with my formality, they'd be more likely to send Madison halfway around the world with us.

"That was perfect!" Madison whispered to me while our parents were making good-bye noises.

"What did you guys talk about?" I asked.

"He showed me the letter," she said. "I know how you feel now. It was weird seeing it again, like it was both familiar and strange."

"Whatever you said, it worked."

"Yeah, I got to show off my reading skills, too. Your dad thinks I'm a genius."

"You're not?" I said.

She smirked and curtsied. She knew she was.

The Chens felt like they owed us one, but we had to work around basketball and medical conferences and one of Madison's cousins' birthdays, so we ended up having dinner together again on a random Wednesday. We went over to their house, and Mrs. Chen taught Dad how to make Mongolian chicken. Or rather, Dad pretended he didn't know how to make Mongolian chicken, and he let Mrs. Chen show off her culinary skills.

While they cooked, Madison and I sat at the dining table and did our homework. Madison had her French book out, and I pulled out the latest crumpled packet from history. Like the ones we'd already read about the decolonization of Africa and the partitioning of India, this packet on Tibet was full of first-person accounts of massacres and abuses of power. Men with their guns and gods and germs and plantations. Who was to blame for all the violence and chaos? Should Tibet have its autonomy? Was information ever completely reliable and true?

"Thank God we're finally doing something worthwhile," I said. "I don't remember Riley getting a concussion at practice or anything."

"What do you mean?" Madison asked.

"I mean second-semester Mr. Riley is way less stupid. It's like he's a different person. No more boring Greeks and Christian crusaders."

"Western civilization is an important foundation for studying other stuff," Madison said. "Didn't you read the course syllabus?"

"But he was so retarded last semester. These packets are so much better." I gestured at mine, which had lost its staple and was spread out over my half of the kitchen table. "Why didn't he have packets first semester?"

She looked up from her French book. "Because we had the textbook."

"Which sucked."

She refocused on her book.

"You're not disagreeing," I said.

She looked up again and tapped her pencil against her cheek. "Probably there's no textbook for the more modern, non-Western stuff we're studying now."

"But if there was, it would suck," I said. "And then Riley would still seem retarded, too." Somebody should have told him first semester not to stick to the textbook so much. He hadn't given us a chance to see this more interesting side of him until now. I hadn't given him the benefit of the doubt, either, but that wasn't my fault. He'd insulted our intelligence for so many months that it was hard to believe that he actually wanted us to think now.

"I'm the retarded one," I said. "Retarded for caring about school at all."

Madison glanced at me again, exasperated. "Vee, you just care about the wrong things."

"What, like because I hate how teachers grade based on whether or not they like you? Because I actually want to learn stuff?"

"Chill out," she said. "You only want to learn certain things. You think you're better than your teachers."

"Better than Riley," I said.

"Case in point," she said. "You've been out to get him since the first day of school."

"It's not my fault he's a shitty teacher."

"Really?" Madison said. "Because I don't have a problem with him."

"That's because you're getting an A plus plus."

She smirked. "And this is the guy who doesn't care about grades?"

I lowered my face to the table and breathed damp air onto its polished surface. Then I banged my forehead against the table a few times. I couldn't explain it all to Madison—how Riley had forced the issue of my family history with his stupid essay assignment, how he'd felt sorry for me even though I didn't want his pity, how he tried to be superdad to people he thought were broken.

I looked up in time to see her shake her head and return to her French book.

I knew she'd blow a fuse if I interrupted her again, so I finished the reading and got ready to write one page on what I thought countries' current foreign policy should be toward Tibet.

I wrote:

> *Tibet should be recognized as an independent country. In the 1960's Cultural Revolution, China was like a bulldog in a china shop, destroying religious treasures and national history.*

But that was stupid. The country was at civil war whenever it wasn't being invaded. Tibetans killed each other even though they were supposed to be Buddhist and all about nonviolence.

I got out a fresh piece of paper and wrote:

> *Tibet and China share the same area and religion. Other countries should recognize Tibet as a territory like Puerto Rico. The reading says that Tibet never ruled well on its own and therefore, if they were conquered, that's just how it works. Like*

And then I couldn't think of any examples that I liked. Like the conquistadores? Like the crusaders? Like Britain in India or Japan in China or the U.S. in Iraq?

I couldn't do my homework. I wadded up both pieces of paper and missed the trash can twice.

"Mads," I said, "what did you write?" I was certain she'd already finished her history homework. It was due tomorrow.

"*Vee*," she said. "Ohmigod, seriously."

"Seriously," I said.

"You can't steal my idea."

I rolled my eyes. "There are only two ideas out there. It's not like you own one."

"Tibet deserves its independence."

"Even if that means everyone's always poor and fighting?" I ran my fingers along the scratched surface of the table.

"Sure."

I sighed dramatically. How was she so confident? How was this so easy for her?

Madison said, "Just make sure you choose a side. That's what he wants." Riley loved to mire us in ambiguity during class discussions, but somehow for homework we were supposed to choose right and wrong.

"What if I can see what's a little right in both sides?" I asked.

She leaned forward and her pencil fell out of her ear. "Don't you want to get a good grade? You're supposed to pick a side."

"Even if it's bull and I don't believe in parts of it?"

She sighed and twirled her pencil like a baton.

"So what do you really think?" I asked. "I mean, if you didn't have to write a paper on it."

"I don't know," she said. "I don't have time to think that much about it."

For a long moment we listened to the clinking and murmuring in the kitchen.

Finally she said, "It's impossible to be totally on one side.

Most things go right down the middle, but that makes a weak argument."

She was right. You could almost never say right or wrong, yes or no, good or bad. Lying was bad, but so was silence, so was not saying anything. Making up a life was wrong, but so was not knowing about a life you deserved to know. Freedom was good, but Dad's freedom took him away from his parents, who then shut him completely out of their lives. Love and marriage were sometimes good and sometimes not, and sometimes you couldn't tell until it was too late.

I couldn't turn to history for any answers. Freedom—physically, emotionally, politically—was a modern concept. The Mongols and crusaders and conquistadores had traipsed around raping women and owning people's lives. Women used to be property because they were weaker and could be pushed around. Black guys used to be property because they didn't have sophisticated guns and disease resistance. Anyone who didn't worship your god in your way was fair game. Who were we to call this violence right or wrong when there was no other model to follow?

23

Knowing Riley wasn't such a dumb-ass at history made it easier for me to keep my mouth shut at practice. The team's record had improved steadily since Christmas, and some of the tension had leached out of everyone's issues with him. He was still aloof with me—as if my calling him a pervert had killed whatever genuine emotion he felt toward me. And I still watched him closely whenever he was with Adele, hoping for more clues to their relationship.

Clue number one: he did call a lot of free throws in her favor. Lily was right to have gotten pissed about it. I kept stats while they scrimmaged, and percentagewise, she got to shoot way more often than anyone else. Of course, I also watched them play, and she really put herself out there. It was why she got hurt so often.

Clue number two: Adele sitting next to Riley on the bleachers after practice one day, and when I got close, they stopped talking. My ears burned as if they had been talking about me, but that would be ridiculous. Who was I to them? Their lowly manager. Underachieving student and failed athlete. I wondered what else they could be talking about that would be private, and of course my mind went to all the unanswered questions I had about their relationship. They hadn't been touching. At least, I didn't think so. The more I thought about it, the less sure I was.

Clues three through infinity were all the looks, pauses, innuendos, and silences that meant everything or nothing. They never added up to anything but more confusion. Was Riley really just a coach-slash-dad? He was too young and sporty. She'd stayed at his house. How could nothing be going on? I didn't have the guts to ask.

The last weekend in February the team had an end-of-the-season party at Steffie's. I'd been invited. Or actually, Steffie had ordered me to be there. Steffie didn't know how to ask for anything without issuing an ultimatum, and maybe I struck her as the kind of guy who would flake on a party with a bunch of older girls.

Dad had to drive me over, since my GPA was still in the no-driving-lessons zone. Madison would be getting her permit in early May, after we got back from China, and we both agreed that she'd probably be driving me around before I ever got to put my foot on a gas pedal.

For the entire ten minutes of the car ride to Steffie's house, I fiddled with my basketball tie and wondered if I'd look stupid and out of place. I didn't know what else to wear. I knew the girls wouldn't wear their warm-ups, but I knew they liked my tie. So I clung desperately to the one thin piece of fabric that announced, *I fit in.*

"I'll call you later," I told Dad.

"You can call me whenever you need me," he said.

"That's like the title to some really bad country song," I said. "Don't worry about me, okay? I might be able to get a ride back anyway."

"Buckle up," he said, which was code for "Be safe." He rarely said it when I climbed into the car, since I instinctively put my seat belt on first thing, but he'd been saying it more and more when he dropped me off at the gym or at school or at the movies. I was worried that all the humor would wear out of it. I was embarrassed that he was expecting me to be tempted by all the bad things some kids did. *I'm not your average bad kid*, I wanted to say. *I'm fucked up in a whole different way.*

As soon as I got inside Steffie's house, I knew that there were more people here than just the girls' basketball team. The air was thick and humid like in the gym. There were other boys. And there was beer. I tore off my tie and shoved it in my pocket.

"Vee-Dawg!" Steffie yelled from across the room. "Vee-Dawg in the hiz-ouse!"

I smiled at her and blushed up to my eyeballs. Steffie picked me up and swung me around and left sweat marks on my shirt. Then she smacked my forehead with her lips.

"Hah! Check that."

I rubbed my forehead.

"No, Vee-Dawg! Leave it!"

I stopped rubbing my forehead.

Lily brought me a red plastic cup. "Libations?"

"Sure," I said. It was already in my hand anyway.

"Okay, have fun," Steffie said, "and don't do anyone I wouldn't do."

I drank my beer. A few people waved at me, but no one left their group to come talk to me, and I didn't want to butt in.

I drank another beer because there was nothing else to do. I felt full and tired. I looked at the pictures inside a glass cabinet. Steffie with her parents at a baseball game. With grandparents at Six Flags. With the basketball team.

I walked down an empty hallway and heard giggling behind a closed door. I jumped back just as the door burst open and three girls came teetering out. I went into the bathroom after them. Steffie's parents were probably very cool, not only to let her have a raging party, but also because the bathroom was all shades of black and white. The sink rose up from the counter like a wide, marble salad bowl. The mirror hung behind it by invisible threads. The toilet was black. There was no trash can and no medicine cabinet and no vat of yellow antibacterial soap. It didn't even smell like a bathroom. It smelled like nothing, like people didn't actually crap in here. I put my beer cup on the edge of the sink, and then I pissed. The watery sound echoed strangely off the shiny black tile.

The echoing made me think about the Chavín temples in Peru, the twisting underground caves and irrigation systems running over them with carvings of people with fangs and claws and snot running out of their noses. The caves had been used to hold human sacrifices. Or animal sacrifices. Or hallucinating priests. No one knew what the temples were for, actually. The whole civilization just kind of sprang up like they were Cabbage Patch Kids, and they built underground temples with water that tumbled over rocks in ditches above them. Then they disappeared. It was spooky. And weird. Archaeologists were still wildly guessing.

It was like trying to guess the right answer on an SAT math question when you didn't know the first thing about variables or logic.

Question:

On a basketball team with eighteen members, eleven are drunk on beer and five are drunk on liquor and two are pretending to be drunk but aren't. How many members will need to puke in the black and white bathroom?

    a. Fewer than thirteen but more than three

    b. Fewer than seventeen, but did you count the manager?

    c. More than one, but how many bathrooms are there?

    d. Beer before liquor, never sicker

    e. Lick her? I barely even know her!

Question:

If you walk out of a bathroom and the girl right out of your fantasies hands you a full shot glass and says, "This has real gold flakes in it," and you say, like a dumb-ass, "Wow, that's cool," and she says,

"You gonna shoot it with me?" and you nod, what are the odds of you knowing what you're getting into?

    a. Pretty good; the Force may be with you.

    b. Fifty-fifty; you have no idea what you're about to drink.

    c. Not good; you're already light-headed.

    d. The odds against you are statistically approaching infinity.

    e. It's too late to call your dad.

The liquid and gold went down like a lump of cinnamon gum. I leaned against the wall of the hallway and knocked a picture crooked.

"Oops," I said.

Adele was staring at the flakes of gold in the bottle.

"Is that really gold?" I asked. "Or just gold-colored plastic?"

"It's seriously real gold," she said, "one hundred percent karat."

Maybe twenty-four karat, but whatever.

"Why do they put it in there?" I asked.

"Because we're worth it," she said. "Want another?"

I shook my head back and forth. "I'm recovering from the first."

"Did you know," she said, "that this is what Shania Twain drinks before she goes on stage?"

"She does?"

"Yeah, I read that somewhere."

"You like Shania Twain?" It sounded like an accusation, like I *didn't* like Shania Twain, but I couldn't even remember who she was.

"Shh," she said, pressing her forefinger against my closed lips.

"I know it's so uncool to like country, but I do. Don't tell anyone."

Who would I tell?

She held the bottle neck like a microphone and sang into it. "'That don't impress me much. So you got the brain but have you got the touch?'" Her voice was husky, and she rocked her hips beneath her skintight jeans.

I said, "Hey, that's greats."

"You just said 'greats,'" she said.

"Whoops."

"Are you drunk?" she asked.

I wasn't sure. My brain and tongue were disconnected, that was all.

"Dance with me," she said. She took my hands and held them up in the air, along with the bottle, and swayed back and forth to the rap song that was blaring in the living room.

"You're a good dancer. Too bad you don't go to school dances," I said. I thought about her dancing with Mark, her long, shiny hair swaying with the beat of the music, her breasts pushing up against his sweaty chest.

"Duh," she said, "I do."

"Not the Halloween dance."

"Yes, the Halloween dance."

"Yeah? With who?"

"Me, myself, and I," she said. She closed her eyes and swayed toward me. "Wanna know the truth? I wasn't gonna go, but then Richie was an asshole again, and I dumped him for good, so it was like go or stay home and have Medusa nag me for everything I always do wrong. So I went."

"Yeah, I know. I saw you there," I said. She didn't even remember that I'd asked her to go with me.

Two more girls tottered down the hall and into the bathroom.

"Richie. Huh," I said. Her older guy. "I had to go with this girl who's a total, you know. Head case." I couldn't believe I was telling her all this.

She opened her eyes.

"Madison set us up," I said. I was talking too much. Diarrhea of the mouth.

"I know who Madison is," Adele said. "You're both in Neil's history class. She's smart as shit. Plus, let me tell you a secret." She leaned toward me and spoke into my neck. Her breath tickled and condensed against my skin. "She totally likes you," Adele whispered.

"No," I said.

"Sure," Adele insisted. "You went with her boring, safe friend. She'd never let you go with someone like me."

"Someone like you?"

"Unsafe," Adele said. "Fun but totally not safe." She put an arm around me and grabbed my cheek. "Anyway, you're absolutely a cutie. You should go for her."

My entire body flushed.

We stood in the hallway and I drank my beer and she poured herself another shot. She drifted farther down the dark hallway, and I followed her, glancing back toward the living room, where everyone was still just standing around with big red cups. Adele opened a door to her right and walked in. I stood in the doorway. No one cared if we disappeared from the party. No one cared if I disappeared into a dimly lit room with a dangerous girl.

I took two steps into the room. I looked out into the hallway, then I reached out into it and grabbed the door and closed it. *Don't think,* I said to myself, *don't think. Be brave. Don't say anything stupid.*

"This is Steffie's room," she said.

"No way," I said, and meant it. The walls were light green, and the white furniture all matched and looked like it belonged in a catalog. Even the pictures on the desk were lined up in a neat row of matching silver frames. There was no basketball hoop taped to the doorjamb, no sports posters, no denim bedspread. This was not Steffie's room. Did her parents even know she was an aggressive, potty-mouthed, butt-slapping jock, or did she hide it when she came home? It shocked me, the idea of Steffie having secrets, of being one way in the gym and another in her seafoam green room.

Adele sat on the emerald bedspread and patted the spot next to her.

"Tell me everything," she said.

"About what?"

"About you. About everything."

I couldn't help it, but I started laughing. Did she really mean it, and if so, where would I start? With my messed-up family?

With my fantasies of her? With my questions about her and Riley?

She laughed and put her hand on my neck. "Come on," she whispered. Her breath tickled my ear this time.

"What happened when you stayed at Riley's? Seriously? Because he knows I know, and he's weird about it." Finally. It felt good to put it all out on the table.

"Oh God," she said. "I don't want to talk about all that."

My ear. She was kissing my ear, and it was like a wet willy but good. Then she laughed. It was a sharp, hurt laugh.

"Everyone's weird about it," she said. "But I swear to God all he did was save my ass."

I bit my lower lip and waited. She closed her eyes, swayed into me, and kept talking.

"It was just more of the same bullshit about me and Richie," she said. "Because he's in junior college and has his own apartment and everything, but with roommates, you know, and I used to stay over there a lot. When I needed a place, you know. But then Medusa found out where I was going, and Steffie found out I was using her place as a cover, and she can't stand Richie to begin with. She always threatens to bust him for drunk driving or pot dealing or statutory rape or something. Anything. Just because he doesn't have anyone looking out for him and because she's had a crush on me since eighth grade."

Her fingers were tracing my lips and running over my ears and my shoulders.

"Yeah," I said. I didn't know why I said that.

"Steffie won't admit she's jealous. And then Medusa kicked me out of the house because she found out about Richie and thought I was, like, out of control and doing all the shit he does." She took a deep breath and blew it out on my face. Tangy cinnamon breath. "And then Richie and I had another fight, and he told me to go home, but then I had nowhere to go. And I couldn't even call Steffie anymore, and I was drunk and seriously wanted to just kill myself, but then I thought about calling Neil. So I did. And he picked me up and drove me around for a while, and then I ended up crashing on his couch. Just until I got my shit together again and Medusa realized she was out of line and I promised to dump Richie."

Then my shirt was open, and she took my hands and brought them up to her ribs. I inched my hands up until I could feel her breasts through her sweater. They were thick and heavy. The sweater was thick. I didn't know where I was allowed to go. I moved my hands in little semicircles around her breasts. I was too nervous to even enjoy it. What if she didn't like what I was doing? What if Steffie came in here and found us? Would she kick me out of her house?

"And Steffie's still pissed. As if she's got any idea what it's like to have a fucked-up family and a psycho-bitch stepmom and a mom who acts like she's the teenager."

"I get it." My mouth felt cottony and my blood roared and sang in my ears. I wanted to be different from Steffie or Richie or even Riley, who just drove her around when she was drunk. I wanted her to know about my family, how fucked up it was. "I get it," I said again. "My mom's parents hate her. And she told me all about them finally because I faked a letter to them about her death. And I invented my whole family history paper because my dad's family was oppressed by the Cultural Revolution and he's too permanently scarred to even talk about it."

I could tell Adele was having trouble processing everything I'd said.

"Oh," she finally said. "Oh, Vee, I'm so sorry." She put a hand on my forearm and rubbed the hairs back and forth. I wanted to close my eyes and lie back on the bed. We were talking about such private things, and I didn't even feel bad about it. My mom and her secrets and unhappiness. My dad and his quiet, tenuous freedom and pride. This was stuff I wouldn't even tell Madison. I was slimy. Disrespectful and slimy. I shouldn't ever have opened my mouth, but Adele had told me everything and she was so close I could smell her sharp, sweet breath, and she was rubbing my arm and saying, "I'm so sorry," like these things had actually happened to me.

Then she said, "Do you want to mess around?"

Yes. No. Yes. Why was she asking like this? Didn't things just happen without all this talking? I remained frozen.

"Not sex. Duh. But . . . you know . . ."

That unfroze me. Excited me. I took a few deep breaths, and the world became a whirling mass of pinpoints of light, and her hand rubbed circles on my belly, and then she threw a leg over me so she was straddling my stomach. My knees were hinged over the bed and my feet dangled somewhere near the floor. I tried to scoot up, but she had me pinned with her long thighs, and her shiny hair fell around my face and got into the corners of my mouth. She flung her hair back and leaned down to kiss me. She tasted like cinnamon gum and smelled like dried flowers. Her tongue pushed against my teeth, and I opened my mouth and let her do whatever she wanted.

"Kiss me back," she said.

I didn't know how. I stuck my tongue out to meet hers and encountered teeth and gums. She ran her tongue along my lower lip. I had a bunch of saliva in my mouth and couldn't swallow it. It was like being at the dentist and waiting for the little mouth vacuum to suck it all out. I had to swallow, but I didn't want to bite her tongue. Just when I was about to gag, she paused to fling her hair back again, and I choked down the warm saliva.

She kissed me for a while without tongue, thank God, and I put my hands on her jean-clad thighs. I could feel the muscles flexing as she bent over me. Her kissing got more aggressive. Then her body sort of collapsed onto mine, so that my hand was trapped between my stomach and her leg. She wiggled down and pushed her crotch against my hand. I couldn't feel what was under her jeans. It was warm and bony, and my knuckles jabbed rhythmically into my gut.

"I want you," she said, "right now. Come on." She rolled off me and began undoing her belt. Faster than I could follow, she had her jeans off, and she was pulling the comforter down and pulling me down next to her. "You like me, right? Right?"

"That's an understatement," I said.

"You want to touch me, right?"

"Huh," I said. My brain wasn't working. I'd become a Neanderthal. I grunted again, and my hands went to her breasts again, but she took one and guided it toward her thighs. "Go ahead, touch me," she said. Her panties were lacy. Under her panties there was hair, wiry hair like mine, hair that confused me. I didn't know what I was doing, it was wet, it felt like blood on my fingertips, like maybe I was hurting her. Should I keep going? Down? Inside? Were my fingers inside? They felt inside. My finger felt like it was inside an orange. She had her head against my chest, so I couldn't see if I was hurting her. Why would she let me hurt her? My arm was starting to feel sore, but I kept jabbing my slimy finger around down there. I was afraid to stop. I was afraid to keep going.

Then she moaned a little and threw her head back. I looked down at her lacy panties with my hand moving underneath, then up her long body to her face, flushed, blotchy, she was crying. She was crying. My entire body went cold and still. I was hurting her.

"Keep going," she said.

"Why are you crying?" My finger was still inside her. I didn't want to move and hurt her.

"I'm just drunk, that's all." She covered her face with both her hands.

My finger lay inside her panties, skinny and wet and limp, on her pubic hair. I felt defeated. It wasn't just about being drunk. I knew there was more to it, and maybe she couldn't put it into words, but it wasn't about me, it was bigger than me. I took back my finger and wiped it on the bedspread, and she sat up and smoothed down her hair. It looked dull and dry, and wisps of it clung to her wet eyelids.

"Will you lie on top of me?" she asked.

I didn't want to.

"Please?" she asked. "Just as a friend?"

I did what she asked. All my clothes were on, and I buttoned up my shirt before carefully lying back down next to and then on top of her.

"Am I crushing you?" I asked her.

"Yes."

I lifted myself off her, but she put her hands on my back and pulled me back down.

"I like it," she said.

She scared me. I rolled off her and sat up. I put my hand gently on her stomach. "I don't know you," I said. "I really don't know you. I have to go."

I wasn't stupid. I knew I was just someone to make out with when she was sad and drunk. I'd been a temporary stand-in for Richie, for Steffie, for her parents, for Riley. I stood up and pulled the covers the rest of the way over her.

"Thanks," she said.

I would never have imagined that, given the chance to lie in bed with Adele Frank, I'd tuck her in and walk away. But that's exactly what I did. I even gave her a dry kiss on the cheek and whispered, "Good night."

Then I was back in the pounding party, but all the party felt drained out of me. As I moved toward the front door, Steffie found me.

"Where ya been, dude? You look a little worse for the wear."

"Been doing my thing," I said. My voice sounded flat and tired.

"You wasted?"

"No."

"Good. Good man. Drinking should be done in moderation."

"Bullshit," said Jen, coming up behind her and grabbing the belt loop at the back of her jeans.

"I'm gonna go outside," I said, "maybe call my dad."

"You good?" Steffie asked.

"Sure," I said, "why wouldn't I be?"

She laughed. She had no idea. I wasn't good at all. This was as not good as I'd ever been, and there was no one I could talk to about it.

24

I'd been wrong about Riley. I imagined Adele calling him, drunk and hysterical, threatening to kill herself, certain that she'd never have a place to sleep off her headache and heartache. What else could he have done? He probably tried to take her home. She probably puked gold-flecked vomit all over his car. It seemed absurd, now that I knew the whole story, that I'd ever imagined him seducing her. That he'd want anything to do with a messy, messed-up teenage girl.

I thought about apologizing to Riley. I'd turned him into such a dirty scumbag. I'd been so certain that he deserved my loathing. I wanted to talk to Madison, but she'd thought all along that my opinions on Riley were irrational and immature. And I'd have to tell her about my essay, and Adele, and what just happened with Adele, and I couldn't do that. I hadn't purposefully left her out of the loop, but I was just never sure how to bring up my feelings for Adele, or how to explain Riley's child molester potential. And now that I was the one who looked stupid and childish, it was better to keep it all to myself.

I couldn't talk with my parents. They weren't good with these things—girls, sex, beer, sports, ingratitude, and a big mouth. They'd tell me to apologize, and I didn't want to be told what to do. They'd ground me for life. Bye-bye, China trip. Bye-bye, trip where Dad would learn that his parents were dead or that he was dead to them. I couldn't even tell them about the letter. Somewhere in the back of my mind I'd expected it all to fall apart and become some joke. Hey, Dad, remember that time when you believed your parents were speaking to you again? That they wanted to see you and me and be a part of our American lives? When we went all the way over there, and then you finally got the joke, hundreds of dollars too late, thousands of miles too late, and by then it wasn't funny?

It wasn't funny now. It was already too late.

We had our tickets: a plane to Beijing, a bus to Madison's family up in the hills, and a few days after that a train to Qinhuangdao, which was a taxi ride's distance from Dad's hometown. At night I lay awake and played the movie in my head: the way the taxi would shudder over a narrow, dusty road, past a muddy, slow-moving river, all of us crammed in the back and peering anxiously through the smeared windshield and windows. The road would climb into the mountains, the river would turn thinner and clearer, and suddenly we'd be in a little town, just one main street with an open-air produce market, an all-you-can-eat buffet, an opium den, and my family's fish market. Dad would narrate and tell us stories of where he used to run as a kid and where his friends lived and what owners of what shops would give him little candy treats if he did errands for them. Madison would notice other things, like the kids our age playing with firecrackers or gutting fish in the Wang Fish Market. Mom would notice the colorful peasant outfits on the ladies and the quiet happiness of old couples playing checkers on their porches. I'd notice an oddly shaped hillside behind the market, and we'd get out of the taxi. We'd go explore, and Dad and Mom and Madison would laugh at me and say it was only a hillside, but I'd take a little shovel and scrape away some of the dirt and old fish bones, and there'd be engraved turtle shells and bones of saber-toothed tigers.

"Dragon bones," I'd say.

"Is this what my grandfather was grinding up and drinking as medicine?" Madison would ask.

In my daydream I was always smarter than Madison.

"It's another name for ancient oracle bones they cracked in fire to tell the future, like a Magic Eight Ball," I'd say, while immediately blocking off the site for further excavation.

We'd take the dragon bones with us and walk farther down the road, to where it curved and sloped toward the river's edge. An older couple would stand in the doorway of my father's house, looking like they'd just stepped out of a historical exhibit about immigration and Angel Island. They'd hug us and shower me and Madison with gifts and old family relics, carved boxes like the one Dad already had, jade bracelets for Madison, and an old, rusty samurai sword that had been in the family since the tenth century. My grandfather would lift the bones out of my hands and tell me that there were mountains of these behind their house. Their house would become a renowned archaeological site, and Madison and I would work on the excavation and never come back. We'd stay in Yihuangkou, and for weeks we'd dig and uncover and piece things together, all the while cracking jokes about everyone we'd left behind in our previous, boring lives.

I asked Dad at breakfast one morning if we could visit Dragon Bone Hill, which was an actual site just like the one in my daydream and also the famous place where they'd found Peking man. "Also, it's near Beijing," I said.

"Let's see where the wind blows us," Dad said.

"Okay," I said. Now was the perfect time to tell him the truth.

"Dad, I—" I said. Where could I possibly start?

He calmly chewed his granola and waited for me to spit out the words that were lodged in my throat.

"Why do you think," I asked, "they want to see us now after so many years?"

"That's easy. It's because of you."

"Oh." I pushed my cornflakes around until I had a well of milk in the center of my bowl. I watched the soggy flakes slowly circle. I tried to see how many cornflakes I could get on my spoon at one time. Four. Seven. One. Three. I asked, "Are you nervous to see them?"

"No," he said. "I don't feel I know who they are anymore. It will be like meeting strangers."

"Do you think they'll like us?" I asked.

I looked up at him. He was looking at me.

"You are family, and you've made them proud. This is what it said in the letter, and I believe it."

He was telling me about the grandparents I'd invented. He talked about them like they were real people.

He wasn't worried. That was my cop-out every time. It didn't matter that much to him, and it mattered so much to me, and so, my logic went, it was best to stay silent for the time being.

When I saw Adele during the last week of basketball, which was the second week in March, she acted like everything was normal and nothing had happened between us. Nothing *had* happened, really. A little rubbing. A little tongue jabbing and finger poking.

I settled for letting everything blow over, like a confusing fight or a silly misunderstanding. I kept my mouth shut and ignored Riley's constant under-his-breath commentary, which wasn't meant for the girls, but that somehow I was allowed to hear. It was like he was trying to win me over by doing guy bonding against the girls. I didn't want to guy bond with him, especially if that meant I had to apologize for calling him a pervert. I figured my accusation hadn't actually hurt him, and I knew that there were always other scandals, other tragedies in the world, bigger than the ones I'd been inventing.

I argued to myself that Riley would have been proud of my insight here, my realization that the stories of history are only ever temporary, that they shift and surface and then can be covered up again. I already knew, from the lessons of archaeology, that the world stretches and breaks and folds over itself, and what is new and obvious one instant can be forgotten as the edges of other, more exciting discoveries emerge.

I was just hoping that these rules, these forces of nature, could apply to my life, too.

On the day of our last basketball game I watched the girls warm up. I watched Adele pick at the tape on her knee, and Shelley play with the rubber bands on her braces, and Jen tuck her shirt under the tight elastic of her sports bra. I realized that they didn't intimidate me anymore. They weren't real friends, but I liked most of them okay, and they didn't make me jittery with hormones or blurry with self-consciousness.

Everyone came by to slap my basketball tie before grabbing water and going into the huddle. It had become a good luck tradition. Steffie and Jen always whacked me pretty hard, and Shelley always giggled, like she was embarrassed to be touching me. Today everyone was nicer and more serious. Steffie gave me a great big bear hug. Shelley didn't giggle and actually gave my tie a good whack. Adele brushed her hand against my tie and didn't look me in the eyes. She somehow sensed she didn't matter as much to me anymore. She was just a girl—yes, a hot girl—but I'd seen her practically naked and touched her, and it hadn't opened up the heavens and changed my life. She didn't have power over me anymore, and I was actually glad that I could reallocate some brain space for more important things.

After the game, which we won, as I was dumping the water bottles and stacking them next to the ice machine, Steffie came in to get ice for her eye, which had caught an elbow during the game.

"Yo, Vee-Man," Steffie said. The ice machine, as if in response, sputtered and roared to life.

"Hey," I said. I watched her pick up small handfuls of ice and put them in a plastic bag. "There's a scoop, you know."

"I don't like doing things the easy way," she said. "Do you know I just read this book where these dudes hike around their village and discover ice for the first time." She picked up a single ice pellet and held it up to the light. We watched it melt between her fingers. "Wouldn't that be weird? To see this for the first time and wonder where it came from? It makes me think that there's a shitload of stuff out there that I've never seen and can't even imagine. You know what I'm saying?"

I knew exactly what she was saying. It was the way I felt about girls and my family and China. It was like wondering about who Mom was with her parents, or what Dad would be like in China. It was what defined archaeologists and their lens on life: their ability to look at the extraordinary and find everyday objects, or their ability to look at something they'd seen their whole lives and recognize it differently, allow themselves to be amazed that they'd taken it for granted this whole time.

"Yeah," I said.

Steffie shrugged and chewed on some ice and began tying up her bag. Madison would have understood my "yeah," that it wasn't a brush-off. That my brain was going too fast for my mouth and I couldn't say all that I was thinking.

"So what now?" I asked her. Basketball was her life. She was going off to play somewhere in the Midwest, though she admitted she was bench-warming caliber by their standards.

"Now we go on with our lives," she said. She put the bag of ice over her eye and said, "Rrrggh. Damn that hurts."

That wasn't what I'd meant. I looked at the unfinished row of Gatorade bottles. They were still sweating.

I said, "He didn't sleep with her, you know."

She pinned me with her one good eye and shrugged. "I know that. He's not that stupid."

"I'm not even sure he's as bad a coach as you make him seem."

She chewed another handful of ice. "You're entitled to your opinion, I guess."

"Why do you hate him?"

"I don't."

"Then why did you threaten him?"

"How did I threaten him?"

Was Steffie really going to stand here and rewrite history? She'd told me she'd talked about going to the boosters. She'd had no reason to lie to me.

"You told me—"

"I was motivating him, babycakes. Motivating him to be better. That's how motivation works."

"That's like saying white people motivated Native Americans with the smallpox virus."

She laughed. "Good one, Vee-Dawg. That's a good one."

"But did you want him fired?" I asked. I didn't flinch from

248

her single-eyed gaze. "I'm not an idiot," I said. "I know the truth."

She lowered the ice bag. "So what if he didn't actually fuck her?" she asked. "Do you even know the truth about losing your best friend? About how one day she's sleeping on *your* couch and telling you *you* saved her life, and then the next she's sleeping at *Coach's* house and acting all weird about it, like he's her daddy or her boyfriend or something? And then he decides to play favorites and starts to tear the team apart."

"It starts tearing *you* apart, you mean."

"I am the team."

"Of course," I said. Maybe she thought she was trying to motivate Riley to be a better coach, but she was really just bitter and jealous. Did Riley see me the same way? Had I been the same way? I had to talk to him. I at least had to let him know that I wasn't as self-centered and delusional as Steffie. I wasn't Steffie. I didn't want to turn into someone like Steffie.

I turned away from her to stack the water bottles. I didn't want to run people over and play God and navigate that sketchy gray area between righteous and horribly wrong. It was easy to be self-righteous and full of advice as long as you didn't care who you hurt along the way.

25

I had too many secrets. My conscience kicked me every time I saw Riley—he'd let me assume things about him, things that were mean and wrong. I wanted him to know that I didn't think these things now. I didn't hate him or consider him a horrible teacher. I wanted him to know that I wasn't someone like Steffie, someone who would bully and threaten others for her own benefit. I'd called him a pervert when I was mad. I hadn't been thinking. Steffie was calculating and cold. I knew I'd continue to feel horrible, and hate history class, and even hate him a little, until I could tell him the truth. There was never a good time, though. We were never alone. I should have taken advantage of all those solitary moments in the gym with him, all those awkward moments when I ignored him and his buddy-buddy jokes. Hindsight. As Dad would have said: Hindsight is twenty-ten.

I needed to tell Dad the truth about the letter, even if that meant we never got to China. I bit my nails and developed nervous habits, like tapping my foot and rubbing my chin so often that a bunch of zits broke out on it. But I couldn't kill Dad's family right in front of him. I kept them alive one day at a time, I kept my mouth shut and let all my mistakes swirl around me, and we rushed toward March 26. My stomach stayed in a tight fist beneath my lungs. I couldn't breathe, and because I couldn't breathe, I certainly couldn't talk. My life was one part adrenaline and two parts imminent train wreck.

Packing was a nightmare. Mom wanted to take a first aid kit the size of a small animal.

"There are drugstores," Dad said, "and hospitals. Please, Pam."

"You haven't been there for decades," Mom said. "Do you watch the news? There's a pandemic flu breaking out there every few weeks, it seems."

I actually enjoyed sitting back and watching, except I was afraid that one of them would take it too far and declare that they weren't going, or that we all weren't going. One night, over a dinner of leftovers that Dad called Anything You Like (which was only true in this case if you liked leftover meatloaf or left-over fried rice), we came close to calling the whole thing off.

Dad was talking about staying off the beaten path.

"What's wrong with a little modernity, Kenny?" Mom asked. "Hot water? Reliable electricity?" Mom was not an adventure-some traveler. She wasn't a traveler at all. Her idea of a wild vacation was a dinner out in San Francisco, maybe a play, maybe even spending the night in some cheesy tourist hotel near Fisherman's Wharf, where the rooms always smelled a little like clam chowder.

"We are in search of an authentic cultural experience," Dad said. "We can't get that in a Best Western."

"What about staying with my grandparents?" I asked. I enjoyed playing my clueless card. "I mean, we could stay in Dad's old room." They were both looking at me. "I mean, they did invite us, right?" *Shut up, shut up now*, I told myself. "I mean, if they came here, they'd stay with us, right?"

Mom put down her fork. "That, honey, is a wonderful idea. We invite them here. Problem solved! We'll pay for their tickets, everything. Think about the medical care they could get here. Your father, Kenny. He could go to a real doctor, not one of those ones who just prescribe herbs and things. That could make all the difference."

Oh God, no.

"That's not a bad idea," Dad said.

"Wait," I said. "No."

"Why not?" Dad asked.

I shoved a huge bite of meatloaf in my mouth, on top of the eggy fried rice that was already in there, just to give myself a second to think. I couldn't breathe and had to chew with my mouth open, and half the meatloaf bite came tumbling out again, fortunately on my plate.

"*Vee*," Mom said.

I nodded. I tried to say "sorry," but it came out gurgly and incoherent. They were both looking at me, so I covered my mouth with my hand until I was done chewing. "Sorry," I said again. "Seriously."

"That's disgusting," Dad said.

"I know," I said. "Sorry."

Neither of them were eating, like I'd just completely ruined the dinner experience.

"I want to go to China," I said.

"To visit your grandparents," Dad said.

"Yeah." With my fork I dissected a piece of spinach that was on my plate. The stem. The watery, bruiseable leaf. "But I'd kinda like to see them at their place, you know, in their setting." I impaled the leaf bits on my fork. "Like a diorama."

"They're real people, Vee, not something in a museum," Dad said.

"Of course. But I just don't know anything about their lives. Not just them, but what's around them, and things like, I don't know, the smell of their house. Their street. Where they like to eat lunch. I want to know those things. I want to be there." I looked at Dad for a long moment. "Please."

He picked up his beer bottle and peered through it, then took a long time bringing it to his lips for a sip. "We have Madison to think about," he said finally. "We have promised her a trip to her family. It would be cruel for her to lose this opportunity twice in a row."

I nodded.

"Okay," Dad said.

And then they went back to arguing about where to stay, and I wisely kept my stupid mouth shut.

• • •

"You saved my ass," I told Madison on the way to history class the next morning.

"Of course," she said. "What did I do this time?"

I gave her the abbreviated version of our dinner conversation, and she slapped me on the arm. "You're so dumb! Stop trying to show how innocent you are. You're a horrible liar, and you'll just blow it."

"You're right," I said. "Of course." I pulled the classroom door open and gestured for her to go in, and the three girls behind us thought I was also holding it for them. "It shows," I said over their heads, once I'd gotten through the door myself, "that we're really just going for you. Dad doesn't care about China, and he doesn't care that I care."

"So I shouldn't feel guilty for lying?" Madison asked.

"Shh!" I said.

Her eyes got wide, and she quickly looked around the classroom. "Ohmigod, what?"

"Everyone thinks you're perfect," I whispered dramatically. "Don't blow your cover."

She slapped me again, harder this time. "I feel guilty all the time, Vee. I don't even know if I can go."

"You can. We are."

"I didn't think this would actually work. Your parents will hate me forever. We won't be able to be friends anymore."

"Listen," I said. "I take the fall for this. When, *if*, Dad figures it out, it's all on me. Scout's honor." My chest puffed out with pride at being so chivalrous.

I could tell she was thinking and that she had a lot of questions and that she didn't quite believe me. "As if you were ever a Boy Scout," she finally said.

"It comes down to picking a side," I said. "You're in, or you're out. Either we tell my parents the truth, or we see it through."

She sat down in her seat and got out her pink pencil case and lined it up neatly at the top of her desk.

"And if we tell the truth, you're never going to China. You know that," I said.

"At least not until I don't need my parents for anything anymore."

"Even then," I said. "Your parents have cornered the Asian guilt market. You'll probably never go."

She waved at Emily and got out the latest packet, this one on nuclear proliferation.

"Never, ever, ever," I reminded her.

"Okay," she said.

"Ever."

"Shut up already."

I opened my mouth, like I was going to cough up another "ever," and she raised her hand like she was going to hit me again. I smiled. She sighed.

"We'll be horrible people together," I said.

A few days later Riley got us in small groups to discuss whether or not the U.S. was justified in dropping nuclear bombs on Japan. "Remember not just the facts that you've read," he said, "but also the moral questions." I hated moral questions.

My small group consisted of me, Thor, and Mark White. If we were going to need a team name, I was ready to suggest the Oafs. Or maybe the Ruffians, though that sounded British and therefore pansyish.

"Definitely a good call," Mark said.

"Why does your opinion never surprise me?" I said.

"Okay, you'd prefer to get into a ground war and lose a ton of American lives?"

"Like the Japanese lives don't count?" I said.

"Let's discuss," Thor said.

"We are discussing," I said. "If we had no difference of opinion, there would be nothing to discuss."

"So you're just playing devil's advocate?" Thor asked. He brushed his shaggy blond hair out of his eyes.

"Maybe," I said.

"You're so annoying," Mark said.

"Since it's a theoretical question," I said, "it doesn't matter what I actually think. What's done is done."

"But what about implications for the future?" Thor asked.

"Any nuclear war is a zero-sum game," I said. I wasn't quite sure what this meant, but it sounded good.

"Sort of like your social life?" Mark said.

We needed a girl in the group, to help keep the testosterone in check.

"Back off the anabolic steroids," I said.

He smirked.

We weren't thinking about nuclear proliferation anymore; we were thinking about girls, girls like Adele, and weighing one another's abilities to have girls like Adele. I wanted to wipe the smirk off his face by saying, *Been there, done that,* or something equally obnoxious. But he wouldn't believe me anyway. And Adele had been drunk and weepy and desperate for anyone. More than anything, though, I didn't want Adele ever finding out that I'd talked about our awkward encounter. She'd be angry, but also hurt. There was no point in hurting her. This was actually a good secret to keep. My good deed of the day was keeping my trap shut and letting Mark continue to think I was a total loser.

March 25. T minus one. Wasting time at the end of history class.

"China?" Mr. Riley said. "How exciting."

Other kids were going to Cancun, Honolulu, Sacramento.

"China's a wonderful place," he said. "I've been there a few times. The geography reminds me of Canada."

Canada? It was like Canada? It was the place where we'd invented writing, gunpowder, paper, compasses, astronomy, and calendars. Where *Homo erectus* had settled and become more human. Where people were still digging up unimaginable remainders of the past and putting the puzzle pieces together. It was a place like no other place in the world. Canada? Funny Frenchmen obsessed with hockey and lacrosse? He was off his rocker.

"That's great," I said. "Canada. Okay."

Then I remembered I was supposed to be nicer to him. That I'd screwed him over, at least in my own mind, and he knew it, and now I knew I was wrong, and so being around him just made me feel guilty, guilty, guilty. I was supposed to be nicer to him.

"Why were you in China?" I asked. The bell rang, and everyone rustled with all their papers and zippers, and Riley sauntered toward my desk so I could hear his answer.

"After college I backpacked around for a while, taught some English, you know. It's a good thing to do. Travel. It helps me keep perspective on all the silliness around here."

"Silliness?" I said. He was talking about me.

"The money, the narrow-minded focus on grades and college, the kids and their partying." He sat down in the seat in front of me and absentmindedly rubbed out a graffiti mark on my desk. I wanted to tell him I hadn't put it there, but I didn't want to interrupt. I could see he was thinking.

"I know this maybe sounds weird to you, coming from a teacher. I'm supposed to give grades and help you get to college. I'm not supposed to know about all the crap you kids do on the weekends."

"That doesn't matter," I said quickly.

"But people talk to me. And I listen. That's just who I am." This was why he'd helped Adele. This was why she'd called him and stayed with him.

"I know, I know," I said. "I'm sorry."

He smiled. "Sorry?"

"Yeah," I said. "I—well—I said some stuff, remember?"

"I do," he said. "You were going through a rough time, I think."

"That's no excuse."

"Well," Riley said. His hands stilled on the desk. "It is if you want it to be. I appreciate the apology, though."

"Steffie was out to get you all season, did you know that?" I said. "She told me everything. And I was as bad as her. I'm a horrible person." I was upset at myself, and my voice sounded angry. I was almost yelling at him.

"No, Vee," Riley said. "Take a load off. You're all good. Don't worry so much about it."

"Don't worry? You freaked out on me!"

"I did?" Riley laughed. "I was probably frustrated, sure. Steffie frustrates me. Adele, too. I'm only human. But that's the game I've decided to play, as a teacher. Always trying to balance helping you guys and having you figure things out for yourself."

I smiled at him, probably the first genuine smile he'd ever seen from me. "You sound like someone's mother," I said.

He threw back his head to laugh this time, and he pounded the desk a little with his open palm. "I think I'd make a great mother," he said. "Maybe someday."

His laughter petered out, and we were left in this awkward silence. Friends would have hugged. We weren't going to hug. I stuck out my hand, and we shook on it. Peace. Water under the bridge. It had taken me long enough, but maybe I was finally pulling my head out of my ass and growing up. Maturing. Becoming someone my parents would be proud of. I thought this way for maybe half a second, and then I remembered that what I was doing to my parents was a whole lot worse than what I'd done to Riley.

"Canada," I scoffed to Madison at lunch. She certainly didn't need to know about my touchy-feely moment with Riley. It wouldn't make any sense to her anyway, since she didn't know the whole ridiculous story.

"I love how Riley compared China to Canada," I said. "I mean, are you kidding me?"

"You've never been to Canada," Madison pointed out.

"Which is just fine with me."

"You're being snippy," she said.

She was right. Maybe I was getting sick. I prayed that I'd come down with malaria, cancel the trip, and be able to explain everything while fevered and delirious. Mom and Dad wouldn't be able to hate me if I were on my deathbed.

26

Then it was March 26, and the plane took off with us aboard. Madison read aloud the entire SkyMall catalog, and Mom—across the aisle from us—fell asleep almost as soon as we were at cruising altitude, her ginger ale balanced precariously on the edge of her tray table. Dad watched *National Treasure* on his miniscreen and laughed randomly and loudly. I wanted to hug him, to tell him everything was going to work out the way he wanted it to. I wanted to be able to promise him this, but I'd already told him so many lies.

The plane hummed along steadily, but my fear and regret knocked around as if buoyed and trampled by violent, volatile air currents. My only hope was that my grandparents were still alive and our letter to them had simply gotten lost. I watched Mom sleep and thought about how the mess I'd made with her family could be overshadowed by my success with Dad's. Mom was such a selfless person that she probably found the greatest happiness watching us be happy anyway. That was the whole reason she was coming along. It wasn't like she belonged in China.

Madison interrupted my brooding by asking me if I wanted a feng shui compass. I pretended to seriously consider it.

"It will help with your positive life forces," she read.

I actually seriously considered it.

"It's only four hundred bucks."

I shrugged. "I guess I'll have to go with crossing my fingers and hoping for the best."

She put the catalog down and looked at me. She knew what I was talking about. "Vee," she said, "don't freak out. Not now."

"I'm trying," I said.

"I know." She glanced across me, at Dad, and we watched as he snorted at something on the screen. Then she picked my hand off my thigh and wrapped her hand in it. Her hand was smaller than I'd expected, and cool and soft and very girl-like. The gesture was supposed to be comforting, but it just made me more nervous. I pulled my hand back and sat on it.

"I'm okay," I said.

She nodded and smiled and picked up the catalog again. "How about a fifty-dollar talking translator?"

"I actually could use one of those," I said. "No joke."

"Not if you have us," she said smugly.

My brain was telling me: *Pay attention! This is* home! *This is where your ancestors lived for millions of years! Do you recognize it? Do you feel at home? Is there a bond like an umbilical cord, like gravity, that tugs you toward the ground?* My brain screamed at me, but my body felt fuzzy, like I had cotton balls stuffed in my mouth and ears, and lead weights on each of my legs.

"Look," I said to Madison from the taxi, pointing to people and buildings and traffic and food carts and the dull, gray sky. We zoomed past stores that could have been anywhere in the world: McDonald's, Pizza Hut, KFC, Starbucks. The wide streets had sidewalks that were missing their curbs. Every now and then a wing-tipped temple appeared in the reflections on glass towers. The glass towers leaned toward us at uncomfortable angles. We turned onto roads that were like parking lots, and we sat for ten, fifteen, twenty minutes before creeping forward to a side street that we'd zoom down just so we could repeat the whole thing again on another road. There were people on bikes everywhere, and tour buses, and scooters, and crowds on every square inch of sidewalk. Everyone was Chinese, which was so incredibly obvious that I couldn't exactly point this out. But for the first time in my life I was completely surrounded by people who looked like Dad and Madison and like parts of me. They didn't seem self-conscious about how they looked. It was amazing to think that all of them had been brought up thinking that they looked normal, that they looked like what people were supposed to look like.

Mom stood out like a Hollywood star. Her blond hair seemed blonder, and she'd grown at least six inches on the trip over. People had stared at her in the Beijing airport. She couldn't wipe the dazed, polite smile off her face, and I worried that people would look at her and think she was sad and alone.

"Goodness," she said from the taxi, pointing to a store with huge gold and black Buddha statues out front, and later a store window stacked with bolts of silk, and later a billboard with red Chinese lettering and then in English below: WELCOME ONCE MORE TO THE PRESENCE.

"A church?" I asked.

Madison leaned into me to see out the window. "A shopping mall," she said, "I think."

Dad was in the front seat chatting with the taxi driver, an old guy with a flat felt hat and liver spots on his neck. Maybe they were talking about the traffic. Maybe Dad was telling him about the purpose of our trip. Maybe the guy would know something, and Dad would figure it all out and snap his fingers and take us right back to the airport. Maybe this old guy was my grandfather. I stared at his liver spots and tried to follow the cadence of the conversation despite the foreign words. I couldn't figure out a thing, but I had the door handle in a death grip, just in case the car suddenly whipped around.

Then the driver did swerve onto another street and lurch to a stop. I looked around in confusion. We'd left the KFCs and glimmering buildings. This street was more like an alley: narrow, curving, and lined with skeleton-like trees. A man on the sidewalk just ahead of us had apples loaded up on a cart behind his bike. Dozens of people hustled down the middle of the street, as if the whole alleyway were in fact a sidewalk. I could see a few rooftops above the crumbling stone walls that ran the length of the alley. Dad pointed to a wooden door that was painted bright red and decorated with Chinese characters.

"Here we are," Dad said. "We are staying in the original part of town."

I wondered if we'd have real toilets and warm water, or if this was going to be a difficult, dirty cultural experience. As much as I wanted to love China, I didn't want to live like a peasant. I wanted nice, clean sheets and a steamy shower and a place like Tom Fat's just down the block.

I scooted out the door behind Mom and Madison, and it was like being assaulted. Cold, dry air blew through my jacket and flung Madison's ponytail against my face. Someone clipped me in the shoulder and kept plowing forward without glancing at me or saying sorry. Everyone wore black and shuffled rapidly toward the massive, boxy concrete buildings that loomed over this older part of town. It smelled like a city, part trash and part steaming, frying food, part body odor and part chemical perfume. The wind that swept down on the city from the snowy mountains we couldn't even see smelled like dry ice and felt like little, cold knives.

I grabbed my bag and yanked Madison's pink rolling suitcase from her hands, just to be gentlemanly. Dad pushed open one of the imposing red doors, and we had to step over the bottom of the doorframe and cross a courtyard paved with uneven cobblestones. The hotel office was a tiny glass-walled room that only fit Dad and the manager, who looked like he was trying out for a marching band—shiny shoes, stiff jacket, hat with tassel; all he needed was a trombone or a baton. Mom, Madison, and I waited outside and inspected the empty bamboo birdcages that hung from a leafless tree in front of the office.

"I know Dad said charming and authentic," I said, "but this place borders on depressing." Wasn't there a Motel 6 in Beijing? A Hilton with a glitzy foyer and marble columns and impressive pictures of the Great Wall? I felt too disoriented to deal with all this run-down, foreign grime.

Mom gave my shoulder a squeeze. "Maybe he's trying to show you what his life was like," she said, "growing up."

"I prefer the cute-little-fishing-village image," I said. "You know, the one in my head."

"Then why travel all the way here?" Mom said lightly.

"I don't know anymore." I was ready to fight, to argue, to defend, to throw my words around to hurt. Whose fault was it that I was so cold and tired and irritable? This place didn't exist because of me. Dad hadn't grown up here because of me.

"Vee, chill out," Madison said. "I mean, holy cow, this is amazing. We're actually *here*." She swung one of the birdcages, and the whole fragile tree seemed to dip and shiver.

I had more to say, but just then Dad and the manager squeezed themselves out of the office and led us to our rooms, which were open to the courtyard, like at a motel, and were dark inside and decorated like an antique shop: polished wood and brass and red tassels on the lamps, and bedspreads and curtains like thick silk robes. No TVs or telephones or minibars. The beds were lined up against one wall, little twin-size beds like the kind you'd sleep on at summer camp, and only two or three feet between them.

"A beautiful room for the ladies," Dad said, and ushered me on.

Mom and Madison were sharing a room, and Dad and I had another. This was an arrangement that had been worked out a long time ago, but I was still embarrassed by the implication. Madison and I were teenagers and everything, but we weren't like that. We'd never been like that.

In our room I climbed over the beds and looked out the window. The view was of another small alleyway and then a rickety brick wall. Boxy concrete buildings loomed above the wall. I peered up at the sky, which was a swollen gray that pressed down on us and the dirty buildings and the twenty million people swarming through the city. I felt the pressure on my eyelids, the brightness and heaviness of that gray, and when I turned back to look at Dad, I couldn't even see him because of the bright dots that had burned into my eyes.

"Nice view," I said.

"This is an authentic part of town," Dad said.

"You said that before."

Dad didn't answer but blinked like his eyelids were burning too, and he began to carefully unpack.

"What are we doing now?" I asked. I didn't feel like taking everything out of my suitcase, especially since we were only staying here one night.

Dad paused, one hand on the lacquered dresser, and said, "We will unpack and then do the next thing."

I had no idea what to expect from the next thing. Tomorrow,

I knew, we were leaving Beijing to visit Madison's family for a few days, but tomorrow seemed lifetimes away.

"We could take a nap," I said, stretching out on my cot. Being horizontal felt delicious after the long, cramped flight.

"No," he snapped. "Get up now."

"But we're on vacation," I said.

"Just listen to me," he said.

I reluctantly rolled off the bed. Dad was snippy and worried, and I couldn't exactly blame him; he imagined he'd be seeing his family again soon. How stressed would he be when he found out they didn't exist? How devastated? How disappointed in me? Every time I thought about this, a literal wave of anxiety broke over me. I felt it tingle my scalp and tighten the muscles in my neck and turn my stomach. This whole trip was a hoax, this whole happy-family trip some mirage, some Disneyland theme park—*Chinaland!*—with actors dressed up like poor Chinese men and this hotel carefully constructed to look old and cold and uncomfortable.

I unpacked quietly and later followed Madison to the manager's office to call her parents. The place smelled like burning carpet, and the ancient floor heater spit fire out at our knees that somehow escaped through the dusty glass or cracks in the door before getting to our hands and cheeks. Madison giggled at the old-fashioned telephone with its circle of numbers. She got out a card from her mom that had all the instructions on how to make a phone call in China.

"Um, okay," she said. "Here I go."

It took eons for her to dial, then eons more for her parents to pick up. I could tell the line was full of static because she was almost shouting into the receiver. She switched back and forth between English and Chinese, and she did the same when she called her local relatives. I watched the birdcages swing in the dusky courtyard and listened to Madison's voice rising and falling. It was hard to pick up her tone when she wasn't speaking English; Chinese always sounded abrupt and angry, but I didn't think she was arguing with her relatives, people she'd met maybe once or twice in her life but who represented everything that could have been her if her grandparents had been the sort of people who stayed put.

When we got back to our rooms, Mom was asleep and Dad motioned us outside into the courtyard. In a low voice he said we'd be going to dinner but Mom wanted to keep sleeping.

"Isn't that bad for jet lag?" I said. "Dad, let's wake her up." A part of me was afraid to leave her alone in a room, a hotel, a city, a country where she didn't speak the language and didn't look even a smidgeon like anyone who belonged here. Another part of me was afraid of venturing out as the foreigner, the oddball of the group. Having Mom by my side at least helped me make sense. People could look at her, and at Dad, and put two and two together. Without Mom, I was completely out of context.

"She's a grown-up, Vee," Madison said. "She can make up her own mind."

I shrugged. "You all would have woken me up," I said.

Dad pretended to think about it for a minute, and then he grinned and nodded.

"It'd be no fun without you, anyway," Madison said.

The three of us went out into the cold, dank alley, down the cobblestones, and onto a larger street. This larger street was filled with noise—cars, ringing bicycle bells, laughter, yelling, the old man with the apple cart calling out to passersby. And smells—grease, trash, stir-fries, sewers, mangy dogs, baked sugar—all of it congealing in the wintry air, making the night, briefly, feel warmer than it actually was. We passed the open door of a housewares shop and heard a few old men arguing just inside. One held the lid of a wok; and another, something that looked like a long-handled spoon. They held them up like a sword and shield. Then, just when I thought they'd attack each other, they laughed and disappeared around the corner of an aisle. We walked into the foggy-windowed, neon-lighted restaurant next door. It smelled like flour and air freshener inside, and the round table where we sat had a tablecloth and was missing the greasy residue of film I was used to at Tom Fat's. Why did I expect Tom Fat's? We were really in China. Dad looked at the menu and scratched his head.

"This is an authentic part of town," he said. This time I wasn't going to remind him he was repeating himself. He said, "I wanted us to stay here so you see what life is like for everyday people." He gestured around the room. "See, no tourists." He tapped the menu. "Which means good food."

"Is the food safe?" Madison asked.

"Safe?" Dad asked.

"Like the way we have to drink bottled water. Is it, like, sanitized or something?"

Dad laughed. "They cook everything real hot, and you'll be fine."

Madison shrugged, and they began talking about the menu like I wasn't even there. Dad encouraged Madison to order, which she did, though I could tell she was embarrassed. Dad gently corrected her a few times, and at one point they and the waiter all laughed, and I felt like the joke was on me. I sipped some hot, bitter tea and watched other people dig into their noodles and soups.

Madison practically bounced in her seat. "That was my first Chinese conversation with a stranger in China! I'm only going to speak Chinese from now on."

"Me too," I said.

Dad raised his cup of tea. "A toast," he said, "to being here and discovering more of our families and ourselves."

"To discovery," Madison said.

"What you guys said," I added. I wasn't confident that I wanted to discover anything else. Just being here was already enough to deal with. My stomach flopped, and I felt the tea bubble up toward my esophagus, and I wasn't sure if it was nerves or poisonous, unsterilized water already going to work on my insides.

"Very poetic, Vee," Madison said, and swung the revolving

tray around to pick up a piece of something she'd identified earlier as lotus flower root.

Our table was soon covered in little dishes: steamed dumplings and crispy roast duck and fried tofu and little sides of mushrooms and cucumbers and stacked lettuce leaves with a Thousand Island–like dressing. I took a deep breath and realized, stomach flutters aside, that I was starving. I dug in. The duck was so good I could have eaten the whole thing, and the sauces for the dumplings and the tofu were thin and spicy. Even the lettuce tasted different, like it had soaked up the flavor of the soil and the water of the muddy village where it had grown. Maybe it had come from Dad's village. Maybe my grandfather had pulled it out of the ground. Everything seemed so much closer, so much more possible, now that we were here.

27

The morning was so dark and cold that it didn't feel like morning.

Dad said, "We must adjust ourselves to this time," and turned on the light.

As if on cue, the shower started singing next door, and I wondered if Mom and Dad had completely synchronized their watches.

"Up, up," Dad said.

During the night I'd cocooned myself in blankets, ripping them out of their neat tucks and burrowing into them to stay warm. The room snapped with morning cold. Apparently, the word "heated" in Chinese roughly translated to "the perfect temperature to see your breath in the air." I dreaded unwrapping myself to change into clean, cold clothes.

"Shower," Dad said.

I sat up, and the flickering antique lamp threw my shadow against the opposite wall. The walls were thin, and I could hear the shower next door. The water didn't patter down in a steady stream but splashed intermittently in heavier cascades, like it had collected in someone's hair or a washcloth and then been wrung out over the echoing tiles.

Maybe Mom was showering just on the other side of the wall. It made me uncomfortable. Mom was Mom, and she wasn't supposed to have a naked body. Thinking of her naked made my stomach flop the way it did when I thought of her parents screaming and maybe even hitting her. I wanted to go back to seeing her as this goofy, happy lady who just happened to be my mom. Not as someone so fragile who I had no choice but to love and want to protect. I flopped back down on the bed and covered my head with the thin pillow.

But maybe it was Madison in there. Thinking about Madison naked didn't make me feel better. It made me feel like I was doing something wrong. Madison was supposed to be a buddy, a brain on a Popsicle stick. She was not fragile and did not need protecting. I took a deep breath. Madison was just Madison; she hadn't changed overnight just because she'd been sleeping ten feet away. Still, as I tiptoed along the frigid tiles to the tiny bathroom, and as I stood under the scalding water that squirted out of a bulbous detachable showerhead, I wondered if Madison ever thought about me naked. I felt flushed and embarrassed. The shower suddenly didn't feel safe or private, as if thinking of Madison had conjured her up, as if she were perched on the toilet—which was a normal toilet, not a hole in the ground like I'd feared—and daring me to use the mini soap bar that smelled like a flower basket. I shook my head to make her go away.

I closed my eyes and imagined Adele under the spray with

me. But in my fantasy Adele had no interest in showering with me. She was interested in Madison, and the two of them wanted me to get out of the shower altogether. But then Adele got needy and Madison got brainy and sarcastic, and I realized I couldn't imagine a lesbian shower scene with two girls who had no respect for each other. So I stood solo under the spray and scrubbed with the perfumed soap and tried to wake up.

When I emerged from the bathroom, Dad was dressed and waiting for me. "Should I wear jeans?" I asked. "I only brought jeans."

"The symbol of America," he said, which was not exactly an answer.

My jeans were wrinkled, and despite the shower, my hair stood up in strange, pillow-influenced waves, but overall I felt clean and warm, and I started thinking I could do this thing. China. I could survive it. Enjoy it even. I felt like giving Dad a bear hug, but he was counting his Chinese money, laying it out in neat piles on the dresser, so I left him alone.

We crossed the courtyard and met up with Mom and Madison in a thick-walled room that smelled like greasy doughnuts. The tables were plastic and plastered with scratched Pepsi logos, and the other guests—an old couple and a set of parents with young kids, all Chinese of course—nodded and bowed to us with wide, genuine smiles on their faces.

"How are you feeling?" I asked Mom.

"Oh, don't worry about me," she said. "Isn't this an adorable little tearoom?"

"Adorable," I said. That wasn't the right word for the chaos and strangeness of everything, but I wanted to agree with Mom, so I left it at that.

The manager—the same one from the night before, his band uniform as crisp as ever—served us breakfast: bitter tea, soupy congee, fried breadsticks, and a big black egg cut in half and sliding around on a thin white plate. It looked like a diseased eyeball.

"A century egg brings good luck," Dad said.

Madison sniffed cautiously at hers, and it made me feel better that she didn't just dig in like she ate these all the time.

"Is this what you get here when you order eggs?" I asked.

Dad laughed. "This is sunny-side up!" he said.

I ate a doughy breadstick, which was oily and tasteless, and I poked reluctantly at my rotten, jellied eyeball. Breakfast didn't make sense. Eggs weren't yellow and salty and yolky; they looked like swollen, naked eyeballs and smelled like stinky cheese. My sense of adventure was diminishing along with my appetite; I wanted to crawl back into bed and wake up in Liverton.

"Eat up," Dad said. "Who knows what can happen before lunch."

He always said things like that, and I never took them seriously before, but today he could be right. Today we'd be with Madison's family by lunchtime. Would they expect us to be brave eaters? I picked up my chopsticks and stuck them in the rubbery brown jelly around the eyeball. I touched the tip of the chopsticks on the tip of my tongue. Nothing. Madison copied me. I picked up a pile of the shredded ginger and carved off a section of the bruise-colored yolk. The ginger burned my nose and I didn't taste a thing.

"Delicious!" I said.

"I'm not going there," Madison said.

"You're there," I said. "You're here."

"And taking all day," Dad said.

"I give up," I said.

"You can't give up," Madison said. "It's too late for that."

I glared at her. She wasn't just talking about breakfast. What right did she have to bully me? "Back off," I said, and I took the rest of the egg and shoved it in my mouth. I wanted to gag, I did gag, at the creamy sweetness of it. I'd expected it to taste like rotten ass, but it was rich and soft and had a burning aftertaste. I fought down the urge to puke it up all over the table. I drained the entire pot of tea and then had to leave the table for fear that thinking about the egg floating in my belly would bring it up again.

We packed and got ready to leave, but Mom wasn't feeling well again, and we decided to catch a later bus. The idea of Mom puking her way through the three-hour trip to the mountains made me feel sad and queasy too, so I was perfectly content to sit in the courtyard and wait. The sun was dusty but warm because there was no wind.

"Is she going to be okay?" I asked Dad.

"It's just the food," Dad said. "She's not used to the flavor."

"We're not used to it either." I shuddered at the memory of the century egg.

"It's in your DNA to accept it," he said. "It takes thousands of years to make DNA that loves things like kung pao chicken."

I knew he was making a joke, but I didn't feel like letting go of the subject. "But if you go back far enough, we all ate the same things," I argued. "You know, grubs and berries. Woolly mammoth steaks. Giant panda kebabs."

"*Vee*," Madison said.

"Your mother," Dad said, "she is most happy when she has a routine she knows. You know, she has never been this far away from home."

I wanted to mention that I hadn't either, but I didn't want to make it a contest. Mom was tired and woozy, and aside from my breakfast antics, I was just fine. Was it really the Chinese half of me that could handle all this? That felt adventuresome and alive? It seemed like it was more than Mom's DNA that made her sick. It had to be bacteria or her dislike of change or both. And her parents didn't love her. Wasn't that enough to make anyone scared and sick for all of eternity?

The courtyard was drowsily comfortable, and we sat in silence and listened to the noises of the street outside and the chirping birds. The chirping came from the bamboo cages, and I moseyed over and found two birds where yesterday there had been none. They were talking to each other, warbling and twittering and bobbing their heads back and forth.

"They appeared out of nowhere," I said. "It's a miracle!"

Madison stuck her face near one of the cages and made cooing baby noises.

"It's more miracle than you think," Dad said. He stroked the bamboo bars, and the birds hopped over and tried to peck at his fingers. He laughed and clucked at them, and then his smile slowly faded. "Since the Chinese have destroyed many sparrows," he said, as if he were trying to spit on his own words.

I looked at him, surprised. Was this part of an ancient Chinese fable? A disturbing family secret? A clue to the buried past?

Dad watched the sky. "I will tell you the story. It started the year I was born. Mao began something called the 'Kill a sparrow' campaign. We would all go in the fields and hills and bang pots so the sparrows could not land and instead fell dead from the sky. A rain of dead sparrows, and this was something we celebrated."

"Why would someone *do* that?" Madison asked.

"Not someone. Everyone. They ate the grain that was for the people."

"Don't birds eat bugs?" I asked. "I'm pretty sure they do." It didn't make sense. Dad was losing his mind, making up stories, mixing myth and fact and fiction. His English was starting to sound choppy, too, like he was thinking in Chinese and translating, poorly, as he went along. If he came totally unhinged, if he began speaking in gibberish, it would be my fault. I'd brought him back to his difficult memories.

"They do, mostly. Eat bugs. Mao was wrong, his science more from old women's stories than real observation. The campaign ended before I was four, but it still makes my first memory. Banging a pot and spoon and walking up and down the fields. It filled me with such purpose, such joy. It was the wrong thing to do, but how could we know this? We were told what was, and we believed it because we had to and because we were hungry."

The bird pecked at his finger again, but he didn't laugh this time. I watched the bird's beak strike the pad of his first finger, denting and reddening it without breaking through the skin.

"All those sparrows dead," he said, "and for what? One person's guess at how to make the world better? A guess on top of other guesses that led to famine and millions of people dead? This is what we come from, Vee," Dad said, looking at me. "There is no pride in it and no escape from it for me, even if we live an ocean away. Do you understand?"

I didn't entirely, but I nodded. My throat felt swollen, and I clenched my jaw against the pain.

"Then this is good," he said. "This is the good that comes from that shame. I want you to make good memories of this trip and not just hear my bad stories."

"They're not bad," I said quickly.

"You were only four," Madison said. "It wasn't your fault."

"There should not be shame in what you cannot change. But agreeing here"—he tapped his head—"and here"—he tapped his heart—"is trouble."

I could forgive my ancestors for being trapped in a cruel time, but could I forgive myself for my own mistakes? Could he?

28

When we got to the Beijing bus station around lunchtime, I fought to keep close to Mom and Dad and Madison. Even though I could see above most people's heads, I was worried that if I got swept up in an unforgiving tidal wave of black coats, black hair, white faces, high-pitched chattering, people carrying massive plastic bags, people not slowing down or yielding to anything—corners, turnstiles, oncoming traffic—I would never be able to fight my way through to them. I couldn't ask anyone for help. I didn't know where I was or where to buy a ticket or catch another train. I was tempted to let myself get lost, to drift away from Dad's looming disappointment, and that was what scared me. I read once that the fear of heights isn't actually the fear of falling, but the fear of jumping. The fear of going insane for a split second and wanting to fly off the edge. The temptation to do something stupid and harmful. I felt the pull of it, which made me even more neurotic about staying with the people I knew. I almost reached out for Mom's hand or Dad's jacket.

The bus was clean and practically empty and not at all

heated. We bought tangerines and spicy noodles from the food cart and eagerly breathed in the steam that floated out of our paper bowls. Mom didn't want food and just lay down in an empty row of seats. I contemplated a nap and watched the countryside drift by. For a long time nothing looked particularly exotic except the road signs; the endless, sprawling Beijing suburbs looked strangely like the gated communities and ticky-tacky houses of South San Francisco or Santa Clara.

I watched Dad stare out the window, and I could tell that he wasn't really seeing what was out there. Maybe all his memories from here were about regret. It was a mistake—my mistake—to be here and force him to remember all this. There was nothing I could do now but watch him remember things and pretend like I didn't notice his unhappiness. Showing my own fear and unhappiness would only make his worse.

We crossed a reservoir with ice crackling in the empty wheat fields; then the road wound between frosty, crumbling bluffs; and then craggy mountains, a thick, wrinkled range of them, rose like fans out of the desert. Dad roused himself out of his reverie and said, "The sky is clear and we can see far. The countryside always has so many memories."

He sounded like a fortune cookie. I wanted to point this out, but he was already back to his silent pondering. Was this place so poisoned with bad memories that we couldn't even share jokes anymore?

Mom woke up just as we pulled into our stop, and as we waited for the driver to unload our bags, a thin, bald man bustled up, saying, "Hello! Hello, Ming-ming! Hello, Mr. Wang!" He bowed, then shook everyone's hand. He looked vaguely like Madison's father, but maybe I was just as bad as everyone else back at school who thought that all Asian people looked the same.

"Kenny," Dad said, introducing himself. "Thank you for having us."

"Tim," the man said. "Not a problem. It's so good to be seeing you, so good." I looked around to see if anyone else was surprised. Tim? His name was Tim? What Chinese name was that butchering? No one asked; everyone shook Tim's hand enthusiastically. Tim was Madison's father's cousin, and we were staying with him for two nights. I was looking forward to something warmer and more modern than the ancient, authentic motel Dad had found in Beijing.

Uncle Tim had a silver Audi A4 and drove without much regard for traffic lights or lane markers. Mom sat between Madison and me and clutched at our arms whenever we swerved or accelerated quickly. I felt sorry for her; we could never go to Texas and show up on the Crawfords' doorstep. It would make all our lives better if Mae and Wayne would just disappear the way Dad's parents had. I put my arm around Mom, even though what I wanted to do was punch her in the arm and say, "Toughen up!" She smiled at me, the tired lines around her eyes softly creasing, and I was glad I hadn't punched her.

Uncle Tim traveled all over Asia selling Chinese wine, and as we drove into town, he tried to sell us on China as well. He took both hands off the wheel to point in either direction and explain that the city had developed in a narrow valley. "We are nicknamed Beijing's Northern Gate. See how the mountains come together? Which is where the gate falls. And here you see the first pile of ruins, that's the Great Wall." He spoke without breathing, his accent thick in the rush of words.

The pile of rubble in the distance looked like the remains of a demolition site or an avalanche, and Dad said something in Chinese, and everyone laughed but me and Mom. We looked at each other, and I shrugged. She shrugged back, and we laughed together, our own private outsider joke.

"We visit the wall tomorrow maybe," Uncle Tim said. "We have big party now, see."

We passed glass-faced towers and concrete plazas, then drove over a river the color of olivine, then pulled up in front of a restaurant. It had dusty red awnings and steam-coated windows.

At the door, a round woman with a flat bun on top of her head bowed to us.

"My wife, Mother Chen," Uncle Tim said. "Her English is not so practiced."

She bowed to us again and waved us in, and then we were in a room filled to bursting with steam and chatter and people. Madison's family. They were all here to celebrate her visit, and she was immediately smothered with hugs and giggling, clucking great-aunts and presents wrapped in shiny red paper. I remembered my daydream about Madison being lifted up on the shoulders of her relatives and carried around like a beauty pageant princess; this actually seemed possible, except she wasn't smiling and waving. She looked overwhelmed, like she was about to cry, as she was completely engulfed by her family.

Politely, I scooted through the crowd, saying *"Dway-boo-chi"* over and over—a phrase I'd learned that supposedly meant "Excuse me"—until I reached Madison. Instinctively, I put my arm around her shoulders. She seemed so tiny. How many times had I walked with her to class and never noticed that she was at least six inches shorter than me?

"I'm okay," she said.

"I know."

"I'm happy," she said.

"I know."

She didn't shrug away from my arm, though.

One of the older women tried to give me a present, but before she could, Madison shoved something in my hand. "Give this to them first," she said. The package was heavy and lumpy and wrapped in thick, shiny gold paper.

I bowed instinctively and offered my gaudy package the way they had—two hands on the gift, a deep bow—and then, somehow, the package slipped from my hands and exploded on the floor. Like a piñata, Hershey's Kisses and mini Milky Way bars pinged people's ankles and scattered. The ladies giggled, embarrassed for me, and I flushed with shame. I knelt down and crawled on the spotless white linoleum to pick up the candy.

From out of nowhere—probably from behind the skirts of their giggling mothers—a handful of little kids emerged to help. They ran around their mothers' and grandmothers' feet and found the candy and practically yelped with joy. One boy, smaller than the rest, barely stable on his chubby legs, toddled toward me with a Hershey's Kiss. He held the candy with two hands and carefully deposited it into mine. His mouth was wide open, and three small teeth jutted crookedly from his gums. He looked like he was laughing silently, hysterically at me. I couldn't help laughing back. His silent laughter turned into a cackle, and he reached over and took the Hershey's Kiss back out of my hands. A woman knelt down and put a restraining arm around the boy.

"I see you've met my son, Fang," she said.

I wanted to laugh and point out that the toothy boy seemed to understand his name, but I couldn't because Fang's mother was gorgeous—gorgeous and not old enough to be a mother; she looked like she could be Madison's older sister. Fang reached out and wrapped a hand in her thick, shiny hair, and she clucked at him and kissed him on the forehead. Still squatting behind her son, she extended a hand to me.

"I'm Liling," she said, "but my friends call me Lily. I'm Tim's daughter."

I took her hand. It was small and soft. "Vee," I said. "I'm . . ."

She smiled. "I know who you are."

"Why is your nickname Lily?"

"It's modern and American. Someday my husband and I are going to move there. America is modern and exciting."

Not to me, I thought.

"Is that why your dad goes by Tim?" I asked.

She nodded. "He has been to Texas and Milwaukee," she said.

"And he still likes America?" I asked.

She didn't smile or laugh, and I understood that she had no idea what I meant. Texas and Milwaukee, to her, were hotbeds of trendy American culture.

Lily took the foil off the chocolate, and Fang gnawed at the Kiss with his front teeth, drooling chocolate down his chin and smearing it in her hand. It was disgusting, but she didn't seem to mind. When he started grabbing for it, she clucked her tongue at him and scooped him up, looking apologetically at me before disappearing into the crowd.

I got off my hands and knees and looked around. I couldn't see Madison or my parents, and I pretended for a minute that I was here on my own, that this was a welcoming party for me. I moved nonchalantly toward the wall of windows. It was getting dark outside, and winter grime crusted around the edges of each pane. All I could see was mist.

"*Woo*." An old lady with sagging jowls and yellowing fingernails stood next to me and pointed out the window.

"*Woo?*" I asked, pointing with her.

She nodded, delighted. I had no idea if she meant the window, the fog, our gritty reflections, or the town we couldn't see.

"*Woo*," I said again, nodding, like I was delighted too.

People began lining up for the buffet, crowding each other out and cutting in line and chattering at a volume that made my ears ring. I tried to stand toward the back of the line, but I kept getting pushed forward until I was right behind Mom, Dad, and Madison.

Madison looked giddy and flushed. She giggled and pointed. "Peking Duck," she said. "And that's lamb, and noodles, and I don't know what. Probably something else delicious." She was talking as if in translation. Dad's accent was always there, just under the surface, but I'd never heard Madison's voice like this before.

I followed, putting on my plate exactly what Madison had on hers.

"Copycat," she said.

"Whatever," I said.

Mom and Dad grabbed seats at the huge, round table, and Madison's excited relatives crowded around them. Madison went to sit a little farther down the arc, and I took a deep breath. I could hang on my own. I didn't need to shove a folding chair between my parents. I didn't need to follow Madison. Feeling like I was back at a school dance, I found an empty seat where the huge table almost butted up against the front window. Before I'd even unfolded my scarlet paper napkin in my lap, an army of older relatives descended on me. They clacked at me until it became clear I couldn't understand them, and then they just smiled goofily and gestured toward the wide, shallow bowls of sauces clustered around the table, then continued talking with one another even as they shoveled food in their mouths.

I wielded my chopsticks and picked up a piece of duck and hovered it over something I hoped was hoisin sauce. "Careful for the spicy one," someone said behind me. I turned. It was Lily; she was pulling up a chair for herself, balancing her son in one arm and her chair and bowl of food in the other hand. My duck splashed in the spicy sauce, we both laughed, and I grabbed at the closest thing to help her. The closest thing happened to be Fang. He reached willingly for my nose and hit me playfully near my collarbone.

"Sorry, thank you," she said. She sat down and took him back.

I rescued my drenched piece of duck and ate it awkwardly. The heat from the sauce shot straight up my nose and made my eyes water. Embarrassed, and looking for distraction from the burning that was engulfing my entire face, I asked Lily, "What do you do?" Was she in college? Was Fang an accident? Did they even have birth control in China?

She giggled and fed Fang a lump of rice. "I take care of Fang," she said, as if that were the only obvious answer.

"Huh," I said. I shoveled rice into my mouth too and then sucked down half a cup of tea.

Lily said her husband worked with a tour company that took people all around China. He was on a three-day tour covering the Forbidden City, Tiananmen Square, and the Temple of Heaven.

"He tried to take off," she said, "to be here for family. But he have to work because it is the week." She meant that it was a weekday. Tuesday, I thought, though I wasn't sure. It was hard to keep track, given the entire day shift we'd gone through to get here.

She asked me where we'd visited so far.

"We just got here," I said. "Madison's family is the most important thing to see." I made the family sound like a tourist attraction, like we'd paid our admission and now wanted to take pictures and check them off our to-do list.

I glanced at Madison, who was smiling politely at an old relative and probably not understanding half of what he was saying. I watched Mom and Dad, who were holding hands and laughing with Uncle Tim. What kind of genuine experience could we expect in two days? Wasn't this a kind of sightseeing for us? A carnival of new cultural experiences?

"What do you do?" Lily asked.

"I'm in high school," I said. "I play basketball."

"Basketball!" Lily said. She said something to Fang, and he clapped in goobery excitement. "Fang loves basketball."

I felt a little guilty about my white lie. "I'm not very good," I said.

"Ttzz," she said through her teeth. "Of course you are."

"No," I said, "I'm not kidding. I pretty much suck."

She looked at me blankly and smiled. I wondered how to say "suck" in Chinese, and if it meant the same thing. I felt stupid that I could only talk with Lily and Uncle Tim and maybe one other person. I should have gone to Chinese school. I was one of those arrogant Americans who expected everyone else in the world to learn English.

I watched the men near us slurp their tea. A little later Mom came over and asked if she could hold Fang, and it was strange seeing Mom with a little Chinese kid in her arms. This was what she would have looked like with me, when I was a baby. She seemed so happy, cooing down at him, and he reached up at her and cackled and showed off his teeth. She was a good mom. It wasn't her fault that I'd turned into a lazy kid and a liar. She'd done the best she could with me.

We went back to the buffet for dessert, and I took a plate of what turned out to be cloyingly sweet almond Jell-O. Mom, who was sitting next to me now, tried a bite and made a face too. We shared the milky, gelatinous cake she'd chosen until Fang knocked it over with his flailing hands. Our laughter joined the happy chaos around us. I realized I was having fun. As long as I could forget about all my lies that had gotten us here, I could have fun. I could only forget about things for a few minutes at a time, though, and in the middle of a bite of cake, or midlaugh, or midsmile, that's when I'd remember that I wasn't destined for my own festive family reunion.

By the time we left, it felt like the sun was just about to rise. Like zombies, we piled into the Audi, drove for less than two minutes, then stumbled out in front of a dirty concrete high-rise.

"Eighth floor," Uncle Tim announced. "The most luckiest number!"

We took a slow, claustrophobic elevator to the luckiest floor, and we filed into the smallest apartment I'd ever seen. Uncle Tim sighed and lamented that he didn't have better accommodations for us. We all murmured about how wonderful it was. Dad cleared his throat.

"Well," Uncle Tim said, "I should say this place seems smaller without my Lily living here." His sadness was palpable. Lily lived with her in-laws, which was common, but clearly it wasn't easy for her dad. He loved her and wanted her around. After this trip I didn't know if Mom and Dad would feel the same about me.

Uncle Tim shook his head and showed us the spare bedroom—Lily's old bedroom, I quickly realized—which looked more like a prefab closet. The bed was smaller than my bed at home.

"Parents goes here," Uncle Tim said.

I looked at Dad.

Dad cleared his throat. "This could be a lovely ladies' room," he said. "It's too nice for me."

"No, nonsense," Uncle Tim said. "The kids can take some blankets. Put them in the living room, just like camping."

"Please," Dad said, "you are too kind. Vee and I enjoy camping."

Dad and I had never been camping. Ever.

"Oh, do not refuse my hospitality!" Uncle Tim said. "You're an old man, anyway," he said, laughing. "You must sleep in the real bed."

Dad laughed too, a forced guffaw. Maybe teenagers in China weren't considered sex maniacs; maybe their parents trusted them to have a little self-control. I was mortified that Dad would say anything, but he didn't continue his protest. He didn't know how to politely demand what he wanted without seeming rude.

Dad and Uncle Tim pulled a few quilts out of the closet and

into the living room. I couldn't look at Madison. I didn't want to know what she was doing: rolling her eyes, blushing up to her eyeballs, maybe looking at me in horror.

"Madison can sleep on the couch," I said. It looked more like a love seat, but it was better than the quilt pile.

"This is big enough for everyone," Uncle Tim insisted.

"Okay," I said, but didn't meet his gaze. It was not okay. The quilts were not big enough for me and Madison and the proper space between us. But here I was being agreeable, doing the same polite, dishonest dance Dad had just performed.

I made my escape to the bathroom to brush my teeth and change into sweatpants and an old seventh-grade basketball T-shirt. The bathroom was stuffy and overly bright and had a washing machine right next to the sink. Next to the toilet was a bucket with a mop, and I wondered if I was supposed to clean the floor or the toilet with it. I was very, very careful not to pee at all on the seat, thereby avoiding the whole mop issue.

When I returned to the living room, Mom and Madison had disappeared, and Dad was sitting on the love seat.

"Off the guest bed," I said.

"Perhaps we should have stayed at a hotel," he said.

"No, this is the authentic experience, right? Living like the locals? I love it. I mean it, Dad."

"She is too big for the couch."

"She probably sleeps curled up." I had no idea, but I wanted him to feel better about things.

"You promise me to stay out of trouble," he said. He stared at the ceiling, as if he were lecturing it. I was embarrassed that he was embarrassed.

"Madison and I aren't *like* that," I said. "You don't have to *worry* so much."

"You are not children," he said.

"Right. And I'm telling you, there's nothing to worry about. I promise. Can we not have the . . . the birds-and-the-bees talk right now?"

Dad sighed and looked at me. Then he jumped up, slapped his thighs, and said, "Okay! Okay, I trust you. You are a good man. I trust you. Be good."

He trusted me. I wanted him to, even though I had never done anything to earn it.

29

Nothing would happen. Of course nothing would happen. I wasn't going to succumb to some hormonal rage and attack Madison while she was sleeping. I wasn't the kind of guy who forced himself on people. The idea of anger and violence being a turn-on scared me. How could anyone think it was sexy to have someone tell you no? I hadn't even been able to do things with Adele, and she'd been saying yes.

I pretended to be asleep on the floor by the time Madison tiptoed back from the bathroom. Something soft hit me on the shoulder, and I ignored it. I snuffled and curled into a tighter ball. Something hit me again harder, and I opened my eyes. Dusty beams from the streetlights filtered in through cracks in the blinds, and I could see Madison about ten feet away, sitting on the sofa and throwing wadded-up socks at me.

"Oh, did I wake you up?" she whispered.

"Ew," I said, picking up one of her socks and tossing it back.

"Do you like my family?" she said. "They're sort of over-whelming, huh?"

"I like Lily and Fang," I said.

"Of course," she said. I waited for her to say more, but she didn't, and I wondered if she wanted to fall asleep.

"I'm jealous," I finally admitted. "I wish this were my family."

"Awww," she said.

"I'm serious. This is the happiest he'll ever be—my dad, I mean. He thinks he's going to get a soppy reunion with his parents."

Madison lay down on the sofa. I couldn't see her expression. I regretted bringing up my problems. This was her celebration, her homecoming. I didn't need to ruin it with my own issues.

"I don't even care about my grandparents anymore," I said. "It's not like I know them. It's not like Dad even knows them. My parents really are my only family, and it sucks, but I can't change that. No wonder Dad offered to take me to Chinatown instead."

Madison snorted.

"What?"

"Just that it took you coming all the way to China to figure that out." She laughed into her pillows.

"I'm such an idiot," I said.

"Come here," she said.

"Why?"

"Let me give you a hug."

"No," I said.

"Why?"

"Your honor and reputation, you know," I said, and gestured

grandly in the almost dark. I turned onto my back, my knees bent and the quilts wadded up under my feet.

"Good God. I'm going to give you a *hug*."

"I promised my dad."

"That you wouldn't hug me?"

I thought about what I'd promised. A hug wouldn't get me in trouble. Madison was my friend. Friends hugged each other all the time. I searched for a sarcastic response but came up with nothing. I'd changed. Madison had changed—her voice had a lilt and poetry to it that I'd never heard before, and she seemed older, more mature and full of Zen. Madison in China was as mysterious and exotic as Lily, and the thought of Lily rising up from her sofa, which Madison was doing, and sitting next to me and wrapping one arm around my shoulder and putting her face in my neck, well, that was different from a friend's hug. That was something more. That was butting up against what I'd promised.

"Hey," I said, trying to sound lighthearted.

"Hmm," she said. Her breath tickled my neck. Were her lips against my neck? She picked her head up and just looked at me. Her face was a few inches from mine. She was going to kiss me. I looked at her frankly. Did I want her to kiss me? Of course I did.

Madison. I wanted Madison.

I reached up to touch her cheek with my fingers. I waited for my kiss.

She smiled. I could barely see it, but her cheek muscles contracted under my fingertips. "Thanks for the hug," she said.

"Thank *you*," I said, which was completely stupid.

She giggled and rocked back on her heels. I could have sworn she'd been about to kiss me, but she was turning and crawling back to her sofa. "Good night," she said. "Sweet dreams."

I rolled onto my side and almost off the quilt pile. "Mmm," I said, faking incoherency. I had a lot to think about. She hadn't kissed me. I watched her root around in her sheets and get comfortable. She'd wanted to kiss me. I watched her shoulder and the outline of her body through the covers and thought about what I'd do if I were brave enough to get up off the floor and break my promise to my dad. But somewhere in the ensuing hours I did drift off, and my dreams were full of flushed Chinese girls who smelled like clean sheets and tasted like onions.

Onions? I realized I was dreaming and the smell pervading the apartment was Mother Chen's breakfast. Onions. My stomach grumbled. My legs were twisted around each other and the quilts, the circulation completely cut off. I straightened and wiggled them painfully and lay still while the pins and needles attacked and then subsided.

Madison was still asleep, and I thought about my revelations from the previous night. This, of course, was why Dad didn't want us out here alone. He knew things about me before I knew them. Things about Madison and me. He understood me. He was being all parental because he was older and wiser and didn't yet hate me. I started bombing Madison with her rolled-up socks that she'd attacked me with earlier. One bomb hit her flat on the ear, and she jerked awake and almost rolled off the sofa.

"Onions!" I whispered to her.

"What?"

"Smell! Breakfast!" I knew I was being silly, but I wasn't going to march over there and kiss her good morning. Not with Dad lurking right around the corner and my breath smelling like a deadly fungus.

She sat up. "Oh God," she said, "this thing is so saggy." She rocked around on the cushions. "I feel like I'm in a hammock."

"Nope," I said. "No palm trees to string you between."

"Good point," she said. She smiled at me a little longer than usual.

We had oily, oniony pancakes and watery congee for breakfast. Then we piled into the Audi again and drove toward Madison's grandfather's grave site, toward mountains like mossy fangs that cut into the cloud bank above. The graveyard was carved into a hillside—"For the dead to have a view," Uncle Tim said, with a grand, two-handed gesture—and the driveway wound its way around elaborate concrete tombs. Some had pagodas on them; others had huge headstones that curved around like cozy benches for visitors. We drove slowly, and Dad read aloud the birthplaces, names, and years of the tombs near the road: "Schwen Hua," it sounded like he said. "Wu Gong Shun. The dates are from the old lunar calendar. Shee Yen Wah. She's from Jimingyi." I wanted to tell him to be quiet and respect the dead, but who was I to talk?

We pulled off the narrow road, and Uncle Tim led us on a path between the monuments. I was nervous about following, about stepping on someone's grave, but there seemed to be no other way. Madison clutched a bouquet of white lilies we'd stopped to pick up, and Dad held on to the incense that we'd light at the grave site. Mom and I had little jars of rice and sunflower seeds, which her grandfather apparently had loved. Madison's eyes were bright, and I wanted to put my arm around her and protect her. I also wanted to kiss her. I also wanted to run off with her and roll around in the mossy grass between the ancient graves. I also really, really wanted to know if she felt the same way.

Her grandfather's grave was simple, just a concrete platform with a granite marker. Uncle Tim bowed to it and pressed his fingers to his forehead. Madison did the same, then dropped to her knees and placed an open palm on the concrete slab. She said something in Chinese to Uncle Tim, then nodded and put the flowers down so she could put both palms on the concrete. I wanted to ask so many questions: Was he cremated or buried? Did they have a real Chinese funeral with wailers and gamblers and burned papier-mâché Audis and eighth-floor apartments that he could enjoy in heaven?

This was not how I wanted people to mourn me. Why had we decided that burning someone or sealing him in an airtight box was the right way to go? Why didn't we offer ourselves to the vultures or grind up the bones of the dead and eat them? Some cultures did that. The Egyptians built huge triangular mausoleums, and Emperor Qin had eight thousand soldiers molded out of clay just so they could be buried alongside his dusty remains.

Why did we all think we were so important when we died? Especially since when we were alive, we were often so mean and imperfect?

I thought of who would come to my funeral if I died tomorrow. Mom, Dad, and Madison. Emily. The basketball team, probably, out of a sheer desire for drama. Adele would cry because she knew me and because her life was sad, not because she wouldn't be able to see me again.

Madison didn't cry. Uncle Tim lit the incense, and we stood around silently in the cold. I couldn't help it, but soon I felt tired and bored. Disassociated. I tried to imagine what I'd do if Mom or Dad were under there, but it was too hard to fathom; they were right here; they were too obviously alive. I imagined it was my grandfather under that slab, but even that didn't move me. I imagined Mae and Wayne under there and felt smug. They were mean and selfish, and they wouldn't have any family at their funerals. I glanced at Dad, whose head was bowed as if in prayer, though I'd never in my life seen him pray. Was he thinking about his parents? They'd been dead to him for so long, and now they were alive again in his memory. And he'd been dead to them. He'd abandoned them just as Mom had run away—both with good reasons, both so they could live their own lives—and their parents had just continued on without them, as if they'd never existed.

This is what Mom and Dad could do to me. I felt the sadness thick in my chest, the sadness that had eluded me when I'd thought about other people dying. I wasn't a nice person. Riley was right that I needed help. I'd manipulated Madison and my parents so I could get here and find my family, but at what cost? What did I really need to know about other people, when in the process I could find out so many horrible things about myself?

I looked up at the blurry sky. I wanted Madison to turn around and see me crying, and then I hated myself for thinking that. I wasn't crying for her or her grandfather. Again it was all about me. Stupid, hateful me.

Madison kissed the grave marker and arranged the flowers and rice and sunflower seeds one last time. Then she stood up and nodded to us and began to meander toward other grave sites.

Dad and Uncle Tim chatted for a while about wine. I listened to Uncle Tim argue that Chinese wines were better than Napa wines. I heard Dad, in an effort to be polite, agree with him. I watched an ant crawl over one of the lilies we'd placed on the gravestone. I watched Madison wander back from wherever she'd gone. Somewhere to be alone and remember her grandfather in peace. Dad asked Madison if she wanted to stay.

Madison looked around, as if maybe there were something she'd missed. "No," she said, "I'm good."

"What I mean," Dad said, "is that you can stay with your family when we leave tomorrow. We can return for you after a few days."

A few days? If we didn't find anyone in Dad's village, we'd be back the next day. And even if we did, then what? Would we be invited in? Would we have a genuine family reunion? It wasn't likely.

Madison looked at me, then at the ground, then at her grandfather's grave, then back to me, then to Dad. I couldn't blame her—this was an easy out. She could skip all the shit hitting the fan when we found that my grandparents didn't exist and hadn't invited us here. I didn't want her to be blamed for any part of it anyway. It was all my doing; I welcomed the chance to shoulder the blame.

"I'm good," she said. "This is all good, but I'd actually like to meet your parents, Mr. Wong."

She was signing herself up for a fiasco, and she knew it. She was doing it for me, to be with me. I wanted to kiss her right there, in front of my family and her dead grandfather. I made a big show of picking the ants off our flowers and smearing them on the long, wet grass. I used the ruckus as a smoke screen, so no one else could tell what I was thinking. As it was, I almost started crying again anyway, right there, with everyone watching.

30

"You're brave," I whispered to Madison. We were back to our sleeping assignments from the night before. We'd spent the afternoon walking through downtown, stopping here and there to take a picture of the muddy river or buy a trinket for one of Mom's colleagues. Madison and I bought Emily a bracelet with little jade baubles on it. For dinner we'd gone to a restaurant owned by one of the distant Chen relatives, and they'd made all sorts of special dishes just for us, and Madison had valiantly tried every bizarre delicacy, even the deep fried scorpion that I could barely look at as it had circled around the lazy Susan.

"Nothing tasted as strange as it looked," she said.

"I wasn't talking about the food."

"Oh." She turned on the boxy television, which cast an eerie glow around the room. She flipped through the muted channels and settled on a documentary about giant pandas. "Oooh," she said. "My favorite. Hooray."

"You could stay here with your family, these nice people you didn't invent," I said in a low voice, "and instead you want to join our miserable dead-end journey."

"You don't know that."

"What are the odds?" I said.

"Look at my family. You can't throw a stone in this town without hitting someone I'm related to. The same could be true for you."

"Throwing stones," I said. "Not a recommended method for making friends."

She laughed obligatorily.

"Seriously, why do you want to stay with us?" I wanted her to admit it was about me, about being with me, even though my life was a mess.

"What did you and Lily talk about?" she asked. Lily had been at dinner and had sat next to me again, which worked out perfectly, since Fang obediently ate things I put on my plate but was too squeamish to try.

Lily wanted to move to America and have three or four children. "You are an only child," she'd said. "Fang is an only child. This is not the best thing to be, I think, and in America, Fang can have brothers and sisters." She thought her husband's travel company could expand to places like San Francisco, and I told her all about the Golden Gate Bridge and Alcatraz and Angel Island.

"We talked about America mostly," I told Madison.

Madison laughed.

"You don't believe me?"

On the screen, pandas lumbered around inside their cages. Tourists gawked and pointed; kids reached out as if to pet them.

"Are you jealous?" I asked.

She snorted again. "Yeah. She's old and married."

"That doesn't matter. You're jealous, aren't you?"

"Shut up, I'm trying to watch this."

I tried to keep my laughter quiet, but I ended up snorting like a rhinoceros. Somewhere in the midst of my wheezing I rolled off my quilt and crawled over next to the sofa. I reached up and put my arm around her, on top of the blanket she was all wrapped up in.

"What are you doing?" she asked.

"Shh," I said. "I'm making sure you don't fall off. I'll be quiet so you can watch. . . ." And I started laughing again. The blanket shook as she giggled. I sat up and put my head on her pillow, my nose practically touching the top of her head. Her hair smelled oily and spicy like the restaurant. It smelled wonderful. I kissed her head through her hair, and she shifted under my arm and arched her neck to look at me.

"You're missing your pandas," I whispered.

"Okay," she said.

We looked at each other for a long second, tongue-tied and cheeks flaming, and then I leaned forward, and just when I thought we'd be kissing, she pulled back a little and said, "Wait, Vee, it's just me. I'm not Lily. Or . . . or Adele. Or anyone like that. I'm just me."

I felt her breath on my lips and brought my hand up to cup her cheek. "Okay," I said, which was my way of saying I wasn't mistaking her for someone else. Lily and Adele were old and complicated, and no one was as wonderful as Madison. I wanted her to know this, but I didn't know how to say it, so instead I kissed her. I really just brushed my lips over hers and then let her make the next move, which she did, which was more like a real kiss, our lips moving, and then briefly our tongues, both of us careful and shy.

I kissed her nose and cheek and jawbone and ear, and she giggled and sighed, which made me kiss her neck, which made her pull a hand out of her blankets to touch my shoulder. I waded through the hot, heavy deliciousness of what we were doing. I wasn't in a rush. This wasn't a one-night thing—my only chance or a pantomimed fantasy or something out of my league. This was Madison, and we could go as slowly as we wanted to go, even though parts of me wanted to do everything and go everywhere now.

"Mads?" I asked. I was kissing her eyelids and petting the covers over her waist.

"Hmm?"

"Will you go to prom with me?"

"Prom?"

"Junior prom."

"That's next year."

"So?" I kissed the corner of her mouth, and she turned into the kiss. I smiled, then she smiled, and we kept kissing, smiling, which made it difficult but still very worthwhile.

"Okay," she said.

"And winter formal?"

"Still okay."

"The Halloween dance?"

"That's some serious commitment," she said. Her laugh tickled my chin. "As friends?" she asked cheekily.

"As us." Then I kissed her seriously, the blood roaring through my ears, and we didn't talk for a long time.

In the middle of the night I woke up freezing. I was lying on the ground, next to the sofa, ten feet from my quilts. I'd been afraid of going too far, too fast, so I'd only let myself kiss her— and let her kiss me back, of course. I was going to be chivalrous; I wasn't going to push; I'd put what Madison wanted first, not out of fear or ignorance, but instead out of love. Love. I did love Madison. The word seemed too big and scary, and I pushed it away and thought about "like" and "lust," but those didn't capture everything I wanted from her: her smooth skin, her sarcastic jokes, her respect, her desire. . . . The flickering TV scrolled through typical Chinese images: the Great Wall, misty mountains, some mountain people in face paint and silly red hats, the Great Wall, a field of rice, the Great Wall again. I loved everything about Madison, even the way she snuffled lightly in her sleep. It made me want to kiss her again. But I was also happy to watch and listen to her sleep. I knew I was grinning sloppily in the semidark, but I couldn't stop myself; I was that happy.

My quilts were musty and cold, and I couldn't seem to wrap

myself in them without either my shoulders or my feet sticking out. I curled into a ball and watched the idealized, stereotyped images of China and wished that Madison and I were on a pre-planned, prepaid tour instead of this messy wild-goose chase. We could look at the Great Wall and the caves at Dragon Bone Hill and hold hands while wandering through the crowded, stinking markets. We could tour around and not worry about what we'd find, not care about how we got here. We could just focus on us, on the new us.

But that wasn't an option. It had never been an option. China was vastly more dirty and chaotic and contradictory than I'd ever imagined, and anyway, I never wanted to be someone who could just look at something and click some pictures and move on. I wanted at least some part of me to feel like it belonged here.

I fell asleep thinking about how each square foot of soil we'd trampled today had been Chinese for at least six thousand years, and before that it had belonged to nomads and Neanderthals and Peking man, and before that, apes and dinosaurs and jelly-fish and the big bang. When I remembered this, it was impossible not to be enthralled by the dust and chaos. My whole life—my happiness but also my fear, my mistakes—didn't seem so over-whelming by comparison.

31

I'd come all the way to China to appreciate my parents and kiss my best friend. What was most surprising was my sense that it had all been worth it, despite the fact that I knew doomsday was approaching. Even as we said good-bye to Uncle Tim and Mother Chen and got on a morning train to Qinhuangdao, and even as it hurled us around fog-tipped mountains and down long stretches of glistening, barren fields, even as it flung us toward some shadowy idea of my grandparents and my father's childhood, I couldn't quash my happiness and amazement at it all. I touched Madison whenever I could—my fingers meeting hers as she handed me a bowl of noodles, my head on her shoulder as I pretended to sleep. In front of my parents we pretended like nothing was new, but it all was. We didn't have to talk about it to know it was. She blushed if I looked at her for too long, as if she knew what I was thinking. I couldn't help touching her, casually, lightly, unnecessarily, as if to make sure she still felt the way I did.

Soon Mom and Dad would know what I'd done—not with

Madison, but with them. With their lives. Even if we found my grandparents, it would be clear that they'd never written a letter to us. That they'd never invited us to arrive at their doorstep. I was starting to accept this as my fate; it didn't throw me into a panic like it had before we were actually in motion toward it.

The train was stuffy and crowded, and we were near the doors, so at every stop people would knock their luggage into the backs of our seats and heads and never even apologize for it. Madison and I sat next to each other, and Mom and Dad sat across from us, our knees all bumping whenever the train lurched into a lower gear. Dad was studying the landscape, and I asked him if he recognized anything.

"Nothing," he said, still looking outside as he spoke. "Not a single thing."

Dad had been in America for almost forty years. What could forty years do to a place? Forty years in ancient Africa or Greece or Rome, or with the Aztecs or Olmecs or Aborigines, went by in a blink. For centuries people used to do the same things with the same technology and the same social expectations. Change happened on a larger, slower scale. But now we were zooming into the future. When Dad left China, there were no cell phones or e-mails or digital cameras. No Facebook or YouTube. Mom was a kid, people were listening to disco, and Episode 4 of Star Wars hadn't even been released. Who was Dad forty years ago? It was no wonder he couldn't even recognize a sliver of himself in the vast, flashing landscape.

I fell asleep and woke up sweaty and thirsty. Madison had

keeled over and was sleeping with her head between her knees, and Mom and Dad were holding hands and looking out the window. I felt like I was invading a quiet, private moment, a moment that reminded them of a time before I existed, and I closed my eyes again as if I'd never woken up. I'd let them be. I'd let them talk about their parents or their childhoods or their marriage, whatever they talked about when I wasn't around.

"Honey," Mom said, and I opened my eyes and realized it was too late. I'd woken up and they'd noticed. I'd killed their moment just by existing, by being conscious.

Mom passed me half a bottle of Coke. I chugged and felt my head clear a bit.

"When I was seven or eight," Dad said, as if picking up mid-conversation, "I decided the world was more exciting than my family, so I ran away and hitched a ride on a boat that had been selling fish to my father. I told the man I was supposed to visit my grandmother in Qinhuangdao, but halfway there I began to cry. The man tried to take my mind off my fear and told me all about the wonders of Qinhuangdao, which is a port city and the summer resting place for emperors. But when I still could not stop crying, he turned around and took me back, about ten or twelve miles, even though I told him I wanted to keep going. He dropped me off where I had met him that morning and told me: 'Maybe someday, but today you are not ready for this adventure.'"

While he was staring out the window and talking, Mom was opening a bag of chips and offering it to me. I took a handful. The chips smelled like sushi and tasted like Styrofoam. I glanced at the label: SHRIMP FLAVOR SEAWEED RICE CHIPS. I wanted to make a face but didn't. I didn't want to interrupt Dad.

Dad dug around in his ear and continued. "I got home to my parents, and they were so mad. More mad than I had ever seen them so far. And I was so angry at the fisherman for understanding and doing the right thing. And I was so scared of my father's anger that I told him I had been kidnapped and had barely escaped alive. After, this fisherman that he knew and trusted and did business with, this man who had brought me home without beating me, my father did not buy from him again."

I stuffed my mouth with Styrofoam and chewed. Mom nodded her head, as if she'd already heard this story before. Dad looked out the window for a long minute. "I do not think he believed me. And yet he never asked, he never forced the truth from me. He was merely embarrassed that I would try to run away. That I was eight years old and did not love my family enough to stay with them." He cleared his throat. "I wish he had beaten the truth out of me. I wish he had not been so forgiving."

"You were eight," Mom said.

"I was wrong," he said.

Mom covered his hand with her own. She rubbed her fingers along his knuckles. "We all have our past regrets," she said. "We all do. That's a part of living." She looked at me. "We understand that."

Was she referring to my letter to Mae and Wayne? Or her parents and her divorce? Why couldn't she just say what she meant? I knew the words weren't easy, but keeping them silent and using them in code only gave them power and made them worse. I nodded. "Right," I said, and the Styrofoam stuck in my throat and made me cough. I pounded on my chest with my fist. "But you get over it, I guess," I said. I looked at Mom, even though the heat crept into my face. "I mean, you couldn't help what your parents were like. They're not your fault. Just because you left, that doesn't mean you don't love them."

"You're right, Vee," Mom said. She kept glancing between Dad and me.

I turned to Dad. "And you were eight. Like I didn't do anything knuckleheaded when I was eight?"

He cracked a smile.

"Of course your parents forgave you for that. That's what parents *do*." I felt my chest tighten, a river of feeling swelling inside me, wanting to leak out my eyes. I held it back. I swallowed it down. I looked out the window until I could take a full breath again.

"I have been around the world but never to Qinhuangdao," Dad said, "and it comes back to this. To me being eight and my father disappointed in me. And the silence always surrounding us until I was suffocating."

"They're not disappointed now," I said.

He gave me a sad smile. "People, they have a hard time changing. We don't know what will come next." He looked at Mom, and I thought of her parents, of their refusal to accept their daughter's happiness. I decided I would never be that way; I would never put people in boxes and not let them change. I'd never hold them to their mistakes. Adele could come out of her self-absorbed-sluttiness box. Steffie could emerge from her self-serving one. Riley, I already knew, I'd misjudged. He was free to be just an overly helpful, slightly goofy guy, without my jealousy or meanness getting in the way. Mom and Dad were free to be themselves in the moment, not a runaway or an unloved child, not Texan or Chinese, not even "Mom" or "Dad." Just themselves. I slammed into Dad's knees while getting up, but I got up anyway and gave them both a one-armed bear hug. People in other seats gawked at us, and I grinned back at them. I didn't have to play by their polite Asian rules; I could touch people in public, especially the people I loved.

I glanced down at Madison. Her head was at a strange, strained angle, and I thought maybe she was pretending to be asleep so we could have this whole family heart-to-heart. But she genuinely was asleep, because when I sat down again, I tickled her ear with a shrimp-flavor-seaweed-rice-chip and she bolted upright and said, "Are we here?" with such focused intensity that we all cracked up.

"We're here," I said, "but we're not there."

"Bleeeh," she said.

I handed her a cold, unopened Coke. "Caffeine. It does a body good." She smiled gratefully. I wouldn't have minded her eavesdropping anyway. Someday I'd tell her Mom's story, since I didn't want us to have any secrets and it'd feel good to talk about it. I knew she wouldn't freak out or judge Mom harshly; I knew she'd feel the same embarrassment and pity I did.

The landscape around us started looking more urban, the giant warehouses and intermittent fields replaced with dull apartment buildings. The streets got narrower, and eventually we pulled into the Qinhuangdao station. I couldn't believe it was only midday. The sun was bright and cold, but my body was so achy and tired that it could have been midnight. The world was lit up inside by a thousand-watt bulb, but it felt surreal—if I blinked, if I looked out of the corners of my eyes, I wouldn't have been surprised if everything was suddenly turned off and black as a moonless night.

The cab looked exactly like the ones in Beijing, but our cabdriver was younger than I'd expected. He reeked of cigarette smoke, and his teeth looked like cousins to the crooked, mossy mountains we'd just left behind.

"You like special tour?" the cabdriver asked. Everyone seemed to know a few lines of English, and they presented those lines to us with careful pride that was hard to say no to.

"No," we spluttered out. "No, no special tour."

The cabdriver also had bad BO and didn't seem to understand that we also didn't want to go to the beach or Old Dragon's Head, a section of the Great Wall that jutted into the ocean, or the best shopping street in the world. Madison didn't seem to understand the cabbie's accent, and Dad did most of the talking. Mom and I stuck together, smiling and nodding like dumb American bobbleheads. I'd chivalrously offered to sit in the middle between Mom and Madison, and I leaned one way and then the other to get the best view as we drove past the beach, where fat waves thumped a pebbly shore, and past the huge port that had the same cranes and container ships as Oakland, and then through the Great Wall three or four times before climbing away from the city and onto roads lined with cheap noodle houses: one-room buildings with red awnings and dirt floors and plastic folding chairs and probably deliciously spicy noodles. We merged onto a bigger road, and I felt a little sick because of the BO, which smelled like rotten century eggs, so I leaned over Madison to crack the window, and a wave of cold air flooded in. It smelled a bit like the ocean—salty, fishy, Fisherman's Wharfy—and also like piss and gasoline and like it was leaving a layer of grease on my face. Everything so far had felt a little dirty and cheap and flimsy, like the whole continent was built of linoleum and plastic Tupperwares from the 1950s.

"Nasty is as nasty does," I said.

Madison gave me a strange look.

"Whatever," I said. "It's just something Steffie says." I'd been thinking about the nasty smells, and the phrase sort of popped out before I could consider how it would sound to everyone else. I wasn't even sure what it meant, except that coming from Steffie, it probably had something to do with sex and girls and acting tough.

"Steffie," Madison said. She stared out the window. Was it possible that she didn't know Steffie? That she was jealous?

"Basketball," I said.

"Oh." She shrugged but didn't turn around to look at me.

I wanted to smack her ponytail and tell her not to be jealous. I also wanted to tell her everything that had happened. It seemed incredible that this whole, huge, melodramatic sector of my life had taken place without her. I wished I could do things over—I'd have joined the debate team with her, or I'd have taken her to the basketball party, or at least I could have told her my suspicions about Riley so she could have laughed at me and made me realize he wasn't that bad. That he'd crossed some lines, but he'd done so out of his boyish enthusiasm, not out of perverted lust for Queen Drama Queen Adele. And that I'd been out to get him all because of the family history essay he'd asked us to write.

Of course, without that essay we wouldn't have gotten here. We wouldn't have met Madison's family, Madison and I wouldn't have kissed, we wouldn't be minutes away from knowing if Dad's family was still alive. I mentally thanked Riley and gave him a tiny raise-the-roof, but everyone in the car was staring out the window, so no one noticed. Even if they had, they all knew me well enough to ignore most of what I said or did.

As we lurched our way toward Dad's village, I wondered what our cabdriver did when he wasn't trying to make tourists throw up in his backseat. Maybe he was a shady gambler and stayed up every night playing poker in some smoky club. Maybe he had a drug problem and shouldn't own a license at all. Maybe he was from the town he was taking us to; maybe he was a neighbor or a cousin. I felt a wave of affection for him. It was possible that I was related to anyone we'd run into so far since getting off the plane. It was possible that my grandparents had more children after Dad left them—which would explain why they stopped treating him like their prized son—and maybe I had half a dozen uncles, or a gaggle of cousins, and when we got to Yihuangkou, I would recognize them.

We passed cornfields and other fields of crops I couldn't identify. Dad pointed excitedly to some signs on the road, and the cabbie swerved toward an exit. We drove down a poorly paved, unmarked road that was lined with large, unmarked warehouses. In less than a mile the road dead-ended at a canal.

"The river," Dad said. He was in the front seat, so I couldn't see his face, but I wondered what he was thinking. Was he anxious? Hopeful? Disbelieving? I didn't want him feeling dread, which was what I felt crawling under my skin. I wanted to fling myself out of the cab and run away. How had I let things go this far?

The river, the ditch, was paved in concrete. Slime-crusted water floated slowly downstream. There were no guardrails, no sidewalks for people to stroll on, nothing that gave someone a reason to stop and enjoy the place.

Dad motioned for the driver to turn right, and as we zoomed around the corner, Dad spoke sharply and the cabbie slowed to a crawl.

"He told him to slow down," Madison whispered.

Mom and I nodded.

Until Madison covertly reached for my hand, I didn't realize how nervous she was. I'd wanted to believe that she wasn't worried, that maybe she'd known something I hadn't this whole time. But her fingers crept over mine, and I turned my hand, palm up, on the vinyl seat between us, and she squashed her palm into mine. Her nails dug into the soft places between my fingers. How many more blocks until we got to the house? Until we knocked at the door and who—my grandfather? a stranger?—opened the door?

We followed the river for a mile or more, as if we were going to trace it back to Qinhuangdao and the Yellow Sea. The river fed into a larger ditch, and then both of those met up with a canal that had a deep, muddy rush of water in it. Warehouse after warehouse lined the opposite side of the street. The sky had turned a deep gray, and the wind smelled like rain and gasoline and our driver's BO.

"Look for Lulong Road," I whispered to Madison. There were no street signs.

It was Thursday but the streets were empty. Where was the village? Where were the houses? The cabbie threw the car in reverse, and we weaved our way back up the street. Dad motioned for him to pull over at the corner. We all got out and stood in the lee of a massive corrugated metal door. Dad walked into the middle of the street. The cabbie lit a cigarette. An old man on a bicycle, a fishing rod in one of his deep pockets, clattered toward us, and Dad motioned for him to stop. Next to the fisherman, Dad looked awkwardly American: his sneakers too white, his jacket too flannelly, his gestures too unrestrained. The fisherman laughed and said something that made Dad spin in a slow circle. The old man pedaled on, and Dad said, "This is the right street. This is Lulong Road West. My house . . . my house must have been right there." He pointed to a dirt parking lot with a few trucks parked haphazardly around it. My voice box decided not to work, and I couldn't speak; I couldn't even swallow. My worst fear was coming true: that his family didn't exist, that we'd never have answers.

Dad walked away, turning the corner and following the river, and when he was out of sight, we scampered after him. Mom gave the cabbie some money so he wouldn't leave with all our things, abandoning us in this warehouse district from hell with no cell phones and no way to get back to our safe lives.

A few raindrops pelted me in the eye and the upper lip as we followed after Dad. Was he putting the pieces together? Would he turn around and yell at me for the first time in his life, or slap me in the face, or disown me as his son? As the rain came down in more steady drops, Dad began to run. He looked like a chicken: his elbows out at all angles, his knees bent high, his head bobbing. Mom and Madison began to run too. I didn't want to go wherever we were going; I walked slowly through the rain, letting it soak me.

Ahead, everyone had ducked under the tin-covered patio of a restaurant. The place was closed and the patio was nothing but a dirt floor. Tables and chairs were stacked and locked inside. A menu on the glass door featured pictures of soupy noodles and their prices. Dad said, "This used to be my father's shop."

I imagined fish guts gummying the dirt floor and perfuming the air with a briny smell. I imagined my grandfather bustling about with pieces of shiny, fat fish and grinning the one grin I could picture on him. The photograph was in my pocket. It was a clue to help me recognize him and to prove we were who we really were. My grandfather had stood here. Right here. I moved to another spot and dripped onto the dirt. And here. I expected to step on a fake rock or touch the right picture on the menu and have a trapdoor spring open and reveal another world, where my grandfather would be singing and gutting fish, and my grandmother, like a Chinese fairy godmother, would serve tea and dote adoringly on us.

"That river"—Dad pointed to the canal—"used to be filled with boats loaded in vegetables and fish. My father was always up before dawn to bargain for the best things. And where is he now?" Dad stared up at the sky. The raindrops were small and fast; I looked up into them, and they looked like stars whizzing by.

"Where is he now?" Dad said again. His voice was shards of glass. "Is this what you wanted?"

"Kenny," Mom said.

"Does seeing this do us any good, Vee? This family is not some ancient, buried treasure. Their lives are their lives. Not an explanation of who you are. Who I am."

I'd never seen Dad this uncontrolled, and it terrified me. He continued to look up at the sky, and I could see him as a stubborn eight-year-old, tear streaks on his face, ashamed that he wanted to go home and lying to his father to hide that shame.

"Dad—" I said.

"No, Vee, no," he said. "Remember, we create our own

happiness. We are not tied to our history. I believe this!" Here he choked up, and I held my breath. "That can't be changed."

Watching Dad come apart made me feel like my insides were breaking. Mom embraced him, and Dad clung to her. I hated seeing him needy; I'd made him weak and needy. I turned to Madison, and her face was all screwed up, like she was about to cry. I'd never seen her cry before.

"What?" I asked her.

"Nothing," she said.

"You don't need to cry."

"Keep your mouth shut, Vee. For once. Just keep it shut."

"Because maybe the mailman recognized their name on the letter and got it to them anyway. Maybe they live right around the corner." I barely knew what I was saying, but I headed out into the rain, my arms swinging with a determination I didn't feel.

"Everyone lives across the river now," Dad called out, pulling away from Mom. His face was dry; he hadn't been crying. "They tore down all the houses to build a factory that makes metal hoses. The men eat lunch here. This is not a fish market anymore." Dad scratched his forehead, leaving red marks running across it like veins.

He whistled to the taxi and said to us, "We can go across the river and find some food and talk about this. About what we haven't found."

I knew it was coming now, my moment of truth. I wanted to drag my feet; I wanted to rest here and take pictures of the old fish market and spend more time with the ghosts of my grandparents and delay the inevitable, but we were already climbing inside the car and winding our way back to the freeway so we could find the bridge over to the other side. The scenery flew by, and we all stared silently at the mountains and the freeway and the bridge and the boats below us and the people crowding the narrow streets and the houses made of stucco and brick and not looking particularly Chinese. No pagodas, no red lanterns or gilded dragons. The silence was suffocating. My grandparents didn't exist, and now we were here in this spot that meant nothing to us and it didn't matter anymore. We knew no one. China meant nothing to us. And Dad couldn't recognize a thing.

32

Madison politely asked Dad if we could stop somewhere to use the bathroom. Once she said it, I realized I needed to pee too, even though I didn't want to have to go. Madison had warned me that sometimes bathrooms were just holes in the ground, holes with footrests, and I didn't want to stand over or around some rural cesspool. Weren't they making metal pipes and tubes just across the river? Couldn't they hook one of those up to a bowl and call it a real toilet?

Dad directed us through the neighborhood and toward the river, and now we could look across at the warehouses and the old fish market. We pulled over—the taxi was getting nowhere anyway, with all the people milling about—so we got out and followed Dad down the crowded street. There were vegetable stands everywhere, and people spitting on the street, and men gathered around cement tables playing chess. And it smelled like the muddy river and dirty rain. And like fish. I could smell the fish market before we even got close to it, but when we did, Dad stopped in front of it.

"What?" I asked. "You want to buy some fish? I don't think that'll make it back to our hotel." We had hotel reservations in Qinhuangdao for the night, but that was as far as we'd planned.

Madison, who was still peeved at me, I could tell, informed me that the name of the fish market was Mr. Wang's Fish Market.

"Old Wang's," Dad said. "Old Wang's Fish Market. This is it."

"Oh, Kenny," Mom said. All her concern seemed to be for him. She hadn't made one comforting, motherly gesture toward me since we left the train station. Maybe she was quietly angry that I'd brought up her parents. Maybe the best thing was never to mention the people we'd left behind, even if our issues with them always dragged us down, weighed on us like overloaded book bags.

Mom had her hand on Dad's shoulder, and Dad took a few steps toward the blue awning and the plastic vats of swarming fish and then paused. We stopped behind him. People crashed into us. Mom guided Dad under the awning and up a few steps into a room full of buckets and tanks of flopping fish, skittish crabs, and ribbonlike eels. An old lady picked up a shiny, palm-size fish from a pile and stuck her nose into it. An old man held up a slender, whiskered fish for his friend's inspection.

Dad cleared his throat and asked one of the older fishmongers a question. The man propped his elbows on an aquarium filled with listless lobsters and moved his lips like he was trying to get something out of his teeth. Finally he called out to a younger man who was massacring a fish the color of rust. The younger man, his knife never pausing, answered back. No one bothered to translate for Mom or me, so I silently made up my own voice-over.

Dad: You guys work for Old Wang?

Old Fishmonger: Old Wang? Old Wang? Hey, Marty, who the hell is Old Wang?

Marty, the Young Fishmonger: Man, he's the moolah.

Old Fishmonger: Right, right. *(Turning to Dad)* Of course. He's the moolah.

Dad *(looking proud)*: Well, he's my old man.

Old Fishmonger: Is that right? Hey, Marty, pass me some salami. I mean sashimi.

Here's where my amusing voice-over ended, though, because even though the fishmongers kept talking, Dad looked like a bullet had hit him, and he put his hands on his stomach and bent over a little, like he was going to throw up all over the tile floor. He said "Oh-oh" over and over, and the fishmongers nodded their heads, then returned to their work, and the customers went back to their chattering, and no one seemed to care that my father was going to die on the floor of their shop.

"I'm gonna ask where the bathroom is," Madison said.

"What?" My voice was too high. "What do we do?"

"I think you should talk to your dad," Madison said. She turned away from me, and I looked desperately at Mom.

"Let's walk outside with him," Mom said. Her everyday job was to deal with crisis—people losing their teeth, people in pain, people afraid of losing their teeth or being in pain—and she calmly put a hand under Dad's elbow and led him across the street, around determined shoppers and rickety bicyclists, until we got to a bench that overlooked the shallow, silt-filled river. The cold wooden slats of the bench bit into my hamstrings.

Dad took a deep breath. "Thank you," he said. "My mother is dead." He keeled over again, and Mom and I both lamely patted him on the back. Mom's eyes filled with tears, and she leaned over to kiss Dad on his head over and over.

"I'm sorry," I said. I was sorry, for almost everything. Strangely, though, I wasn't sorry that we were all sitting on a bench together, looking at the river that Dad had grown up with, sharing our grief over his mother, my grandmother, and all we'd lost and left behind and could never get back.

Having grandparents was sad. Having them meant understanding that they'd die and that you'd be around to watch it happen. I felt the loss of my grandmother as if I'd grown up in her arms. My grandmother. My *nainai*. Ju. Her name was Ju, which meant "chrysanthemum." I'd never seen a picture of her, but I could imagine her in every woman who walked by: the deep gray hair; the powdery, lined skin; the careful, shuffling steps. Dad sat up and stared out at the river. I patted his knee. This was a perfect family moment, with the right mixture of togetherness and shared grief and even a sort of excitement that rose like steam from the bad news.

Dad gestured to the canal. "It used to reflect the sky," he said. "It used to not be so dirty."

"I'm sorry," I said again. Was I apologizing for the mud in the river? I didn't know anymore.

"I never imagined he would outlive her," Dad said.

"Who?"

"My father."

"Oh. Of course," I said without thinking.

"There is no 'of course' about it. He's in a care home. In Qinhuangdao. Those men in his market have worked with him, and now he is too old and has no family to care for him. So three years ago he goes away. To a nursing home. In Qinhuangdao."

"I'm sorry," I said. "This is all my fault."

"No, I am sorry," Dad said, "for not telling you the truth."

Wasn't that my line? What lies had he been telling me?

"I wanted you to experience being here," he said. "But it has surprised me by being so deeply difficult. I feel more like a child myself. I find myself remembering who I was when I called this home, and wondering how different things would be if I had never left." He combed his eyebrows with his fingertips. He continued to look out at the river.

"Kenny, you made your choices," Mom said, rubbing his neck with her fingertips. "You can't live two lives. I did the same thing. I always wonder what I'd be like if I'd stayed home and lived out the joys and sadnesses there. But I did choose to leave. And if I hadn't, I wouldn't have you two. I wouldn't be sitting here now with you two."

"Yes," Dad said, looking from me to Mom and back to me. "Yes, you two."

"Being here is all my fault," I said suddenly. "I wrote that letter. It's my fault. I wrote it. I made it all up. You love me too much. You don't understand all the wrong I've done." It came tumbling out of me. I stood up and reached into my pant pocket and took everything out. My train ticket. A Juicy Fruit wrapper. A one yuan banknote. The picture of my grandfather, grinning, standing in a shallow boat with the ancient, misty hills behind him. Lint from my pants clung to the creases and folds. The stack was warm from my body and felt thick and dry in my icy hands.

"Here, take these," I said. "Take the picture. Take everything."

It wasn't everything. I should have had the letter that Madison and I forged, my letter to the Crawfords and their crappy Christmas card, my report card, the family history essay I invented, and every other little scrap of everything that was evidence of how I'd gotten to this point. The cliques and disappointments of school. Mr. Riley's misdirected kindness. Steffie's misdirected anger and Adele's awkward neediness. All of it had built to this point. If I hadn't been so angry and confused, I would never have caused such a mess.

I imagined I had all the cards and letters and homework assignments and photographs in my hands. I imagined ripping them up and scattering them into the steel-colored water. I imagined dumping them in Dad's lap and running away, getting lost forever in China, just one person in a crowd of a billion people.

Even if I could collect all the evidence, and if I could shred it or dump it, what then? I couldn't go back. I couldn't untell all the lies I'd scattered around. I couldn't give Mom her parents' love or Riley his players' respect or Adele her happiness or Dad his childhood on some dinghy boat. I couldn't give him a life before he was Kenny, when he was still Ken-zhi, just this torn-up teenager who couldn't stand secrets and lies, this smart kid who wanted something to change, this person who existed before America and Mom and me.

"Dad?" I said. My voice was a rusty whisper. "Dad, I'm sorry. Dad, look at me. Dad. I'm sorry. I'm sorry." I held the picture out for him to take.

I felt empty, hollow, like everything inside of me had been dug out and replaced by nothing but air—stale, cold, empty, silent, echoing air.

"Thank you," Dad said. He took the picture of his father and slipped it into the front pocket of my jacket. Then he stood up and took my face in his freezing hands. I stared at his chin. "Vee," he said. I looked up. His eyes were full. "Thank you," he said, "but I already knew."

The wind whipped around us. Somewhere close someone was making sweet bread. The warm, sugary smell drifted down the street in waves.

"You what?" My voice cracked. I licked my chapped lips. "How?"

Dad let go of my face and laughed. "You remind me of me," he said, "always having a plan to get what you want. But I did not just fall off the turnip truck, you know." He laughed at his own joke. "My father's voice is forever in my head. As mine will be in yours." He tapped my skull, and I was too shocked to bat his hand away. "The letter simply was not his."

"Madison," I said quickly. "But it's still my fault. I put her up to it."

"I guessed all that right away. The letter does have a few significant mistakes."

"Don't tell her that," I said, "please. She was really proud of it."

"Come here," Dad said. He folded his arms around me, and even though I was as tall as he was, I rested my head on his shoulder and relaxed into him. "I will not be so hard to reason with," he said. "That is my promise."

"I won't lie to you," I said. I imagined our silences and lies like an endless ocean, and both of us like rudderless dinghies trying to row toward each other against the relentless waves. "At least, I'll try not to," I said.

"That is something," he said. "That is good enough for me." His breath warmed my forehead, and then he kissed me on the head, through my hair, and when I looked up, Madison was standing with Mom, both clutching each other's arms, looking like they were about to launch themselves into the hug circle.

"I ordered us a snack," Madison said shyly, "at the place over there that the fish guy recommended." She gestured to a restaurant that was crowded with older men. They all wore shapeless black jackets and soft, shapeless black hats with small, wide brims.

"He knows," I said.

"I know," she said.

"*What?*"

"I really knew when he asked you over there"—she pointed

across the river—"if this was what you wanted. But I guessed a long time ago."

"When?" I asked.

"A long time ago."

"You know you're pissing me off?" I said.

"You know I enjoy that?" Her hair blew across her eyes, and she shook her head and turned her face toward the direction of the wind. "When we came over to your house for dinner and he asked me to read the letter, it crossed my mind. It just crossed the teeniest back part of my mind. But then I forgot about it because, well"—her eyes flickered over to Dad, then up at the heavy sky, then back to me—"if my dad figured something like that out, he wouldn't even ask. He'd just ground me for the next thirty years. And he'd never forgive me. Never, ever, ever." She smiled brightly, falsely, and said, "But your dad's not my dad. So hooray for that."

"Your Mandarin is very good," Dad said.

She blushed, or maybe the cold was freezing her cheeks off. "It's not that good," she said, "but it's getting better. I'm sorry—"

"No more apologies today," Dad said. "No more. We have all had a part in getting us here. But now we are here." He clapped his hands together and rubbed them. "Here we are."

"Too bad we don't live here," I said.

Everyone looked at me blankly.

"If we lived here? Dad, come on. If we lived here? Guess what?"

Dad chuckled.

"Oh!" Mom said. "I know what's coming."

I turned to Madison.

"What? I don't know. We don't live here." She looked back and forth between Dad and me.

"It's going to be a joke," Mom told her. "You'll see. It always is."

We'd told it a million times, but the more we told it, the less the funniness hinged on surprise and the more it felt like a scripted reason for us to laugh together at the world. I felt a laugh bubbling in the back of my throat.

Dad looked at me and grinned. "If we lived here, we'd be home already!"

33

We spent the majority of the afternoon in either the restaurant or the fish market. Dad pumped the fishmongers for information about my grandfather, and Madison practiced her Chinese by continually ordering us things—tea, of course, and then dumplings and pork buns and rice noodles and egg tarts. It was the best food I'd ever tasted. Even Mom, who'd been careful with the foreign food, tucked away bean flour cakes and slice after slice of pale, tart pear. The more tea I drank, the more giddy I felt, until I was like a kid on a Halloween sugar high, laughing uncontrollably, wanting to run through the streets and dance with the bustling Chinese ladies and hug the old men playing chess. Every now and then one of us would get up to wander around and talk more with the fishmongers, who later joined us for more tea and pot stickers and steamed meatballs, or to check on our smelly cabbie, who'd parked the cab and was taking a nap, or smoking, or eating noodles, and running his meter all the while.

The fishmongers gave us the name of my grandfather's

nursing home, and Dad folded up the paper at least nine or ten times before putting it in the breast pocket of his jacket. Then we left the waitress a ginormous tip, and the cabbie drove us back to Qinhuangdao. We paid him about twenty bucks for the entire day, but he seemed happy with it.

It was dark by the time we got to the hotel, and Dad called the nursing home and spoke to someone who confirmed his father's existence and said we could make an appointment to visit him. We made an appointment for the next day.

We all ended up back in Mom and Madison's room. It was warm, and a little stuffy, and my face and fingers felt hot, like they'd been frostbitten. When Mom got up to brush her teeth and Dad went downstairs to check the train schedule, Madison and I both stood up at the same time.

"I was going over there," Madison whispered, pointing at me.

"Same here, but over there," I said, and pointed at her.

We met in the middle and I stroked her cheekbones before leaning in to kiss her. I wanted full body contact, but I was afraid of forgetting that Mom could pop back into the room any minute.

"Want to go walk in the garden?" I said. We were finally in a nice, classy, Western-style hotel, and it claimed to have an award-winning courtyard tea garden.

"No. Your parents aren't stupid. They'll figure us out."

I threw up my hands in mock horror. "As if we're good at keeping secrets from them."

"There's no rush," she said. Her fingers were at my hips, just above the waistband of my jeans, and I could barely hear what she was saying with all the blood roaring in my ears. "I'm not going anywhere," she said. Her lips brushed my chin and then along my jaw to my earlobe. She was already more confident than she'd been the night before.

For all my failures, I had done right by Madison. She'd finally stood on Chinese soil and met her family. She'd found some breathing room from her parents. And she knew how I felt about her. This was the best part: that even when we left this place, we'd be leaving together.

We pulled apart when we heard the bathroom door click open. I tousled Madison's hair and peered at her scalp.

She giggled. "What are you doing?"

"I'm checking for lice," I said. "Mom, you're next."

Mom looked tiredly amused. "And what will we do if we find them?"

"Umm . . . ," I said. "I haven't figured that out yet."

"Oh," she said, "I thought you were setting us up for a joke."

Dad returned and declared that he was all tuckered out.

"Okay," I said. "I'm leaving." I hugged Mom and said good night, and then I put my arm around Madison's shoulder. I could tell from her rigidness that she was uncomfortable. "Good night, Madison." I turned us around so we were facing Mom and Dad. "Just FYI, you guys know that I'm crazy about Madison, right?"

"Of course, honey," Mom said. "Who isn't?"

"Or just crazy," Dad said.

They were, after all we'd been through today, still very much my parents. I rolled my eyes, and Madison elbowed me in the side, and I thought briefly about turning to kiss her in front of them, to drive my point home, but decided against it. Maybe they did actually understand me and were accepting this without silliness. Or maybe they were genuinely clueless, which gave me the freedom to tell the truth without worrying about their fuddy-duddy judgment.

It would always be a balancing act: what to tell them, what to keep to myself, what they already knew, what they guessed at but didn't need to know. What was mine, what was ours, and what belonged to them that I didn't need to know. For the first time I didn't feel bad about it. I didn't feel like they were keeping secrets from me.

"Come on, Dad," I said. "The ladies need their beauty sleep."

Madison sighed and shook her head.

"No, I mean it," I said. "You look like crap right now."

Mom swatted at my head.

"Just telling it like it is," I said.

"Oh, shut up, Vee," Madison said. She practically pushed me out the door.

"A little honesty goes a long way," Dad said as he followed me into the hallway.

"Ain't that right," I said. We'd probably had enough for one day.

34

The next morning we took a cab to the nursing home. I missed our crabby cabbie. This cabbie seemed like a typical middle-aged Chinese guy, and the cab had slippery vinyl seats and red-tasseled trinkets and a heater with two settings: hellfire and glacier. Dad had to do a lot of talking and pointing, and once, we backed into an alley and turned around, almost killing five or six old guys on rusted bicycles who shouted and tapped the sides of the car and then swerved and almost ran one another over.

The nursing home could have been an office building or a hotel. It was boxy and gray. It had windows with plain white curtains. Most of the curtains were drawn, like the building's eyes were closed and it was shutting down. We stumbled out of the cab, the dry wind whipping around us, and I stared up at it, wondering if my grandfather was peering down from between his curtains right now. Looking down, would he recognize me? What would I say to him? Hello? Hi? What's up? *Ni hao?*

"Dad, how are we going to do this?" The place scared me already. I thought about the third-grade field trip I'd taken to a nursing home. We were supposed to sing carols and play with the old people as a kind of Christmas penance for being so young and healthy. One old guy tried to play cards with me, but the only card game I knew then was Go Fish. And he didn't know how to play Go Fish. I remembered having to pee but being afraid of the big, grown-up toilets.

Dad looked at me, but he didn't focus on me. I was probably a blurry, white blob in his vision. "Just be yourself," he said.

I glanced around and shrugged. "Who's that?" I asked.

"Ha, ha," he said. "I don't know what to expect. I can't tell you what to do, only that he might feel like a stranger but is not. He is all the family we have."

I glanced at Mom, who nodded. Of course she did. We weren't about to go to Ding Dong to meet her parents. I wouldn't be able to lie and trick my way into that.

Obediently, I followed Dad and Mom and Madison into the building. An attendant, a young guy in a starchy nursing uniform, talked to Dad and led us to the tenth floor. He knocked, opened the door, and led us into a bleak bedroom, where my grandfather sat in a small wooden chair.

He was tiny. His shoulders were trying to take over his neck, and his back looked like it had spent too long in a hammock. He could have been one of the kids on the street outside, wrapped up and slung on his mother's back, mute and wide eyed, watching the world go by. I felt like a king who'd just discovered I had to stoop to be at eye level with Napoleon or Genghis Khan. How could someone so small be that scary? The word "grandfather" shrank in front of me. What had been big and bold and terrifying suddenly seemed faded and ordinary and old.

Dad dropped to a knee, took my grandfather's hand, which looked like a claw, and kissed it. He held his head down for a long time. My grandfather's eyes leaked puslike tears. They said things back and forth in a whisper.

The attendant stood by my grandfather's bed. Wasn't someone going to ask him to leave? What right did he have to be here? I stared hard at him, but he kept his eyes on the two men by the window. Couldn't he see that this was a private moment? I couldn't even look at them. I glared at the attendant and at Madison's feet. I tried to avoid looking at the hospital-like bed, with its metal safety railing, and at the little brown bottles of medicine lined up on the bedside table. I tried not to breathe the stuffy, medicinal air. I felt light-headed, like we were somehow on the 110th floor and all that space below us was just dissolving, and any minute everything would start to collapse.

Dad looked up and his eyes were puffy, like he'd just woken up, and the attendant handed him a tissue. Was this guy supposed to be a waiter or a bellhop or something? He needed to back off. I could hand my own dad a stupid tissue.

But of course I couldn't. I hadn't. I hadn't thought of it, and even if I had, I felt stuck, my joints all stiff and afraid to move. I was frozen in place like I was eight years old and climbing up the high dive for the first time. I couldn't go forward; I couldn't go back. The kids below me were yelling at me to hurry up, and Dad had to climb up and grab the rail right above each of my white-knuckled fists, and I rested my back against the wet warmth of his hairless chest, and we backed down together, one rung at a time, until we were again on solid ground.

I never thanked him for that. We never talked about why I was scared or how he helped me. He was my dad. Of course he'd help me. But I should have thanked him for it.

Now Dad couldn't help me. I'd gotten us here with my lies, with my self-pity, with my American entitlement. I was about to meet the man whose fear and silence had provoked Dad to run away from his entire family and culture and history, to run right off the continent and toward the land of opportunity, the land of free speech and self-invention and kids who seemed to pop right out of the melting pot and look like they came from nowhere.

I was one of those kids. I looked like I came from nowhere. I was a spoiled American who was nothing like this small, shriveled man. I could never be genuinely Chinese. I was the Pilgrims and Paul Bunyan. I was Johnny freakin' Appleseed.

Madison put her hand on my back and pushed me forward.

"No," I said, resisting. I glanced at Mom, who stood quietly behind us. "Mom, you go."

"Go ahead, Vee," she said.

"Madison," I said.

"No," Madison said. "Just go, Vee."

Dad turned to me, his face all blotchy and swollen, and said, "Come here, Vee. He knows some English, but he barely speaks it now and is rusty."

"Rusty," my grandfather said. It came out sounding like

"lusty." His voice was old, like his hands, all dried up and cracked like little cakes of yellow rosin.

Dad turned to him and said, "This is Vee, your grandson. *Sun. Sun zi.*"

"No," my grandfather said.

No? No? I wasn't his grandson?

"Yes," I said. "Yes, I am." It felt good to say something that was so simple and true. It was biology. We could do a DNA test right here and prove it.

"Dad?" I asked. What was I supposed to say now?

My grandfather looked at Madison. "Ju?" he asked.

"No," Dad said. "That is Madison. She is a friend for Vee."

Madison stepped forward, but my grandfather's eyes rolled away from her, back to me, and he said, "I remember. We meet before."

"Dad?" I asked. My throat was all thick and tight, and I wanted him to say something to make this right. I wanted my grandfather to look at me and understand who I was.

"No," I said. "We've never met before. I've always wanted to meet you." My voice cracked a bit, and I coughed into my elbow. I didn't want to spray him with deadly American germs.

Dad looked like he was about to say something, but he closed his mouth and leaned back on his heels. Crouched down, he was even smaller than my grandfather. I was the tallest person in the room.

"No Ju," my grandfather said. "Ju sick. Heart sick. No move. Long time."

Dad looked brittle. Disoriented. He turned away from my grandfather and stared through the dusty window at the bright, overcast sky. My grandfather's eyes rolled between us.

The attendant was holding out a tissue for me.

"Thank you," I croaked, and took it.

My grandfather motioned me closer. I leaned in, and he reached up to hold on to my upper arms. He tugged me down until my ear was inches from his lips.

"I learn English and I speak to my son. When he come back."

"He's here!" I said, too brightly. Where was the tug of blood and genes that would tell me we were related? Where was the instant sense of reunion?

"English bad language," he said. His claws were still on my arms. His breath was hot and sour, and his voice sputtered and cracked. "No English. We go way. We speak English get *dai bu.*"

"Arrested?" Dad asked.

"Why?" I whispered back.

My grandfather's eyes slid to the attendant, then back to me. "*Hong Wei,*" he said, "Red Guard."

It didn't make sense, but anything could happen here. And he wasn't lying. He really meant it. His voice was urgent and scared.

"Dad?" I said. I heard the tight fear in my own voice. "Dad, what do we do?"

He put his hand over both my grandfather's and mine. Finally, he looked at me and said, "There is no danger. There are no Red Guards."

"We see them!" my grandfather said. "You remember!"

"Shh," Dad said. "That was a long time ago."

"They take me for telling bad story! For speak truth! For knowing the English!"

"Shh, shh." Dad and I were both saying it now.

"They parade me through streets naked, *ai ya*, take my books, you so shamed! So shamed!" He waved the hand we didn't hold, and the attendant took a step closer. "No let me take them! No take me! You go, never come back! So shame! So shame!" He started bawling and lunging for us with his clawed hands, and the attendant pushed us away and came around behind him, pinning my grandfather's arms to his sides while holding a lemon-scented cloth under his nose. My grandfather struggled to escape. It looked like a sick, twisted wrestling match. It looked like cruelty. I took a step toward the attendant. The attendant spoke quickly and quietly to Dad.

"Vee," Dad said, "let this happen. Take a breath. He is confused about time."

The attendant picked up my grandfather and put him on the bed. He was limp, exhausted looking, like he'd passed out or died. My face felt hot and stuffy.

"Dad? Dad, did that really happen? I thought that happened to your teacher. Was it him? This whole time, was it him?"

"Vee," he said. We both stared at the crumpled body of the man on the bed. "I do not know." His voice was high and tight. "I could have remembered it wrong. He could be right. It could have been him this whole time. It could have been him."

"This is all my fault," I said.

Dad's face reflected every torn-up thing I was feeling. "I wanted this too. I've been afraid to see this, to face what I left behind. As difficult as this is, the fear has been worse. Does this make sense to you?"

I nodded. We would get through this. This was not the end of us. I wanted to laugh or hug him, but all I could do was stand there and take in big, choking breaths.

"I say to you to choose happiness," he said, "and here I have been afraid to choose it for myself. I needed this. I needed to see him again."

From the bed, like an echo, I heard my grandfather say, "Choose happiness."

Dad put his hand over his mouth, like he was trying to swallow back some overwhelming emotion. "That," he said in a whisper, "is where I get that."

The attendant gestured toward the door, which Mom was still standing next to. She'd never moved into the room. My grandfather had never even seen her. I wanted to know if Mom was innately the kind of person who stood near doors or if her family had made her that way. I realized this wasn't a question I could ask, because there was no certain answer—all I could do was accept who Mom was now and hope that she wasn't miserable in this role.

As we reluctantly shuffled past his bed, my grandfather reached out to grab Madison by the arm.

"Ju?" he said. "Ju!"

The attendant lunged for her but stopped when Madison held up her hand. She looked over at me with wide eyes. Then she turned, leaned down, and whispered something in my grandfather's ear. His face melted into a smile, and he stroked her cheek with his rough, old fingertips. She sat on the side of his bed and let him hold her hand until he'd fallen asleep.

The whole episode was probably only two minutes long, but I felt frozen in place, like we'd been there all day. Mom moved quietly from her place by the door and went to stand behind Madison and stroke her hair. They whispered together for a minute, and then my mom gently pulled Madison away. My mom leaned over my grandfather for a minute and fussed with his sheets and gnarled hands, and then she, too, backed away. It felt like a funeral. He looked lifeless. I wanted to touch him too, and deliver some comforting gesture, but I was too scared, and he was already asleep anyway.

35

My grandfather didn't know us, and he never would. I wanted this realization to hurt more than it did, but it didn't, and I couldn't force myself to cry or mourn something I'd never had: a grandfather's love or pride or recognition or whatever else I was looking for.

As we left my grandfather's room, Dad said he wanted to stay behind for a few minutes. Mom, Madison, and I promised we'd wait outside, which seemed like a fine idea until we stepped out into the freezing wind.

"Can you find us a restaurant now?" I asked Madison. My throat had dried up while we were inside, and I had to clear it a few times just to finish my sentence.

Madison waved her hand as if it were a magic wand. "Ta-da," she said, and pointed across the street. She waited for a few cars and crazy men on bicycles to pass by, and then she took Mom's arm and the two of them crossed the street in front of me.

I missed Dad. Mom and Madison had that conspiratorial girl thing going on, and I felt ganged up on. Probably they'd bonded irreversibly while standing over my sleeping grand-father, and now Madison would forget all about how this trip was in a lot of ways about us. It was about having some-thing exciting just between me and her—the forged letter, the shared and confused thoughts on being Chinese, the way people looked at us and saw two weird, smart-ass Nuprins, the way our secret plans and jokes were the only way to survive the tidal wave of the Liverton Lions rah-rah high school cul-ture. This whole trip had been about my family, but also about us. It seemed ridiculous to be jealous of my mom, but I was. I wanted every amazing, meaningful moment with Madison. And if I couldn't have that, then at least I wanted my wing-man, my jokester-in-arms.

I followed them across the street and was so busy sulking that I almost got run over by a moped. The woman driving it had to swerve, and she swerved again when she took her hands off the handlebars in order to gesture at me and yell. I wanted to yell back and give her my middle finger, but I wasn't sure if that was a universal gesture. With my luck, it'd be some secret Chinese way of saying "You turn me on" or "I'd like to give you a million yuan."

The restaurant was dark and smelled like five-spice powder. An old guy stood behind the counter and noisily sipped a bowl of noodles. Mom and Madison sat at a sticky table, but I sud-denly didn't feel good.

"I'll wait outside," I said, "so Dad knows where we are."

"He'll figure it out," Mom said. "Take a seat, honey."

I didn't want to sit down and have crappy tea. "You don't know that," I said. "I just want to be outside."

"But you're the one who wanted this," Madison said.

I shrugged and ducked back outside and let the cold wind whip me in the face and tear through my supposedly windproof jacket. It felt fantastic. I imagined Dad sitting by my grandfather's bed, holding his lifeless hand, wondering what else one or both of them had remembered wrong. Dad would never know unless he wanted to do some weird hypnosis therapy, and I couldn't see him caring that much, especially after all this time. For most of his life he'd been fine with his incomplete or self-censored memories. I didn't want him to change that now, all because of me.

When Dad came out of the nursing home, I waved at him to cross the street.

"They're in there," I said, pointing to the door of the restaurant.

"And we're out here," he said. I looked for tear streaks on his face, and he put a hand on my arm. "Is this helping?" he asked. "To see our family, such as it is—is this what you imagined?"

I shrugged. I couldn't put everything into words. We were on our own, just Dad and me, the last of the Wong men. My family tree was more like a twig or a dead branch. In my gut I'd known this all along—that we wouldn't have some magical family reunion with cousins who looked like Lily and grandparents who spoke like oracles. I'd always known that we were on our own, and surprisingly, there was something close and comfortable about confirming it. I just wanted to know if Dad felt the same way, or if now he was wishing he'd lived his life closer to home, with some woman who wasn't Mom and some real Chinese kids who would never be as awful and sneaky and selfish as me.

"I've got you," I said. "I guess that's enough."

"Too much sometimes!" he said, laughing. "Come on, it's freezing out here."

He seemed okay, and even a little happy. And not at all mad at me.

We all sat around and drank tea that was watery and bitter and that we didn't really want. Because our visit had been so brief, the rest of the day stretched before us. The rest of the trip—all six days of it—seemed like an eternity. I wanted to put my head down on the sticky table and take a nap.

Finally Dad cleared his throat. "Today we go back to Beijing and stay at our *hutong*. I called this morning, and they have our same rooms available. I think the train leaves soon."

"Oh," Mom said. "Let's go, then. We don't want to miss it." She nagged at Dad to hurry up and pay, and we left most of the tea and a ridiculous tip for the noodle-slurping shopkeeper. Suddenly we all had pep in our step. We'd just needed a plan.

On the train Dad asked if we wanted to go back to see more of Madison's family.

"Stay with Uncle Tim?" Madison asked.

"Back to my quilt pile?" I said. "Hoo-rah." I didn't smile or wink at Madison—I didn't even look at her—but I knew she was thinking what I was thinking.

"Maybe for a few days," Madison said, "that'd be nice."

Mom suggested that while we were in Beijing, we could see some of the sights. "You know," she said, "let ourselves be touristy. Why not?"

"We could do something today," Dad said.

"Awesome," Madison said. "I mean, how can we not go see the Great Wall?"

None of us wanted to talk right now about the lies and discoveries and excitements and disappointments of the last twenty-four hours. We wanted to focus on things that had happened to other people hundreds or thousands of years ago. We needed to take pictures and buy postcards and pretend that this canned, safe experience was exactly what we'd come all this way for. At least, that's how I was feeling.

"The Great Wall, of course, and the Ming Dynasty Tombs, the Summer Palace, Mao's Mausoleum." I ticked these off my fingers. "Oh, and Zhoukoudian. That's at the top of the list."

They looked at me blankly.

"Peking man? Dragon Bone Hill? World Heritage site? We could do that today. It's only a few miles outside of Beijing."

It turned out to be a little more than that. "Thirty minute," the taxi driver said. "Thirty minute. No problem." The downtown streets were clogged with traffic, and our driver zipped from highway to back alley to one-way streets and even through a dirt parking lot to get us across the city. I recognized a few intersections—the one with the blinding glass buildings that stacked together like a Tetris game, the one with soaring red gates that looked like an ancient temple—and then we were out of the downtown area and onto wider streets with more open sky.

"If you'd like to, Vee," Dad said from the front seat, "we can take the train back and visit your grandfather again before we leave."

There wasn't enough time to do everything—go back to Madison's family, be tourists, return to Qinhuangdao. I couldn't see Dad's face, so I couldn't tell if he was trying to tell me what he wanted to do.

I shrugged, then realized he couldn't see me. "If you want," I said. "That'd be . . . nice." "Nice" wasn't the right word for it. We'd return and sit in the same room with a grandfather who would only whisper words from a dangerous language, who would barely recognize his son, whose memory was as brief, burning, and unpredictable as a comet. Then we would leave him in the stale, sterile nursing home to live out his days in a cloud of lemon-scented medication. We could not take him with us. He would not take a memory of us with him. We were dead to him, not because of his own stubborn pride, but because his brain had lost its ability to connect the past to the present to the future.

But maybe Dad had gotten more out of it, or maybe he wanted to keep trying. "Sure," I said, more enthusiastically. "Whatever you want."

We entered a town with patches of brown fields and warehouses. It looked exactly like all the other towns we'd driven through. Then we turned a corner and there were rows of identical red-roofed high-rise apartments, and we could have been on the outskirts of San Francisco or San Jose.

"Crazy," I said.

"How big are these prehistoric caves?" Madison asked.

I'd read a humdrum review in the guidebook, but I didn't feel like sharing such lukewarm news.

"Huge," I said. "Ginormous."

"Really?" she asked.

"Maybe."

We were back to our usual sarcasm and indirection, but it felt different—it was playful because we wanted it to be, not because we felt like we couldn't say what we really meant. I hoped this was how it would always be—that when we got home, we wouldn't go back to annoying each other because we didn't know what else to do. I hoped I'd have the balls to do things like kiss her to shut her up sometimes. Guys were always doing that in movies, but I wasn't sure that'd work so well with Madison.

When we pulled up to the front of the museum, we were the only cab in the parking lot. I stared out the window at the hulking bronze head of the half ape/half man whose bones had been found here.

"This is it," I said. "Don't get your hopes up."

"Not too many people enjoying their ancestors today," Dad said.

"No one knows if these are our ancestors," I said. "I mean, no one knows for sure who we were three quarters of a million years ago."

We walked through the tomblike museum, which was just one dark hallway with red carpet and a few glass cases with plaster skulls sitting at awkward angles on thick red felt. Four life-size dinosaurs made of plaster and painted a spotted, moldy brown lurked in each corner.

"You guys know we don't actually see Peking man," I said. "We just see, you know, his cave."

"Right," Madison said. "Because the Japanese stole the bones during World War Two."

"No one knows," I said. "We just don't know."

We walked to the end of the hall, and one of the attendants left a card game spread out on the gift shop display case to open the back door for us. He gestured wordlessly to the pathway.

The path took us back toward the hills where there would be caves and buried bones. One muddy hillside rose steeply next to us, and Madison read its placard aloud.

"'Dragon Bone Hill,'" she read, "'the first site for interest of prehistoric animals such as three-toed rhinoceroses. Many bones from this hill were transported to pharmacies, where they were called dragon bones and cured diseases such as demonic possession.'"

"Maybe Peking man ended up as an elixir," Dad suggested.

"Maybe he ended up in my *yeye*'s liver," she said.

"Nasty," I said.

"How do people even find these things?" Mom asked me. "After they've been buried for so long."

"A lot of times it's a natural disaster—an earthquake or mud slide will shift everything around and reveal a cave entrance or an old burial site or ancient trash pile."

"Out of disaster comes discovery," Dad said. He took a picture of the placard.

"Thank you, Mr. Fortune Cookie," I said. He turned the camera on me and snapped. I made a face, and he snapped again.

And then I added the requisite "in bed" to Dad's fortune cookie phrase. But only in my head, of course. It seemed true, too—that out of my disastrous encounter with Adele, I'd found the confidence and opportunity to make a move on Madison. But maybe one of these events would have happened without the other. Maybe disaster and discovery happened on their own, in bed and everywhere else, without any connection. I wanted to believe that I wouldn't always have to do stupid shit in order to figure something out.

I watched Mom wander ahead of us and stop in front of a feathery tree. She touched one of the leaves as if it were actually part of an animal. "What a lovely plant," she said, to herself or to us.

"Agreed," I said, just to be nice.

She turned to smile at me. It was so easy to make her happy. All I had to do was say something nice every now and then, and not worry her too much with bad grades or unexpected fights. Maybe if I could keep being nice and out of trouble, she'd eventually teach me to drive. Maybe she'd let me go on a road trip to Texas. Maybe she'd even come with me. I was done tricking my parents, but I could always ask and hope they could see how important certain things were to me.

The path took us straight into the side of the mountain. The cave was as small as my bedroom, and a dim set of bulbs that looked like Christmas lights made the stalactites glimmer like icicles or daggers. There were no placards. So much sediment had settled over time that this was all we had, without digging, of Peking man's seven-hundred-thousand-year-old house.

He'd had fire and stone tools, and his grunts would later become words, and his brain would evolve, and he'd become us.

Or maybe he'd struggled along with his venison and grubs, with his heavy, chipped tools, and eventually died out. Maybe Peking man had nothing to do with us.

We couldn't know for sure. We would never know, not just because the bones were lost, and not just because our carbon dating and analyzing methods were limited, but because there were too many variables to ever sort out. There was no one answer. All the fossils and cave sites in the world couldn't tell us why we existed or why we believed what we believed or treated each other the way we did.

We stood in a huddle and felt the damp air leach through our jackets.

"Do you think he's happy?" I asked Dad.

"Your grandfather?"

"Who else? Peking man? I don't care if Peking man is happy."

"What is happy?"

"Oh, come on, Dad."

"No," he said. "No, this is not a theoretical question. I do not know what he's lived through for the last forty years. I know he lost his wife. I know he is locked in a room for as long as he still breathes. But does he know this? One man's happiness can be another man's hell."

Mom gently touched his arm, and he leaned into her.

Dad looked at me solemnly and nodded. "If I get like that," he said, "you must promise me, Vee, you'll . . ." Here he pulled his index finger across his throat.

"No!" I said, horrified. "No, I won't do that, Dad. If you lose your mind, you could still be happy. You could still want to live. I'd come visit you every day."

"I know you would, Vee. Of course you would. I would not want to make you sad, though, by not remembering you. By not remembering all the fun we've had."

I couldn't stand the thought of him looking shriveled and defeated. "Too bad," I said. "That's not your choice. You can't decide how much I can love you." I grabbed his jacket and pulled him up into a hug. Us Wong men, we were very unmacho. We were smart and sensitive and good to other people.

"Plus," I said, pulling away and smiling, "I'd come every day and tell you the same jokes, and you'd laugh like you'd never heard them before."

Dad laughed and slapped his knee. "And how is that different from how we are now?"

"That's a good point," I said. "That's a very good point." I reached down and scooped up a handful of cold, coarse dirt. Maybe I'd come back here someday and look for more pieces of the past. I let the dirt sift through my hands. The cave felt like a temple, like the inside of the earth. Even if this earth didn't have all the clean-cut answers, we were very likely standing in the middle of something extraordinary. Maybe we couldn't even imagine—as wild as our imaginations were—what, at this very moment, could be shifting to the surface all around us.

DISCUSSION GUIDE FOR
THE COUNTERFEIT FAMILY TREE OF VEE CRAWFORD-WONG

1. Throughout the novel, Vee is often sarcastic—sometimes to be funny, sometimes defensively, and sometimes to avoid having to deal with the truth. When does his sarcasm have negative consequences, and how does he respond? How should he respond?

2. Vee is fascinated with archaeology because he likes unearthing bits of the past and using them to understand different worlds and cultures. How does this interest correspond to his search for his own family history? In what ways is he "digging" to find his own identity?

3. Vee struggles to communicate with his parents and often decides to remain silent rather than share his confusing emotions. As his problems deepen, he feels trapped in his silence. Which is the greater transgression—lying by omission, or telling an uncomfortable truth? Where else in the novel does this issue surface?

4. When Vee claims to be a victim of racist insults, his dad unsympathetically remarks, "You decided it was a convenient place to take out your frustrations. If you had laughed, he'd have lost advantage." Is Vee's father insensitive, or is he giving good advice?

5. In discussing the background of the novel, Holland notes that high school students face incredible pressure to conform and fit in, and many look to their ethnicity to help define themselves. Do you think ethnic identity is an issue on high school campuses today? If so, how do people of mixed race, like Vee, find a place to belong? What are the potential positives and negatives of allowing your ethnicity to define your self-identity?

6. Vee loves history but is easily frustrated with its ambiguous moral lessons. How would Vee define the terms "enemy" and "friend," in the context of his own life as well as in his study of history?

7. Both Vee and Steffie use rumors to bully Riley. What is their motivation for doing this? How does Vee finally achieve some resolution with Riley, and do you envision Steffie ever doing so?

8. Madison and Adele are very different, yet Vee is attracted to each of them. How does Vee's interest reveal facets of his own personality, and does he ultimately make wise decisions regarding his love life?

9. Characters in stories often undergo transformative journeys. Does Vee's trip to China fit in this category? In what ways is his external journey a metaphor for an internal one? Does he need to go to China to learn about himself?

10. How does this novel compare to other books you've read about teenagers? Are the ideas and discoveries in this book best suited for a teen audience, or are the insights also applicable to adult readers?